Sherlock Holmes and the Abominable Worm of Fleet Street

By
Miguel R. Rivera, Sr.

Hardcover ISBN 978-1-80424-455-5
Paperback ISBN 978-1-80424-456-2
ePub ISBN 978-1-80424-457-9
PDF ISBN 978-1-80424-458-6

Published by MX Publishing
335 Princess Park Manor, Royal Drive,
London, N11 3GX
www.mxpublishing.com

Cover design by Awan

For my dear wife, Barbara; my sister, Raquel; and my beloved mother, Ann. May you all enjoy the foggy streets of London while walking in the footsteps of the Master Detective.

Among these unfinished tales…is that of Isadora Persano, the well-known journalist and duelist, who was found stark staring mad with a match box in front of him which contained a remarkable worm said to be unknown to science. – **The Problem of Thor Bridge**, by Sir Arthur Conan Doyle

Prologue
(Winter 1895)

The house was just like all the others in this upper-scale side of London. Nothing to set it apart from the other large homes along Kensington Court off Kensington High Street on the west side of London. Victorian in style, light in color, with dark wine-colored shudders and door. A brass knocker decorated the top middle of the door. To the right was a highly polished brass plate that read, "The Gemini Society / Private / By Appointment Only." The street was quiet and well-lit by gas lamps up and down the thoroughfare. Still, the gas flames gave faint light on this foggy winter night in December of 1895. Instead giving a greyish-yellow glow to the air, the street, and casting dark shadows on the house. It was midnight and the denizens of this street were long asleep. All, except those in the house itself.

The house was dark inside except for the light that came off the street and that of a single candle, placed in the middle of a round table, itself standing in the middle of the drawing room on the ground floor. The candle burned on top a large brass candle holder, heavy and deeply carved. The room was richly decorated with books, paintings, statuary, and rugs. It had an air of refinement and conservative, stiff, long-lived decadence – even in the relative dark, lit only by the streetlights and the single candle. The round cherrywood table was covered in a large dark red and black exquisitely crafted textile of cotton and lace – shrouding the entire table and reaching to the floor. The air was thick with the smell of incense burning from a brass bowl in a corner of the room.

The yellow light from the candle revealed thin whiffs of incense as they slowly danced toward the ceiling and filled the room with a heavy aroma of sandalwood.

Around the table sat three people. A man and two women. The man was heavily bearded, large, dressed in evening clothes, and very aristocratic in appearance and in attitude. The woman opposite him was stately, her long hair, now grey with age and mixed with a faded blond, all up in a large crown of well secured locks. She was dressed in finery as if for a night at the theatre. Both sat upright, facing the candle in the middle of the table, with eyes closed, and faces of silent concentration, as if in prayer. The man and woman leaned slightly forward, holding each other's hands across the table, the man's right to the woman's left. Both also holding the hands of the other woman who sat at the table, her head back, her green eyes looking straight up at the ceiling. She was moaning and her head moved around in slow circles, first left and then right. Her back stiff and straight.

This second woman was dressed conservatively in a black dress, with a bright red shawl over her shoulders. She was petite with a comely figure, a tiny waist, a face that was feminine with fine delicate features. Her light brown hair was in an intricate bun with a cascade of ringlets down her back. Her olive-shaped green eyes intensely staring with a wild energy and far-off expression. Her well-formed lips were silently mouthing words that gave no sound and carried no obvious meaning, as her throat emitted light groans. Her breath was short and fast, in little burst of inhalations and longer exhalations. Her body began to writhe in rhythm with her breath and her staccato moans. The man and other woman stiffened at the sudden increase in the woman's breathing and the increased violence of her movements. The room was filled with a sudden feeling of expectation, of dread, of fear, and of reverence.

The table began to slowly shake and wobble. The candle flame swaying to the sudden movement of the table, the tablecloth gently dancing back and forth as the shaking took on an urgency. Slowly the shaking became more imperative, and the man let go of his wife's hand, for just a moment and opened his eyes.

"Do not break the chain! Do not disrespect the presence of the nether world! Clasp! Clasp each other and hold on to this world! Close, close your eyes and stay fixed on his name. The name we are calling up from the depths of the spirit world." Lilith was in rare form this evening.

Sir Eustace Gardner and Lady Gardner both clasped each other's hands again and closed their eyes tight. The table was shaking violently now and the noise of wooden legs striking the floor filled the room and seemed to echo in the dark. Lilith's moaning grew louder, and her body shook as if in spasm.

"Jonathan, we are calling you up from the nether world. There are those here who wish to speak with you. Come toward the light of the candle. Come!"

All at once the candle went out and at the same time the table struck the floor hard and then all was still. Sir Eustace and Lady Gardner were breathing hard and there was perspiration on the man's brow. Lilith collapsed forward and as she did, she let go of the hands of both her clients. Her breathing was deep and loud in the dark room, and Sir Eustace and Lady Gardner both let go of the other's hand and sat back with their eyes wide.

"Well? What is the meaning of all this Lady Tabitha? Is he here?" Sir Eustace was wiping his brow with a handkerchief and his wife was pressing down her dress with shaking hands.

Lilith did not answer right away, breathing hard, she slowly sat up and held her head in both hands. "He was here, for just a second. Something drove him back. I could not hold on to him. He is surrounded by other spirits who hold onto him, swirl about him, and keep him where he is."

"And where in the blazes is he? Heaven or hell?" asked Sir Eustace, and Lady Gardner began to cry into her gloved hands.

"Jonathan is neither in heaven nor hell. He is between worlds. Not here on our plane of existence. Not in heaven. Not in hell. He is caught, trapped by other spirits and not at peace. He needs our help to move on. Something keeps him in between, something that the other spirits are attracted to and desperately need. It will take more sessions to set him free." Lilith feigned exhaustion and leaned on the table with both elbows, her head turned to the side as if resting.

Lady Gardner spoke for the first time, "Oh Eustace! Our poor son suffers so. We must continue our work to give him peace!" She sobbed into the handkerchief that Sir Eustace had handed to her.

"Lady Tabitha, you are exhausted from your efforts this evening. May we come back later and continue our attempts to contact our son, Jonathan?" Sir Eustace looked desperate and worn.

Lilith hesitated as she sat upright and looked toward both Sir Eustace and Lady Gardner and then back down at the table. She reached in the dark and with a match relit the candle. The yellow glow revealing the worn, fearful, and desperate faces of her two clients. "It is difficult. The other spirits cling to him so. He is confused and in terror. I am not sure that we will be able to reach him and bring him fully into our world so that we may commune with him."

"But we must! We must!" cried Lady Gardner. "Eustace, tell her that we must."

"Lady Tabitha, money is of no concern. Our son must be brought to the light. He must find peace, and we must know why he took his own life." At this Sir Eustace, with earnest effort, controlled the grief that shook his strong voice and caused his chin to quiver.

"In a fortnight. I must rest and recover. In a fortnight, we will try again," said Lilith in a voice of capitulation.

"Oh thank you. Thank you, dear Lady Tabitha," sobbed Lady Gardner.

Sir Eustace stood and reaching in the pocket of his evening jacket and took out a small cloth bag, heavy with sovereigns, and placed it on the table in front of Lilith. "We thank you sincerely. There will be more if we are able to contact him directly, get our answers, ease his pain, and bring him to peace."

"We can only try, Sir Eustace. We can only try." Lilith looked sad and hopeless but bowed reverently to both Sir Eustace and the now standing Lady Gardner, who reached out and lightly caressed Lilith's forearm. With that Sir Eustace and Lady Gardner, resuming their regal postures, walked from the room towards the front of the house and to their waiting carriage.

––––––––––––––––––––––––

The bedroom was lavishly and elegantly furnished. The walls covered in a fine thick wallpaper embossed with ornate *fleur-de-lis*, in the style of the Continent. A warm, bright fire blazed in the fireplace, and the windows were covered in intricately woven curtains that matched the linens that covered the four-poster bed. Lying in the bed, naked and barely covered by the sheet, sleeping, was his lady of choice for the evening. Her red hair covering her sleeping face as her slow deep breaths moved the sheet up and down in a slow rhythm. The room lit by the gas chandelier and the light put out by the fire.

He sat at the small oval table in just a dressing gown looking at the light of the fire as it danced off the decanter in front of him. His eyesight blurred, his brain in a stupor, sweat on his brow, and his heart racing. Effects of the mixture of absinthe and cold water poured over a sugar cube turning the green fairy into the white milk colored liquid he drank so often. The hallucinogenic effects were just beginning, and the room seemed to slowly spin as the light danced in refracted rays against everything in the room. He was in the dreamy mental state that he searched so often for. Languid and numb. A mental and physical state that he seemed to need increasingly.

The girl stirred in the bed awakening and turned to her side, her head resting on her folded arm. "I see the green fairy has you in her embrace. You will not have any more need of me for the rest of the night."

Rodrick slowly turned his glassy, dreamy eyes towards her and absently stared. "My lady, the combination of your talented attentions, followed by my dearest fairy are all that I need tonight. You may leave whenever you are ready...My, how the light dances off your fine red locks. How sensuous is your scent and the curves of your body under the sheet." Roderick seemed caught by the image before him, taken away by the green fairy and his momentary lust – but the mood quickly passed. "I wish to be left in peace now. Good night." He turned his head back to his study of the dancing flames, oblivious to her continued presence.

She rose slowly from the bed stretching and reaching for the silk lingerie that lay crumpled on the chair next to the bed and she slipped into the cool silk and was in the act of putting on her robe when Roderick called out incoherently.

"My love, does the fairy bring nightmares this night?"

But Roderick did not answer, still madly staring into the fire with wild eyes. "My father is in hell. In the flames. They consume him," he yelled and then fell silent.

She walked slowly to the table where he sat and ran her fingers through his black sweat-drenched hair. "She has you in her embrace indeed. Go slowly where she takes you, my dear. She can be so fickle." She reached down to the table and took the folded pounds that were her payment for the evening, turned and walked toward the door.

The room she left was one of many on the fourth floor of the Gemini Club, where she served her many clients. As she walked down the long hallway toward the stairs, she could hear the various sounds of other girls and men engaged in what men came here to do – sounds of pleasure, of screams, of lashing, and even talking could be heard as she made her way down the hallway. She descended the staircase to the next floor, one large room that served as a lounge area with multiple small tables, cushioned chairs, and wood-paneled walls, with three small bars serving fine wine and spirits via impeccably dressed waiters and the well-dressed membership. Dimly lit and surprisingly quiet but for the occasional feminine laugh of one of the many ladies who worked the room and the muted sound of the quartet playing in the corner.

The second floor was large and open, set up this evening as a gambling establishment. Men in formal dress, women in gowns, the room fogged by smoke, the sounds of gambling, and the muted talk of the gamblers. She continued to the ground floor which was divided into multiple rooms used for many elaborate parties and sinful deeds, more maze like than the other floors. She passed into a room marked by an ornate sign that read, "Gemini Club Management" and closed the door behind her.

Roderick awakened in a start, at first not knowing where he was. His eyes slowly clearing and the fog of absinthe still heavy on his mind. He stood and got dressed, stopping to look at his pocket watch – it was just after three o'clock in the morning. He would have trouble finding a hansom so late in the night. He stumbled toward the door and made his way downstairs toward the private entrance to the club, past the door marked, "Gemini Club Management," and one of the staff stopped him.

"Have a good evening, sir?"

"Yes, thank you. My coat and hat please."

"Certainly. Miss St. John would like to see you if you have time this evening sir."

"Miss Saint John?"

"Yes, the lady of the establishment. This way, sir."

The maître de, a German man named Steven Sobotta, was known to all the members of the club. As was his twin brother, Scott Sobotta, who shared duties as maître de of the Gemini Club. Members simply referred to them as "the Twins," Steven and Scott, and they knew everyone by name and appearance. Mr. Sobotta led Roderick through the door and into Miss St. John's office.

"Madam, Mr. Hudson per your request. Mr. Hudson, may I introduce you to the lady of the establishment, Miss St. John."

Miss Rebecca St. John stood and walked toward the duo as they came into the room. She was beautiful and finely but conservatively dressed. She was dainty and petite. She had a grace and refinement about her that made one look at her. She smiled seductively at Roderick Hudson, with her feminine, finely shaped face, her head tilted slightly to the side and her left arm outstretched pointing to the settee and twin chairs that stood in front of the fire. Over the fire, hanging from the wall, was a large finely painted portrait of the lady herself.

"Please, call me Becca. It is good to meet you Mr. Hudson. Please, have a seat here by the fire. I understand you are a regular here at the Gemini Club. The ladies here speak fondly of you. It is late, I know. May I offer you some tea? Some coffee?"

"Uh, yes Miss St. John. Some coffee please. What may I ask is this about?"

Becca moved to a small serving table and began to poor coffee for Roderick and tea for herself. Looking up coquettishly she asked, "Cream? Sugar?"

"Oh, cream please. No sugar." Roderick waited for Miss St. John to hand him the cup and saucer and then sat, waiting for her to sit first. He was confused, tired, and still felt the fog slowly lifting from his mind. It was unusual, to say the least, for a lady to be the manager of such an establishment, and even more unusual that she should be meeting with a man, alone, at this hour of the night. He felt uncomfortable and on edge, but Miss St. John's grace and beauty put him in an agreeable mood, even if he was confused.

Becca sat and took a sip of her tea and looked at Roderick Hudson. He was clearly not in the best of form. His clothes were obviously quickly put on, his face was moist and haggard, his eyes tired, and his black hair tousled and wet with perspiration. He looked almost feverish to her. She knew that Mr. Hudson was a regular, coming in at least five nights a week. He preferred two of her girls, both young and red-headed, and when in the mood would share more about his life and work than was customary or wise. They would of course report everything to Becca who kept meticulous notes on Mr. Hudson, as she did many of her members.

She took him all in, thinking carefully about the conversation she was about to start with him. She had to be careful, use her information wisely, and draw him in slowly.

For what she wanted from him was important to her plans and her tireless desire to replace the Professor – whom it was clear, Mr. Sherlock Holmes had dispatched at the Reichenbach Falls. She had survived the demise of the Professor's syndicate and had inherited, as it were, a small percentage of the Professor's organization in London. She was interested in both Mr. Hudson and what he might offer her.

Becca had planned her moves carefully. Patiently getting information about Mr. Hudson. Feeding his desires and his lusts. Instructing the girls that he preferred in the art of getting information while appearing both not to be pushing or leading while maintaining the appearance of being completely disinterred. Teaching them how to draw a man out so that he trusted and spoke about things his better judgment should have prevented. She joined these lessons with the careful use of drugs and other inducements to help draw the target out. In Mr. Hudson's case, by lacing his absinthe with ever increasingly higher amounts of laudanum. His frequent visits to the club and his physical appearance told her it was time to draw him into her web.

Becca laid her cup and saucer on her lap. She looked Mr. Hudson in the eyes, and in her most persuasive voice said, "May I speak with you about a business opportunity?"

Part One

(Summer 1896)

Chapter 1

Watson was asleep. Back at his old rooms with Holmes in Baker Street, now almost four years since the untimely death of his late wife, Mary Watson formerly Mary Morstan. The death had been sudden, but not entirely unexpected to a trained physician like Watson. Mary's heart had given out; she had inherited a heart condition from her late father. Her frequent trips to warmer climates having failed to do anything other than purchase some time with Watson before she succumbed to the inevitable. He had sold his medical practice in Paddington and had repurchased his old, but much less busy practice, in Kensington – to both give himself more time to write and now, though unplanned, to spend his time with Holmes, being a bachelor again.

He was awakened by the sound of Holmes playing his violin downstairs in his rooms. He rolled over in bed trying to drown out the sound with one ear in the pillow and his free hand over his other ear. But it was of no use, he was awake now. He rolled over on his back and with a sigh of exasperation decided to get up. He took his watch from the night table and looked at it. It was only seven thirty in the morning. A Sunday morning. Watson usually slept late on Sunday mornings and Mrs. Hudson knowing his habits, would not have even started breakfast. He stood and grumbled to himself. It was no use; he might as well get dressed and go downstairs to greet Holmes and read the morning paper before Mrs. Hudson brought up breakfast. He walked to the bowl and pitcher to begin his morning ministrations.

Holmes had been up the entire night working on a chemical analysis, finishing his yet unpublished manuscript on the coal tar derivatives – work he had not completed while away after the demise of Professor Moriarty. It had so far been a slow year as new cases went. He almost always had something to deal with, but nothing that taxed his prodigious talents for deduction. Still, he was busy enough to keep away the ennui that plagued him. This morning he played his violin to calm his nervous energy after working all night. He stood playing in front of the cold fireplace with his back to the door and was so lost in his music that he did not notice Watson come into the room until he opened his eyes and saw Watson's reflection in a mirror on the mantle.

"My dear Watson, you are up early for a Sunday."

Watson grunted as he walked over to his chair by the fireplace and as he sat said, "If you must know, it was rather difficult to sleep with your violin playing. Have we the morning paper yet?"

"Ahh, of course. Sorry old man. The paper? I am not sure." Holmes set his violin and bow down beside his chair and sat. Watson was not awake yet and had not had his morning coffee. Holmes knew that Watson would not be in the mood for conversation, so he simply picked-up the manuscript he was writing, his pencil, and worked on edits. Neither spoke for several minutes, Watson slowly awakening and Holmes focused his edits.

"Well, I am going downstairs to get the paper and see if Mrs. Hudson can bring up some breakfast and coffee," Watson stood and began to walk toward the door. Holmes said nothing in answer.

Watson walked back into the room carrying the morning paper, "It seems Mrs. Hudson was awakened by your violin as well. The good news is she is busy making breakfast and it should be up shortly." Holmes looked up from his manuscript and nodded. Watson sat back down and began to read the paper.

After several minutes, Holmes asked, "Anything of interest in the paper?"

"The Germans and Greeks are still crowing over their wins earlier this year in the Olympic games. The Russians are still celebrating the coronation of their new Tzar, Nicholas II. Nothing of interest to you there. Oh, and the mysterious death of a solicitor who went mad and ran out into the street before being hit by a carriage and four horses late yesterday. The sudden madness being the mystery, not the death."

"What of the agony columns?"

Watson flipped through the paper and handed the agony column section to Holmes. "Here, read the bizarre things yourself."

"Really Watson you are in a mood this morning. I trust your losses at whist last night were not larger than you can afford. Should I make you a loan to hold you over, dear fellow?"

Watson dropped his paper in his lap and staring surprised at Holmes said, "How in the devil did you know that? My luck was rather bad last night, and I did come away a bit the worse for wear, if not a wiser man."

"Watson, you know my methods. Come now, you tell me how I came to this conclusion."

"Holmes, I am sure that I have not the slightest idea. Come out with it old man."

Holmes rolled his eyes and made a dismissive gesture, "It is really quite simple. I know that you went to your club last night to play whist. This morning you come downstairs not wearing the signet ring on your left hand. You are in a bad mood and while you sat here earlier you mumbled to yourself. I caught you mumbling something about, 'Bloody spades.' So, I conclude that you lost at whist last night, having run out of money, you were forced to hock your signet ring to save your honor, no doubt with the promise to buy it back next game?"

"You are correct in every respect. It is a good thing that you are not married Holmes. You would drive your spouse to distraction. In any case, sorry Holmes. I am a bit out of sorts this morning. First my losses last night, then your violin playing so early on a Sunday morning, I have not had my coffee yet, and it all just settled on me. I am afraid I took it out on you."

"Quite. Not to worry Watson, I hear Mrs. Hudson coming up the stairs now with our breakfast and your much needed coffee." Holmes chuckled as Mrs. Hudson knocked quietly on the door and came in carrying a tray of breakfast and coffee.

Watson had finished his breakfast and was on his third cup of coffee. Holmes sat smoking, having drank only a cup of coffee for his breakfast. Both heard the bell ring and shortly hereafter Mrs. Hudson arrived in the room with a card on a small silver tray.

"A lady to see you Mr. Holmes. She sends her apologies for coming so early and on a Sunday but insists that the matter is urgent and that she must consult with you."

Holmes took the card from the tray and read the name to himself – Mrs. Brenda Snyder. "Please, show the lady in Mrs. Hudson. Watson, will you stay to see what the matter is?" Mrs. Hudson left to bring up Mrs. Snyder.

"Of course, Holmes."

"Splendid. Here is the lady now."

Mrs. Snyder was indeed a lady in every respect. Tall for a woman, with dark brown hair and a stately and lady-like stature. She was dressed well in the fashion of a well-bred and well-raised woman of about twenty-five years of age. She looked from Holmes to Watson in an inquiring fashion.

"Mrs. Snyder, I am Sherlock Holmes, this is my friend and colleague Dr. Watson. What can we do for you this morning?"

"Mr. Holmes, Dr. Watson, thank you for seeing me without an appointment and so early on a Sunday morning. I come to you as a last resort, not knowing what else to do and in fear that my liberty may at any moment be taken away from me by agents of Scottland Yard." Mrs. Snyder trembled at the thought of losing her liberty and with one hand supported herself on the back of the settee.

"Please, Mrs. Snyder, sit down. You look about to faint." Dr. Watson took the lady's hand and led her to the front of the settee and invited her to sit down. "May I get you something to drink? Tea perhaps?"

"No, thank you Doctor. I am fine. I just need to sit. The events of the last few hours have been taxing." Mrs. Snyder sat down.

Holmes sat in his usual chair by the cold fireplace and looked at Mrs. Snyder carefully, while Watson moved to his chair and sat as well.

"Mrs. Snyder, beyond the obvious, that you are a typist, a well-educated woman, were once married, have yet to put in gas at your place of residence, and are an asthmatic, I do not recognize your name and have no idea why you are here. Please tell me what I can do for you and please be precise as to details."

"Mr. Holmes, it is true that I am a typist and do work on a contract basis for several law firms in the city. I am educated, I received my degree in Continental history but two years ago. I do suffer from asthma, and I fear that the stress of the past day, the quick trip to your rooms, and the climbing up your stairs has me a bit winded. I do have gas in my apartments but as I did not stay there last night and instead stayed with my aunt, and alas she has not had gas put in. How did you know this?"

"You have candle wax on your right sleeve, and just a bit down the side of your dress where you blew out the candle before you left. As for the rest, it is irrelevant to our present objectives. Please tell me why you are here." Mrs. Snyder looked at her sleeve and dress in an embarrassed manner.

Watson looked judgingly at Holmes, "The fingers of your hands, as you took off your gloves, reveal a certain padding or flatness that is common to ladies who type regularly for many hours. If you do not mind my saying, you have a very lady-like and stately way about you that points to education and an excellent upbringing. As for having been married, now that Holmes points it out, I see that the skin on your left ring finger is lighter than the rest of your hand and in a circular pattern, marking where you wore your wedding ring."

"Watson, you have indeed improved greatly. Well done."

"It is true; I was married to a solicitor in my current fiancé's firm. He died some two years ago. Killed by an angry client whom he failed in some case he had with him. I only stopped wearing the ring recently. My fiancé, or my late fiancé, is why I am here." Mrs. Snyder looked down at her lap and reaching into her purse took out a woman's hanky and began to wipe her eyes.

"Please take your time. We are both sorry for your loss." Watson leaned forward, his face a mask of empathy and concern.

"Yes, we are all very sorry for your loss. Can we please get to why you have come to see me this morning?" Holmes was impatient.

"Mr. Holmes, I am sure that you are a remarkably busy man and I have come to see you this morning without an appointment. I am sorry for delaying my account. It is just that things have only just happened, and I am afraid that I have still not adjusted to the fact that my fiancé, Mr. Robert Holcomb, Esq., has been killed in a horrible accident involving a carriage and several horses. It is…It is…just so horrible and grotesque. The whole affair is so…grotesque."

Miss Snyder began to quietly cry, but soon regained her composure.

"My Robby, for that is what I called him, was a good and hard-working man. I of course knew of him before my husband died. He was so supportive and such a good friend after my late husband was murdered. Soon, friendship turned into more, and we have only been engaged this past thirty days, I have not even gotten the ring yet. I simply cannot imagine what happened in the few hours after our dinner last night and this morning when I learned of his death when I read the account in the paper at my aunt's home."

Watson suddenly stood and walked to the table retrieving the newspaper. "I was just reading about the account of this affair in the morning paper. Holmes, this is the story that I briefly mentioned earlier before breakfast."

"Ahh, please read the account to me now, Watson."

Watson stood and read the following account to Holmes and Mrs. Snyder:

> "**Bizarre Happenings on Near East End**
> Mr. Robert Holcomb, Esq., a solicitor, and partner at Avery & Middleton, was killed late Saturday evening around eleven thirty when he ran out of his rooms in a state of madness and into the hooves and wheels of a carriage drawn by four. His mangled and bloody body was dragged for some distance before the driver could rein in the horses and stop the carriage. Blood and body parts were strewn about the street..."

Watson stopped reading at this point and gave a sad look at Mrs. Snyder who sat with her back straight and hands clasped. "I am sorry, Mrs. Snyder, should I read on?"

"Thank you, Dr. Watson. Yes, I have read the account myself this morning and it is what spurred me to come see you and Mr. Holmes."

"You are very brave. I will read on..."

> "...Neighbors of the unfortunate Mr. Holcomb said that he lived quietly, was a fine solicitor, and had recently been engaged to a Mrs. Brenda Snyder, a widow whom he had been seen in the company of that very evening. It is said that Mr. Holcomb was in his rooms and suddenly began to shout and toss furniture about, causing some of his neighbors to come out into the hall to investigate the matter. He threw open his door and running wildly up and down the hall shouting for what seemed like several minutes to those who witnessed the event, suddenly he ran down the stairs and out the front door of the building and into the street. Having run only a few yards, he met his fate when a carriage, drawn by four horses, came around a corner and ran the unfortunate Mr. Holcomb over, killing him instantly."

"There is nothing more of interest, Holmes, save for more lurid descriptions of the scene and its effect on those who ran out of the building and those on the street who witnessed his unfortunate demise." Watson walked backed to his chair, handing the paper to Holmes on the way.

"It says here that the police may be looking for you to question you, regarding the matter, Mrs. Snyder. Has anyone contacted you yet?"

"No Mr. Holmes, I was not at my rooms last night. I was staying with an aunt in London, whom I had promised to visit. The police, as far as I know, are unaware of my whereabouts. Though I doubt that will be true for much longer."

"Pray, begin with Mr. Holcomb and you meeting for the evening and tell me what happened, leaving nothing out, however inconsequential it may seem." Holmes sat back in his chair, crossed his legs under him, and steepled his fingers in deep concentration.

"Robby worked hard and long hours all week, so it was our custom to go out on a Saturday evening. He called on me at my rooms around seven thirty in the evening. I was ready and waiting for him when he came. He was in good spirits, and all seemed quite normal, Mr. Holmes. We took a hansom to the restaurant and had a wonderful dinner. We talked of his work and our plans to be married later this summer. It was a nice evening, sir." With this Mrs. Snyder began to wipe her eyes again, trembling and working to regain her composure.

"Yes, please go on."

"Well, Mr. Holmes, I told Robby that I wanted to go to my aunt's home rather than back to my apartment. He accompanied me there in a hansom and said good night. That was about nine thirty last night. I had no reason to believe anything was amiss. And now, my poor Robby is dead and according to the paper the police want to speak with me. That is all I know Mr. Holmes."

As Mrs. Snyder finished her account the bell rang below and there was the sound of several feet on the staircase. As Holmes opened his eyes in walked Inspector MacDonald of Scotland Yard accompanied by two constables.

"Mr. Holmes, why is it not surprising that we find Mrs. Brenda Snyder in your rooms on so early on a Sunday morning?"

Holmes quickly stood and walked the few steps to where the inspector was standing. "And how may I ask did you trace Mrs. Snyder here?"

"Her aunt was kind enough to tell us that she was on her way here. You are not the only one Mr. Holmes who can learn things that other people know," the inspector looked at Holmes triumphantly and then turned his gaze to Mrs. Snyder. "We will want to ask you a few questions. I am obliged to tell you that anything you say will be used against you at trial. Now, come with us if you please."

"Inspector, Mrs. Snyder was just telling us her account of what transpired last night when you interrupted our interview. Surely a few minutes lost in allowing us to finish our conversation will not disrupt your investigation?"

"I suppose not." The inspector motioned for one constable to stand beside Mrs. Snyder and the other to guard the door. "Please continue." The inspector sat at a chair by the table, took out a small notebook and pencil from his jacket pocket as Holmes went back to his chair and sat.

"Did Mr. Holcomb appear in a hurry to leave last night when he dropped you off at your aunt's home?" asked Holmes.

"No, not at all. He seemed perfectly normal."

"And that is the last time that you communicated with Mr. Holcomb?"

"Yes."

Holmes sat in thought, "Are you aware whether Mr. Holcomb had any cases that troubled him or that put him in danger?"

"No. His practice was primarily civil suits and finance law. Nothing that would put his life in danger."

"Has Mr. Holcomb any history of mania? Was he a nervous and sensitive man?"

"No, not at all, Mr. Holmes. He was a quiet and unassuming man. Nothing to predict this strange and terrible end to his life." Mrs. Snyder patted at her eyes with her handkerchief.

"Very well. I will look into the matter on your behalf. Inspector, this woman knows nothing of the events that transpired after she was taken to her aunt's home by Mr. Holcomb last night around nine-thirty. Surely you can see that."

"Mr. Holmes, a man is dead, apparently driven mad by some event, the very evening that he and Mrs. Snyder had dinner. Surely you can understand that suspicion falls on her as one of the last persons to interact with him while he was alive. Mrs. Snyder, I understand that you are a widow, now single and support yourself in a small way with a business of typing. Is that correct?"

"Yes, Inspector."

"Humm, any experience with chemicals or poisons?"

"I should say not! Mr. Holmes, must I endure this man's questions?"

"I am afraid so, Mrs. Snyder, and better here than at the Yard." Holmes looked frustrated with the inspector. "Inspector, Mrs. Snyder tells me that she was picked up by Mr. Holcomb at about seven thirty last night, had dinner with him, was taken by him in a hansom to her aunt's home, and only learned of the events that led to his death upon seeing it in the paper this morning. She knows nothing more."

"Had you and Mr. Holcomb quarreled recently, Mrs. Snyder?"

"No, we have never quarreled, Inspector. Never."

The inspector sat and studied his notes in thought, "I have no reason to hold you Mrs. Snyder, but I will ask you to stay close to home and not to change your habits as our investigation continues." With that the inspector closed his notebook and motioned the constable away from the door.

"Mrs. Snyder, please give me your address. We will contact you via messenger if there are any developments. In the meantime, do as the inspector instructs."

"Thank you, Mr. Holmes." Mrs. Snyder stood and giving Holmes her address, put on her gloves, and left, stopping for a moment at the door and looking earnestly at Holmes, said, "I am grateful to you Mr. Holmes. Thank you."

Holmes nodded and then turned his attention to the Inspector. "What can you tell me about this affair?"

"Well, Mr. Holmes, the man Holcomb returned to his rooms before ten last evening. About an hour later his neighbors heard him yelling, heard furniture being turned over, and then Mr. Holcomb stormed out of his rooms yelling and running in circles about the hall. No sooner had several neighbors come out of their rooms curious about what was going on, when Mr. Holcomb ran downstairs, out the front door, and straight into the path of a carriage drawn by four. He was dead almost immediately. The street is a mess, and his body is in several pieces along the road. We had a time of it collecting all the parts for the coroner. That is the whole of it, Mr. Holmes. I have a constable standing outside the door to his rooms ensuring nothing is disturbed."

Holmes was standing filling his long-stemmed cherry wood pipe. "A rather strange and unique set of facts, is it not Watson?"

"Yes. As Mrs. Snyder said, a grotesque and mysterious turn of events."

"Well, Mr. Holmes, we are going to the man's rooms, if you wish to accompany us?" The inspector stood.

"Yes, we will follow you shortly, Inspector. Please do not enter the rooms until we arrive." Holmes sat and lit his pipe.

"Well, how long will you be Mr. Holmes? I have not all day. It is Sunday you know."

Holmes looked at the inspector dismissively and continued to smoke.

Watson stood and said, "I am sure we will be there within an hour. What is the address for the rooms?"

The inspector giving Watson the address, looked at Holmes, who was now seated with his legs crossed and eyes closed. "We will await your arrival." With that the inspector and the two constables left.

Watson turned toward Holmes, "How long do you intend to wait, Holmes?"

"Watson, I don't intend to wait at all." Holmes was up and was walking quickly toward the door to retrieve his walking stick. "If we hurry, we may just beat the inspector to the rooms. Come Watson!"

Chapter 2

"I am not sure, dear Watson, if that was not one of the fastest trips I have ever taken in a hansom." Holmes was paying the driver and Watson was getting out of the cab with big eyes and nodding in agreement. They had arrived at Mr. Holcomb's rooms before the inspector. After paying the driver, Holmes began his slow meticulous inspection of the street, the pavement in front of the building, and the steps to the building itself. "Too much traffic and too many footmarks to make any inspection worthwhile, Watson."

Holmes and Watson entered the building and went up the stairs to the third floor, where there were four apartments, two on either side of a long hall. A constable stood in front of the farthest door on the left. Just as they arrived at the landing, the inspector arrived below. Holmes waited.

"What the devil? How? What are you doing here, Mr. Holmes? I thought I was to meet you here later."

Holmes laughed, "I thought it best to meet you here now. After all, it is Sunday, you know."

The inspector laughed. "You are full of surprises, Mr. Holmes. Shall we examine the rooms?"

"Yes, please lead the way."

As they arrived at the door, the constable unlocked it and Holmes said, "Gentlemen, if you please, allow me to enter first." Upon opening the door one was presented with a small sitting room, spartan, and what furnishings there were, were in disarray. There was a large rectangular carpet on the floor beginning just to the left of the entrance and proceeding towards the middle of the room, a fireplace to the right, with two sitting chairs and a small oval table in between. To the left, was a round dining table that was turned over on its side, two chairs on one side of it, and two others tossed about the room. The table and chairs had once been on the left side of the large rug. Holmes took this all in at-a-glance.

Holmes handed Watson his hat and walking stick and surveyed the room with his two hands together just below his face. He let out little sounds of interest as he looked. "A bachelor, indeed. Tidy in his habits. Not a smoker. Spartan in his tastes. Room is functional, but not decorated with much thought. The room of a man whose life is his work, and whose rooms are purely functional. A few law books on the mantle place, bust of Napoleon, drawing of Her Majesty, framed on the wall next to the fireplace."

Holmes suddenly fell on his face crawling along the floor and the rug. He stopped in several places and having taken out his magnifying glass, examined several areas of the rug very carefully. He took out a measuring tape and made several measurements. After his crawling, he stood and turned his attention to the chairs, examining the cushioned area on the seat of each, the backs, the legs, and the tops of each chair. The inspector and Watson stood watching. The inspector with a serious look on his face, as if memorizing every move that Holmes made. Holmes stepped carefully on the tips of his toes, as he moved about the room, eventually stepping off the rug and making his way toward the two chairs by the fireplace. He examined the chairs and the table and then turned his attention to the fireplace itself, using the poker to dig around the remnants of some old fire, and reaching in and sifting through the ashes themselves.

"The bedroom I suppose is down this way?" he asked as he went down a short hall and turned right into a small bedroom. "The bed has not been slept in, as it is still made up. Mr. Holcomb took off his evening jacket and put on a dressing gown, as the evening jacket has been placed over the foot of the bed and there is an empty hangar behind the door. His shoes likewise are laid on the floor. When found, did he have on his slippers and dressing gown?" Holmes opened the armoire and quickly searched through the pockets of the few clothes inside.

"Why, yes Mr. Holmes, though the dressing gown was ripped and trampled, and the slippers strewn about. He did have his socks on his feet." The inspector consulted his notes as he answered Holmes's question.

"There is nothing more to be gleaned from the bedroom." Holmes returned to the sitting room. "Constable, you may pick-up the furniture and otherwise tidy up the room. I have learned all that there is to know."

"Do you mind sharing what you have learned with me, Mr. Holmes?" The inspector looked at Holmes demandingly.

Holmes looked at the inspector with a far-off expression, "Oh, have you not seen what was here? Of course not. There were three people here last night. Mr. Holcomb, another man, and a woman. The man, with square toed boots, stood at the head of the table for quite some time, as his impressions in the rug are rather deep. Mr. Holcomb sat in that chair also at the head of the table. The woman walked back and forth along the other side of the table. The man is large and heavily built. The woman petite and of average height. You might ask the neighbors if they saw a large, heavy man and a woman here last night either before or after the unfortunate Mr. Holcomb met his end. The rest of these rooms are unremarkable. Some legal papers on the small desk in his bedroom. Nothing of interest in the pockets of the clothes in his armoire – I checked those quickly while in the bedroom."

The inspector was writing quickly in his small notepad as Holmes outlined what he had seen. "You say two other people in this room last night, a man and a woman?"

"Yes. They were either here waiting for Mr. Holcomb or he let them in." Holmes was examining the doorknob and keyhole. "No signs anyone forced the door, and no scratches from lock-picking tools."

The inspector had finished his notes and was giving orders to the constable in the hall. "Constable, ask about to see if anyone saw a man and a woman here last night. Go on." The constable began knocking on the door to the apartment across the hall and a conversation ensued. He went down the hall to the other two apartments and returned.

"Inspector, no one saw anybody of that description here last night. I was a talking wif one of them earlier and he told me Mr. Holcomb was quiet in his ways and did not have visitors. Kept to himself, and was a hardworking man, keeping late hours at his office." The constable stood upright as he delivered his report.

"Very well, thank you. Now get on with your duties." The inspector dismissed the constable who began to walk down the hall.

"Before you go, Constable, is there a back entrance to this building?" Holmes was standing with his hands in his trouser pockets and his chin on his chest.

"Yes, Mr. Holmes. On the third floor there is a door that leads to some metal stairs and to the alley in the back."

"Show me," said Holmes, taking his chin off his chest and once again full of energy.

As the inspector, Watson, Holmes, and the constable approached the back door on the second floor Holmes stopped the group and began to examine the floor in front of the door and then the door itself. "Nothing," he said to himself. Holmes quickly opened the door and inspected the landing and the stairs leading to the dirt alleyway behind the building. Holmes was quickly on his knees and had his lens out examining the ground.

"Square toes and the lady left their marks in the dirt. They came by dogcart, and I can just make out their steps."

"Holmes, what do you think these two people could have told Mr. Holcomb that would have driven him mad in so short a space of time?" asked Watson.

Holmes stood with his hands in his trouser pockets and his chin on his chest. He did not immediately answer, standing staring down at the ground instead. Watson looked at the inspector and they both looked back at Holmes.

"There is nothing more for us to learn here, Inspector. Come Watson, let us visit the aunt. Have you the name and address, Inspector?" The inspector scribbled on a blank piece of paper in his notepad, ripped it out and handed it to Holmes. "Thank you, Inspector." With that Holmes walked swiftly down the alley. "Are you coming, Watson?"

"But Holmes, it is Sunday."

Lilith sat at a large table in the dining room at the house on Kensington Court, having just finished her late breakfast. Becca was sitting across from her, drinking her tea, and reading a newspaper. Neither was dressed for the day, and instead wore their night clothes and dressing gowns. A servant girl stood discreetly in the corner looking for any chance to serve the two ladies as they finished their meal.

"Will you be going to the club today, or will you take an afternoon off?" asked Lilith.

Becca looked up from her newspaper, "I will take the afternoon, but will go in this evening. Do you have plans for this afternoon?"

"I thought we might take a walk in the park and have afternoon tea out."

"That sounds lovely." Becca returned her attention to the paper and frown lines appeared on her forehead.

"Is there something disturbing in the paper?"

Becca dropped the paper to the floor. "It is just that damn Fleet Street rat, Isadora Persano, and his incessant investigations into the clubs and parlors of London. Why he finds it necessary to delve into the private affairs of the patrons of these establishments is maddening to me. If we are not careful, he will be into our affairs soon. He bears watching." Becca was lost in thought staring down at the table.

Lilith knew from experience not to interrupt Becca when she was lost in thought. It had been five years since the death of the Professor and the great purge that Scotland Yard had made decimating the Syndicate and leaving her without a job, and if not for Becca, without a home. They had met during one of Becca's visits to the Professor toward the end of her time with him. Lilith remembered that last day well. The dozens of constables that suddenly burst into the warehouse, the noise and chaos as those who were not in the know began to be arrested and the warehouse searched. She remembered going down the back steps into the alley as she escaped the scene only to be caught by two constables in the alley. After hours of questioning, it was determined that she was a simple domestic, as far as anyone could tell, innocent of any crime. It was as she was leaving Scotland Yard, that she saw Becca across the street, and she had been with her since that day. Lilith was sister, confidant, friend, business partner, and lover to Becca. Yet, she only knew what Becca confided in her about her larger business and the plans and schemes Becca carried out.

Becca, for her part, had managed to gather a small group of the Professor's old organization – those who had escaped the purge. Gone was the art store. Becca now managed the Gemini Club, Lilith's spiritualist business, and a growing criminal enterprise whose focus was blackmail, illicit entertainment, prostitution, gambling, and other more complex crimes still in the planning. The house and the building housing the club had both come to her through illicit blackmail schemes and the deeds had been signed over to her as part of the payment for her silence.

Becca was set-up well, and just small enough not to catch the attention of Scotland Yard. Her clientele was rich, established, publicly respectable, and very concerned to keep their public reputations intact, while availing themselves of what she had to offer at the club.

It was the larger plans and schemes that taxed Becca. She was intelligent, careful, inconspicuous, scheming, and very ambitious. She was ruthless when dealing with anyone who might threaten what she had worked so hard to establish and anyone who got in the way of her schemes. Miss St. John, as she was known to her clientele and employees, was not a woman to be underestimated or crossed.

Holmes and Watson arrived at the home of Mrs. Laurie McKinnon, Mrs. Snyder's aunt; with Watson still chaffing from having to work on a Sunday when he expected to be enjoying a leisurely day in reading, napping, and smoking.

"It is hardly proper, Holmes, to be making a visit to a woman's house on an early Sunday afternoon without an appointment. I do not understand what the hurry is all about."

"Dear Watson, we must strike while the iron is hot. Come, pay the driver, and let us visit with Mrs. McKinnon and see what we can learn."

Holmes rang the bell, and the door was quickly answered by his client, Mrs. Snyder. "Mr. Holmes, so good to see you again so soon. Have you news for me already?"

"I am afraid not, Mrs. Snyder. We wish to visit with your aunt if she is available?"

"Why yes, Mr. Holmes. Come with me. She is in the parlor. Hello, Dr. Watson. It is good to see you as well."

"Thank you, Mrs. Snyder. I apologize for the interruption on a Sunday afternoon." Watson followed behind Holmes as Mrs. Snyder led the way to the parlor.

The parlor was a small room, eclectically decorated, a room very much of a thinking person. It had several windows overlooking the back of the home and the garden. The windows were open and the sound of the birds in the garden gave the room a peaceful and homey feel. Holmes looked around the room quickly and then toward Mrs. McKinnon who was seated in a settee just in front of one of the windows. She put down a book that she was reading as Holmes approached her and stood.

"Mrs. McKinnon, I am Sherlock Holmes, and this is my colleague and friend Dr. Watson. Your niece has retained me in the matter of Mr. Holcomb's death. I would like to ask you some questions."

"Mr. Holmes, it is good to meet you. I confess that I am aware of your reputation, and I was glad that Brenda followed my advice and came to see you. I do not know what I can add, but I am grateful that you have agreed to help poor Brenda. First the death of her husband, and now this horrible accident that befell her fiancé. Please sit."

Watson sat in one of the chairs next to the settee and Mrs. Snyder sat next to her aunt on the settee.

"I will stand, if you do not mind, Mrs. McKinnon. How long have you known Mr. Holcomb?"

Mrs. McKinnon was a slim and feminine woman in her middle fifties. Her hair was a mixed grey and white, but the mixture of colors was attractive, and her hair was thick and well-coiffed. She had a pleasant smile and gray eyes that seemed to always laugh with happiness as she looked at you. She wore a dress of pearl grey, and her hands were graceful and delicate. She had an air of refinement and confidence about her.

"I have known Mr. Holcomb for about eight months, after Brenda introduced him to me. We did not spend a lot of time together, but he and Brenda would sometimes spend a Sunday afternoon with me here in this very room. We had good discussions. Mr. Holcomb had simple taste and though he knew a great deal about the law, he was little read in other matters."

"I am sure that those visits were very enjoyable and looked forward to," said Watson as he looked at Mrs. McKinnon with a smile.

"Yes, they were." Mrs. Snyder's eyes filled with tears, as she sat next to her aunt. She took out a lady's handkerchief and began to dab at the corners of her eyes.

"And did Mr. Holcomb have any unpleasant habits? Was he quick to anger? Did he suffer from bouts of melancholy?" Holmes asked while looking again around the room.

"Mr. Holmes, Mr. Holcomb was a quiet and unassuming man. A respectable solicitor who kept very much to himself. He worked hard and he doted over my Brenda. To suggest anything else so quickly after his horrible death, is quite beyond my understanding." Mrs. McKinnon sat straight with her hands in her lap looking directly at Holmes as he turned his attention back to her with a quizzical smile and a look of wonder in his eyes.

"Mr. Holmes does not mean to offend you, Mrs. McKinnon. He simply needs to understand the situation and what kind of man that the poor Mr. Holcomb was. That is all." Watson spoke in his most soothing and gentle voice. Holmes cleared his throat, rolled his eyes, and took a step or two away from Mrs. McKinnon, looking at some flowers on a tea table in the room.

"Mrs. McKinnon, I advise you to answer my questions carefully and truthfully. I am simply trying to get to the bottom of this very unfortunate affair. Now, did Mr. Holcomb ever speak of any enemies, anyone who wanted to do him harm?"

"No, Mr. Holmes!" Both Mrs. McKinnon and Mrs. Snyder answered at the same time.

"Mr. Holmes, I am answering your questions directly and carefully. I simply do not agree with the insinuations and assumptions in your questions." Mrs. McKinnon was now openly frustrated.

"Did he have any unfortunate habits? Did he drink, for instance?" Holmes returned his gaze to Mrs. McKinnon and looked her directly in the eyes.

"No more than any other man and never to excess, Mr. Holmes." Mrs. McKinnon stood and faced Holmes directly.

"Did he frequent any gentlemen's establishments? Was he a member of any clubs?"

Mrs. McKinnon looked over at her niece as if to say, she was finished answering Holmes's questions.

"Mr. Holmes, I can assure you that my Robby was a hard-working, decent, and well-respected man. His life was taken up with his work as a solicitor and the time he spent with me. There were no shadows on our relationship and nothing of the sort that you are suggesting," answered Mrs. Snyder.

"I am sorry, ladies. I am suggesting nothing. I make no insinuations. I merely ask to get a better picture of the situation between you two and the unfortunate Mr. Holcomb. Now, anything at all that you can tell me further? Did Mr. Holcomb gamble, for instance or frequent women of the evening?"

"What?" exclaimed Mrs. Snyder. "I should say not!"

"I can only say that what I know of Mr. Holcomb and how he treated my Brenda, makes it completely unfathomable that he would be engaged in such activities; and, how his death could have come in so, in so…grotesque a manner." Mrs. McKinnon looked at Holmes very directly and was emphatic in her answer.

"What a lovely garden you have, Mrs. McKinnon. The bees fly about, and the birds sing. How tranquil and peaceful is the garden. And yet, if I were to make a closer inspection of the garden and its inhabitants, I would find the resident spiders with their webs. What a different impression one would get, upon focusing on the hunters in the garden rather than the bees and the flowers. Life in London can be very much like that. On first impression a busy place of business and society, and yet upon closer inspection there are spiders and hunters in our fair city." Holmes fell silent as he contemplated the garden.

Mrs. McKinnon looked aghast, as did Mrs. Snyder. Watson stood and quickly filled the silence left by Holmes's comments, "It has been a pleasure meeting you, Mrs.

McKinnon. Very good to see you again so soon, Mrs. Snyder. We have taken up enough of your time on so nice a Sunday afternoon."

"It has been a pleasure meeting you as well, Dr. Watson. Mr. Holmes, I wish that there was more that I could tell you, but there is simply no more to tell. Thank you for your visit. May I show you out?" Mrs. McKinnon motioned with her left arm the way to the front door.

Holmes broke his reverie and looking around the room as if he had forgotten where he was, said, "Ahh, yes. You are right Watson. Thank you, ladies. Good afternoon." And with that Holmes abruptly left the room leaving Watson to say goodbyes and follow him out into the street.

"Holmes that was both very rude and in bad taste. Those poor ladies are suffering in grief over the death of Mr. Holcomb, and you showed no compassion or understanding at all." Watson was angry.

"Watson, as I have said before, my clients do not come to me for sympathy and understanding. For that they can visit a priest. No, they are not telling me something. They are protecting Mr. Holcomb. A respectable solicitor who, how did she put it, 'keeps very much to himself,' does not come to such an end in the middle of a Saturday night. Not at all. Something is amiss." Holmes had stopped on the walkway outside the house and was frustratingly striking the ground with his walking stick. "They are prevaricating, Watson. I am afraid the only way to get at the truth will be to visit the solicitor's offices tomorrow. We can do nothing else on a Sunday afternoon."

Watson was looking at Holmes with easing discomfort and his demeanor began to relax. "Still, old man, you must be more aware of how you affect people."

"Watson, I do not like being lied to and both of those ladies, including our client, are hiding something to protect the man's reputation. Something that could be particularly important to our investigation. You are too frequently taken in by a woman's beauty and your desire to shield and protect." Holmes stopped tapping his walking stick against the ground and let out a sigh. "Well Watson, back to Baker Street, hey? I have no data, and it is a capital mistake to conjecture and theorize without data. So back to Baker Street and a late lunch?"

Watson scoffed and began to say something, but then relaxed his posture. "Yes, Holmes. Lunch would be much appreciated. And perhaps some peace and quiet. No conundrums to vex us on this lovely Sunday afternoon."

Chapter 3

Late Monday afternoon, Holmes and Watson arrived by hansom in the central part of London, near the western boundary of the City and the Royal Courts of Justice in the legal quarter, where the solicitors' offices of Avery & Middleton were located. Holmes leapt from the hansom and was at the front door before Watson had the chance to pay the driver. "Come along, Watson."

"I am coming as fast as I can, Holmes. The driver needed paying." Watson looked frustrated and did not like to be hurried.

Holmes opened the door, entered the firm, and stopped to look about. The foyer was a small room with a small fireplace, chairs for sitting, and a clerk behind a large wooden desk. Behind the clerk was a half-wall, and behind that was a maze of desks and clerks busy with their work.

"May I help you gentlemen?" asked the clerk from behind his desk.

"Yes, my name is Sherlock Holmes, and this is my friend and colleague Dr. Watson. I would like to see the managing solicitor please?"

"And what may I ask is your business with Mr. Zamarron?"

"We are here regarding the death of Robert Holcomb."

The clerk's face immediately changed as a shadow seemed to pass over his eyes and he looked down at his desk. "Very bad business, what? Poor Mr. Holcomb was a good solicitor, one of the firm's finest, and just engaged to be married too. Very bad business."

"Yes, bad business. Is Mr. Zamarron available?"

"If you will please wait here, gentlemen, I will check to see if Mr. Zamarron is available to see you. He is not always here you know. Clients' demands and court dates take a great deal of his time." With that the clerk rose and opening the swinging half-door disappeared into the maze of desks.

Holmes stood by the cold fireplace as Watson sat in one of the chairs. "Have you considered, Watson, where we would be without the law and Her Majesty's justice? What a barbaric and loathsome place London would be without its laws and its courts. It is a wonder that we get along at all and are capable of even the most basic of ordered society given the work performed in this place, in the courts, and my own contributions to holding back the flood of crime that constantly threatens to overwhelm our fair city. It is a gift that Her Majesty gives us and the world – the law and justice. Still, I wonder at times if our question should not be, 'Why don't people commit crimes?' rather than, 'Why do people commit crimes?'"

"That is a bit depressing, Holmes. Surely, crime is the exception to an otherwise orderly and congenial society."

"I am not so sure, Watson."

Holmes and Watson were interrupted by the return of the clerk bringing along a tall, thin, and respectable man. He was clean shaven, dressed in the black suit of his trade, and had an air of confidence and objectivity about him.

"Mr. Holmes, may I introduce Mr. Robert Zamarron, our managing solicitor here at Avery & Middleton."

"Mr. Holmes, it is indeed a pleasure to meet you. You must be Dr. Watson," Mr. Zamarron shook Watson's hand

and turned his attention back to Holmes. "It is indeed lucky that you find me here, I have one or two matters in the courts this week that demand my attention." Mr. Zamarron stopped and looked at Holmes. "I must confess that I have read about your exploits in *The Strand* and am pleased to meet you. But what would you have to do with Mr. Holcomb's death? I understand from the papers that it was all a terrible accident brought on by a sudden attack of insanity."

"Perhaps if we could talk in your office, Mr. Zamarron?" asked Holmes.

"Of course, just this way gentlemen." Mr. Zamarron led Holmes and Watson through the crowded room of clerks and desks, toward the far end of the building where his office was located. The clerks looked up from their work as the three walked towards the office but remained quiet and focused. For all its people, the large room was remarkably quiet, except for the sound of an occasional muffled voice, the scratching sound of old quills on paper, and the shuffling of the paper itself.

Mr. Zamarron cleared his throat as he walked and soon the three were at his office door. "This way if you please, gentlemen." Holmes and Watson walked into the solicitor's office as he followed and closed the door behind them. Mr. Zamarron took his seat behind his desk and with his hands clasped in front of him looked up at Holmes and said, "Now, how may I help you Mr. Holmes?"

Isadora Persano's office on Fleet Street was a storm of papers. There were papers all over his desk and stacks of papers on the floor around the room. His typewriter was front and center on his desk and surrounding it were note pads, several pencils, pens, several bottles of ink of different colors, empty whiskey glasses, and the bits and pieces from his habit of rolling his own cigarettes. Behind the desk was a credenza that was stacked two feet high with old newspapers. Tacked to the walls were cut-outs of stories he had written, mixed with small ink drawings of famous racing horses.

Unlike the state of his office, Persano was a neatly dressed man in his late thirties. He was tall and had an athletic built. His black hair was well combed and shined with the hair tonic he used to keep it in place. His mustache was long and curled at each end with wax. He was dressed immaculately. He was a handsome man, and he knew it. He sat drinking what was left of his glass of whiskey while looking over the latest edition to his continuing series of stories investigating the private clubs of London and the secret lives of the city's rich and powerful. He took delight in exposing the true natures and habits of the rich and powerful. He especially enjoyed ruining the occasional reputation and delighted in the infrequent suicide brought on by his work. As he sat and read over the draft of his latest expose, he was interrupted by loud voices outside his closed door, and the sound of heavy boots on the wood floor. As he looked up, the door to his office was forced open with a loud bang.

"I beg your pardon. What is the meaning of this?" Persano dropped his copy and stood angrily behind his desk.

The man who entered was a large and heavily built man with a full grizzled beard of red and grey. He was built like a prize fighter and his large hands shook a heavy walking stick in the direction of Persano.

"You, sir, are no gentleman! These damn stories that you are writing about the esteemed members of London society must end and must end now. Your most recent account in last week's paper has ruined me in society. The fine lady to whom I was engaged to be married has called off the wedding, thanks to your meddling and gossip. I have become a pariah in my former social circles. You have ruined me, man!"

Persano smiled, "Sir Lyle Hammersmith, I have done nothing but expose to the light of day the seedy and disgusting habits that you and your kind engage in behind the locked doors of private clubs. You, Sir, have ruined yourself."

"What a man does behind closed doors is his own business. You have no right to expose the private affairs of men and women to the world. You have no right to ruin the lives of those whom you expose to public ridicule and embarrassment." Sir Lyle shook with anger and his voice rumbled like thunder as he spoke.

"I am afraid that my time is precious and that I must ask you to leave my office immediately." Persano pointed towards the still open door and the faces of several men outside who watched as the scene played out.

"So, you will not cease? You will not stand down? You will continue this...this inquisition?"

"My dear Sir, I have no intention of stopping until every one of you is exposed and until the people of London know your true characters."

"Then you leave me no choice. I will have satisfaction. Your reputation as a duelist is well known. This is a matter of my reputation and honor. You have publicly humiliated me. Will you defend what you have written with your body, or will you publicly apologize, withdraw the story in writing, and publish both in your paper?"

Persano laughed, "I will make no apology and no retraction. I stand by my story."

"Do you have a representative with whom I should arrange the matter, or do I deal directly with you?"

"You may deal with me."

"You shall hear from me by telegram within twenty-four hours with the date, time, and place to settle this matter. Are you agreed?"

"I look forward to it. As you are the challenger, it is for me to select the weapons. I select swords. Please make the arrangements accordingly and discreetly."

"You shall pay for what you have done." With that Sir Lyle turned and walked swiftly away.

Persano smiled to himself, satisfied that his story had given him an opportunity to hurt, not only with pen, but now with sword. He sat and continued his work.

———————————

Holmes looked around Zamarron's office as Watson sat at one of the two chairs in the room in front of Zamarron's desk. Zamarron looked impatient as Holmes continued his examination of the room.

"Would you take a seat, Mr. Holmes?"

"No, thank you, I prefer to stand. Tell me, Mr. Zamarron, what kind of man was Robert Holcomb?"

"He was a good and honest man. A good solicitor and lived a quiet life."

"Did he have any bad habits? Women, opium, cocaine, alcohol? That sort of thing?"

"Mr. Holmes, at Avery & Middleton we do not hire that sort of man. Our clients put their trust in us, and we return that trust by being upright citizens of Her Majesty's kingdom. I know of no black mark against Robert. None whatsoever." Zamarron's face was flushed, and he leaned forward as if to drive home his point.

"Mr. Zamarron, Mr. Holmes meant no disrespect to yourself, the firm, or Mr. Holcomb. These are questions that Holmes must ask as we investigate Mr. Holcomb's death." Watson spoke up quickly before Holmes could respond.

"Investigation? What is there to investigate? Who hired you, Mr. Holmes?"

"Mrs. Brenda Snyder asked us to investigate the matter. Don't you think Mr. Holcomb's death is a bit out of the ordinary for a man of quiet habits and how did you say it? Oh yes, 'an upright citizen of Her Majesty's kingdom'?"

"Mrs. Snyder is a lovely woman, but she cannot keep a man. Perhaps you should be investigating her." Zamarron stopped, took a deep breath, straightened his waistcoat, and calmed himself. "Mr. Holmes I am sorry if I lost my temper, but we are all a bit, well, distraught at the moment. I did not know Holcomb well. We did not socialize outside the firm."

"Is there anyone here who did know him well?"

Zamarron cleared his throat and looked a bit uncomfortable. He hesitated and then said, "Well, yes. One of our secretaries, Miss Lauren Pearl, was more acquainted with him. She and Mr. Holcomb were close, it was expected that they would be engaged, that is until our late colleague, Mr. William Snyder, was killed by a deranged client. Mrs. Snyder is the widow. It was then that Mr. Holcomb began to care for Mrs. Snyder's affairs after the death of her husband. It seems the two became close and Mr. Holcomb broke it off with Miss Pearl. Holcomb and Mrs. Snyder have been engaged for a couple of months; I believe."

"Is Miss Pearl here today?"

"Yes, I believe so, why?"

"I would like to speak with her please."

"I will see if she is available." Zamarron stood and walked to his office door, opening it slightly and asked someone outside to bring in Miss Pearl. Closing the door he said, "She will be here shortly, Mr. Holmes. What makes you think anyone here at the firm has anything to do with Holcomb's death?"

"I have not said anyone here has anything to do with Mr. Holcomb's death. I cannot tell what might come of speaking with those who knew him, though."

"Mr. Holmes is very thorough in his methods, Mr. Zamarron. Please do not make any assumptions about why he is doing what he does." Watson stood as the door opened and a lovely young lady entered.

Miss Lauren Pearl was a tall, young woman, with a thin but attractive appearance with blond hair neatly styled like a crown above her head. Her blue eyes looked nervously at the three men in the room, as her fine, long fingers moved quickly from her chest to her waist and back again.

"Yes, Mr. Zamarron. I understand that you wanted to see me."

"Actually it is Mr. Sherlock Holmes here who wants to speak with you. He wants to ask you about Mr. Holcomb." Zamarron motioned for Miss Pearl to sit in the empty chair next to Watson.

Miss Pearl's eyes grew large and her hands began to shake. She stood like a statue looking first at Watson and then at Holmes, her pretty, feminine features showing concern. "About Robert?"

"Yes, Miss Pearl, about Mr. Holcomb. Please sit." Holmes looked at Miss Pearl with cold indifference.

"Miss Pearl, I am Dr. Watson and this Mr. Sherlock Holmes. We have been asked to investigate the death of Mr. Holcomb and we understand that you were, eh, acquainted with him both professionally and, eh, socially. Mr. Holmes just has some questions to ask you. Nothing to be worried about at all." Watson, who was standing as Miss Pearl entered the room, moved the empty chair back to allow her to sit.

"Yes, Mr. Holcomb and I were acquainted and had even discussed marriage. I have been deeply disturbed by his untimely and strange death. I am in fact quite shaken by his passing, as we all are." Miss Pearl took a lady's handkerchief from the sleeve of her blouse and began to wipe tears from her eyes as she sat.

"Miss Pearl, were you not angered by Mr. Holcomb's decision to cut-off his relationship with you and pursue another with Mrs. Snyder?" Holmes looked directly into Miss Pearl's eyes.

"I admit that I was both angry and embarrassed by what happened, but that has all passed, Mr. Holmes. It is surely yesterday's news and has nothing to do with what has happened to the unfortunate Mr. Holcomb. I feel only pity for poor Mrs. Snyder who has lost one husband and a fiancé in such a brief a period of time."

"I am sure. What kind of man was Mr. Holcomb?"

"He was a fine solicitor and a gentleman."

"Yes, I am sure he was. Did you know him to have any unfortunate habits? Drinking perhaps?"

"No! He had no bad habits that I was aware of, Mr. Holmes. He was a very private man. He worked hard, kept to himself, and was quiet in his ways. I knew him only to be a gentleman. We saw each other socially at least once per week – usually Friday evenings and occasionally Sunday afternoons. He went to his club for whist three nights a week and was very regular in his habits."

"Did you know him to ever have any occasional bouts of mania, nervousness, or depression?"

"Absolutely not. Mr. Holmes, there was nothing that I could ever say that would explain his sudden madness or why he ran into the street only to be run over by a carriage. Nothing." Miss Pearl began to softly cry and covered her face with her handkerchief.

Watson leaned forward and putting his hand on Miss Pearl's shoulder softly consoled her. "Holmes, I think the young lady has had quite enough questioning for now."

"You said that Mr. Holcomb was a member of a club and attended frequently. Do you remember the name of the club?" Holmes had steepled his hands in front of his face and turned away from Miss Pearl.

"I do not remember, Mr. Holmes. Mr. Zamarron, may I please go now?"

Zamarron looked at Holmes and then at Miss Pearl, "Mr. Holmes are you quite finished with Miss Pearl?"

"Are you sure you cannot remember the name of the club? Miss Pearl, it is important that you tell me all that you know, even if it seems to count against him."

"I do not remember, Mr. Holmes. Mr. Holcomb went to the club with Mr. Gurel, another solicitor in the firm. I just know that he and Mr. Holcomb would attend whist at the club three nights a week. That is all that I remember."

"Did Mr. Holcomb have any enemies? Anyone that might want to do him harm?"

"Mr. Holmes, I think that this questioning has gone on long enough. I can tell you that Mr. Holcomb had no enemies to speak of and lived a respectable and quiet life. He was a good solicitor and represented his clients' interest well and was an outstanding member of the firm." Zamarron stood and moved toward Miss Pearl. "Lauren, I am sure that Mr. Holmes has no further questions. You may return to your work."

"Thank you, Miss Pearl. I know that these are difficult times and Mr. Holmes and I appreciate your patience and your assistance." Watson stood and helped Miss Pearl to stand, as Zamarron opened his office door to let her out.

"One last question, Miss Pearl. May you lift your skirts just enough for me to observe you shoes?"

Miss Pearl looked at Zamarron who nodded yes, and Miss Pearl complied. Holmes knelt and looked at Miss Pearl's shoes and then stood.

"Thank you, Miss Pearl." Holmes turned away and seemed to be examining an old manuscript, framed on the wall as Miss Pearl wiped her face and stood gracefully regaining her composure and left the office with a quiet swish of skirts.

"Is Mr. Gurel in the office today?" Holmes asked.

"We are a busy firm, Mr. Holmes. I must ask how much more time this is going to take?" Zamarron stood behind his desk very much beside himself.

"Not long, Mr. Zamarron. Please, may I see Mr. Gurel?"

Zamarron angrily stepped across his office, opened his door, and asked that Mr. Gurel be sent for. He closed the door to his office with a bang and walked swiftly back to his desk and sat down staring at Holmes with disdain.

"Thank you, Mr. Zamarron."

Watson sat, uncomfortable with the silence as all three waited for Mr. Gurel. The office door opened and a tall young man with longish hair and a thin mustache and goatee entered the room.

"You wanted to see me, Mr. Zamarron?" asked the young man.

"Samuel, this is Mr. Sherlock Holmes and Dr. Watson. They are investigating Holcomb's death and want to ask you some questions. Do you have a few minutes to oblige them?" Zamarron's patience had run its course.

"Uh, I suppose so. Which of you is Mr. Holmes?"

"I am Sherlock Holmes, and you are Mr. Samuel Gurel?"

"Yes. But why do you want to speak with me about Mr. Holcomb's death? I know absolutely nothing about it, save what I have read in the papers."

"You and Mr. Holcomb were members of a private club, were you not?"

"Yes. We were. Why do you ask?"

"Do you mind telling me the name of the club?"

"Mr. Holmes, private clubs are just that...private. Why should I tell you what club Mr. Holcomb and I were members of?"

"Because it may be important to solving the riddle of what happened to Mr. Holcomb."

"I do not see that there is any great riddle, Mr. Holmes. Mr. Holcomb became insane, by some means or method unknown to anyone, ran out into the street, and was run over by a carriage. That all seems clear. What might our club have had to do with that?"

"Mr. Gurel, I do not know. It may have nothing to do with it and it may be the key to why Mr. Holcomb is dead. Nevertheless, I ask you again, what was the name of the private club that you and Mr. Holcomb frequented?"

"Mr. Holmes, you are a very rude and meddlesome man. You drive hard and inquire into matters that are none of your business. I am a busy man and I have work to do. Mr. Zamarron, if that is all, may I attend to my duties?" Gurel stepped toward the office door and had his hand on the doorknob. Before Zamarron could answer, Holmes stepped toward Gurel, pointing a finger toward his chest.

"Mr. Gurel, you may be aware of my reputation enough to understand that I can have Scotland Yard here and they will not take your lack of cooperation as patiently as I do. I have asked you a simple question, a question that may be important to resolving the reason Mr. Holcomb met his end as he did. You are a solicitor, and I presume you know the law. I am sure that Mr. Zamarron and this firm would find it inconvenient to them and troubling to your clients, to have Scotland Yard here asking the questions. Now, I ask one last time, what is the name of the private club that you and Mr. Holcomb frequented?"

Gurel hesitated, looking at Holmes and studying his face. He looked at Watson who was now standing as if prepared to defend Holmes. He looked at Zamarron who nodded his head.

"The Gemini Club." With that Gurel opened the door and left the office.

Chapter 4

Rebecca St. John was seated at her desk in her office at the Gemini Club. Scott and Steven Sobotta, the "Twins," were seated in the two chairs in front of her desk. They were deep in muted discussion.

"We think we have sufficient documented proof, in the form of written testimonials and the photographs that we took surreptitiously, to have a serious conversation with Lord Beckwith. Given his position at the House of Lords, we think that he will be agreeable to pay a significant sum to keep this news out of the paper," Scott Sobotta finished and looked quietly at Miss St. John. The two twins sat at the edge of their seats.

"Miss St. John, I agree with Scott. Beckwith's taste for adolescent boys could be very damaging to him, his reputation, his career, and his family name. Not to mention the ruin of his marriage and social status. We will hardly need to point these consequences out to him. He will pay." Steven looked over at Scott and both turned back toward Miss St. John, mirror images of each other.

Becca thought about the information that she had. She had testimonials from five different boys in her hire and several photographs of the Lord *in flagrante delicto* – but was it sufficient? She knew better than to take a shot at a dangerous and powerful person without the shot being sufficient to end his life. Simply wounding her target was insufficient and dangerous.

"Do we have anything else that we might add to the soup before we serve it to the Lord?" she asked.

"He has gambling debts, but that's hardly a surprise for a person of his stature. No, we think that this will be sufficient. Lady Beckwith is a very devout and conservative person, from an equally devout and conservative family, she would publicly denounce him, it would surely end in divorce with the Lord not nearly so rich as he is now." Scott folded the file in front of him and simply waited for Miss St. John to make the decision.

"All right, let's set-up a meeting with his Lordship and make the pitch. Have we arrived at an appropriate figure?"

Steven looked down at his notes, "Yes, we think five thousand pounds should be sufficient and something that will hurt him a bit but is well within his current means."

"Do we use one of our intermediaries or is this one that you want me to handle personally? I am not sure I want to part with the usual ten percent fee for the intermediary, but I also want to protect the reputation of the club and my anonymity."

"We both discussed this, and we agree that an intermediary would be wise. We know that His Lordship is a member of more than one club, and he will likely not know from which this information comes. The other club he attends frequently is Smithwick's Gentlemen's Club – the one recently exposed by Persano, but His Lordship's name was not associated with Persano's story." Scott smiled to himself; he knew that much of the information about Smithwick's, used in Persano's story, came from sources under Miss St.

John's hire – a tactic to increase membership in the Gemini Club and reduce the competition.

"Okay, let's get this done. I want a report on the outcome within the week. Anything else, gentlemen?"

"Yes, we had a recent inquiry from Sir Lyle Hammersmith. It happens that his name appeared prominently in Persano's recent article, and he confronted Persano asking for a retraction. When Persano refused, Sir Lyle challenged him to a duel. He would like to hold the duel here. We understand that the choice of weapons is swords, so we can set-up one of the larger rooms as a fencing studio. He is willing to pay a handsome sum for the use of the facilities and of course for our expected discretion." This was an unusual request, Steven knew, but it was an opportunity to make a nice profit and gain something on the famous dueler himself, Persano.

"Interesting proposition. How much did he say he was willing to pay?"

"Two thousand pounds, and the room fee of five hundred pounds."

"Men and their egos. I am assuming that this is just the ordinary practice these days – first blood and it's over?"

"The way that Hammersmith described it and the level of vitriol I saw in him, I am afraid that either or both men may get carried away. This may be to the death."

"Even better for our crusade against Mr. Persano. But we will need to be careful. I want this staged so as not be come back on me or the club. Understood?"

"Yes, Miss St. John. Scott and I will make the necessary preparations ourselves using our usual tact and discretion."

Holmes and Watson were back at Baker Street having finished their late lunch. Holmes was pacing the room as Watson sat in his usual chair by the unlit fireplace. The windows facing Baker Street were open and a breeze blew the curtains into the room like sails on a ship.

"Holmes, we should take advantage of the beautiful day and go for a walk in the park."

"Not at the moment, Watson. This case, it intrigues me. Something is amiss, I feel it in my bones. Gentlemen solicitors who live quiet, unassuming lives, do not come to such ends. There is nothing to support the theory that Holcomb was of a nervous and sensitive disposition. Nothing, so far, to indicate that he had brain fever or that anything happened in his life to drive him to sudden madness. There was nothing in his rooms to indicate some illicit drug. No one says that he took opium, cocaine, or some other drug that might lead him to experience a bout of insanity." Holmes stopped his pacing and looked toward the windows and Baker Street. "A hansom has just pulled up in front of our doors," Holmes walked quickly toward the windows. "It is Mrs. McKinnon. Interesting."

"Holmes, your ears are positively inhuman."

The bell rang below, and Holmes walked toward the door to his rooms and opening it said in a loud voice, "Mrs. Hudson, please show Mrs. McKinnon up. Thank you."

Holmes walked toward the fireplace and stood alongside Watson as they waited for Mrs. McKinnon to arrive. She came into the room presenting a lovely, confident, and feminine pose. With a smile she approached Holmes with an outstretched, gloved, hand.

"Mr. Holmes, I trust that you are not inconvenienced by my unannounced visit? Returning the favor, as it were."

Holmes gently shook the lady's hand, as did Watson, and motioned for Mrs. McKinnon to take a seat on the settee.

"It is good to see you again, Mrs. McKinnon. To what do I owe the pleasure of your visit?" Holmes sat in his own chair, crossing his legs, and looking relaxed, as though he expected Mrs. McKinnon's visit.

"I would very much like to speak with you alone, Mr. Holmes. I am sorry, Dr. Watson, but what I have to share I share is only with you Mr. Holmes." Mrs. McKinnon was in the act of taking off her gloves, and having finished both that and her statement, looked Watson straight in the eyes.

Watson rose to leave, but Holmes stopped him with a gesture. "I am afraid that it is both or neither of us, Mrs. McKinnon. Dr. Watson shares everything with me." Watson stopped in mid-attempt to sit back down as Mrs. McKinnon continued.

"Mr. Holmes, what I have to say is both personal and professional. The personal part I will share with you alone. If you wish, the professional part can be shared with both of you. Oh, I see you are confused, Dr. Watson. Please sit." Mrs.

McKinnon let out a little chuckle as she saw Watson in the middle of sitting or standing.

"Thank you, Mrs. McKinnon." Watson sat down.

"Mr. Holmes, I will get right to the point regarding the professional matter I wish to speak with you about. Neither my niece nor I was completely truthful with you when you visited earlier. In part to protect Mr. Holcomb's reputation, and in part because we simply didn't know you well enough. Brenda and I discussed it at length and came to the decision that I would come around and fill in the deleted details."

"I appreciate that, Mrs. McKinnon. I was aware that you and Mrs. Snyder were keeping details from me. It is refreshing, is it not Watson, that you have come of your own volition to amend your interview."

"Well, yes Holmes. I am sure that this fine lady was only acting with the best of intentions."

"Indeed I was, Dr. Watson. My late husband left me well off and of independent means. I find that…liberating, Mr. Holmes. I am in need of no one, and I do not rely on anyone but myself. I educate myself according to my own interests and I am engaged in society to the extent that I wish. I am not your typical woman at the arm of any man. I hope you can appreciate that, Mr. Holmes. I make my own decisions."

"I can see that, Mrs. McKinnon. You are indeed a formidable personality. Now, what have you come to tell me?"

"Mr. Holcomb was as we described him and lived very much as we described, but there was a shadow on his life. That shadow was women and drink. He could go for days without a drink, but when the mood struck him, he would spend the night at his club, drinking and womanizing with that friend of his, Mr. Gurel. There were frequent Saturdays when Brenda and I would go to his club to retrieve him, and he would convalesce at my home.

"He was always very contrite and apologetic once the drink wore off. He would swear never to do it again. His oath would last a few days, until the need for both drink and women would strike him again…and Mr. Gurel's demands finally broke him down. No, I blame Mr. Gurel as much as I do Mr. Holcomb."

"And how did Mrs. Snyder respond to these fits of immorality and drink?"

"In her stride, Mr. Holmes. Brenda was convinced that once married, when Mr. Holcomb could have access to her, that he would get over the need for other women. She was convinced that her attentions and her love would take the place of the alcohol and the women. She could not be convinced otherwise. Believe me, I tried.

"You must understand, Mr. Holmes, Brenda was lonely and afraid. She is very much the opposite of me. She needs a man and feels very much incomplete without one. She wants children, Mr. Holmes. To the world, Mr. Holcomb was a quiet and unassuming man of the law. Very respectable and to be trusted. And for the most part he was, save for this one weakness. She envisioned a quiet life of respectability, married to a solicitor, with two children and a fairly easy way of life. She is not getting younger and felt the cold embrace of age gaining on her. Mr. Holcomb, she believed, was her last chance at the life she wished for. And so, I helped her hide his weakness from the world and to protect his reputation."

"I see. We have met Mr. Gurel, and he informed us of this club. It is the Gemini Club. Correct?"

"Yes. That is correct. It is no different from a hundred other clubs like it in the city. Where men go to meet their needs and to engage in their habits. Men are weak, Mr. Holmes. Oh, they act strong and in charge, but they are slaves to their lower instincts. Mr. Holcomb was no different and he was better than most.

"Well that is the professional part of my visit. Now I must ask Dr. Watson to leave us so that I may pursue the personal reason for my visit." Mrs. McKinnon looked at Watson with an expression of both strength and request.

"Mrs. McKinnon, I will leave you with Holmes. No, Holmes. I am happy to acquiesce to her request. I will be upstairs in my room. It was a pleasure to see you again, Mrs. McKinnon." Watson stood and left Holmes and her alone.

Holmes looked somewhat ill at ease. He stood in front of the cold fireplace, choosing a pipe with his back to Mrs. McKinnon.

"Mr. Holmes, please sit and allow me to speak to you, person to person."

Holmes left his pipe choosing and sat down again, looking at Mrs. McKinnon with trepidation. "Please, get to the point, Mrs. McKinnon."

"I will. As I said, by way of introduction, Mr. Holmes, I am a single woman, my husband having died several years ago. I am independent financially and I do not need a man to support me. But I am also a woman who likes the company of a man from time-to-time. You, sir, if you do not mind my saying, are an intelligent and very eligible bachelor, are you not? I mean to say, I would be very much agreeable with having dinner and conversation with you, if you too are interested."

Holmes's eyes grew large, and he sat up very straight in his chair. "I am not accustomed to a woman being so straightforward with her intentions, Mrs. McKinnon."

"I am not surprised, Mr. Holmes. I am not a typical Victorian woman. But surely others have been interested in you? You are a prodigious intellect, a well-known man, by reputation you are honest, and you are a professional. A man who has created his own profession. I have read Dr. Watson's stories about your exploits, and they show you to be a brave, resourceful, strong, and hardworking man. What I propose, is a friendship and companionship. Where it may lead, we cannot know. Do you not find me attractive?"

Holmes stood and offered his hand to Mrs. McKinnon.

"Mrs. McKinnon, my work is my life. If you have read of my exploits, you will know that I find a relationship of the kind you describe at best a distraction and at worst the destruction of what I have worked so hard to maintain – a mind free of emotional commitments and pleasures that serve to distract from that which is necessary for me to ply my trade. Even for one such as yourself. I thank you for your visit, but I must hasten this interview to its conclusion."

Mrs. McKinnon stood while Holmes held her hand. She looked Holmes very carefully in the eyes, as if to understand the man. She turned to go, still holding his hand.

"Mr. Holmes, I am sad for you. You have chosen a life of solitude. A monk's life really. I sense that this is the cost of your prodigious talents and what you give to the world?"

"Yes. I am afraid so, Mrs. McKinnon. Such is the cost."

Mrs. McKinnon let go of Holmes's hand and walked gracefully toward the door and stopped as she opened it. "I am much taken with you, Mr. Holmes. You are someone to be admired. I will always consider your response very much a lost opportunity. I will honor your decision, but if you ever feel the need for conversation and a woman's intuition and company in service to your work, or just for personal reasons, I am available. Please tell Dr. Watson good day for me. And I wish you a good day as well. Thank you, Mr. Holmes."

A swish of skirts and the door closed. Holmes fell back into his chair, his face flushed. He looked about the room as if not knowing what to do next. He retrieved his violin from beside his chair and began to play. A piece very much slow, sweet, and melancholy.

Watson had fallen asleep laying on his bed while reading a book. It was just beginning to get dark, and he was very hungry. He looked at his watch, it was nearly half pass eight in the evening. He stood and shaking the sleep out of his limbs, began to walk down the stairs to the landing in front of Holmes's sitting room. He looked down the seventeen steps just as Mrs. Hudson opened her door and stepped into the foyer.

"Oh, there are you are, Dr. Watson. Are you ready for dinner? I have already eaten myself, but I can bring up your dinner shortly. Mr. Holmes is out."

"Yes, Mrs. Hudson, I am famished. Thank you." Watson walked into the sitting room and turned up the gas. The windows were still open, and Holmes's violin and bow were sitting on his wicker chair. He went over to close the windows and saw a poor beggar hobbling in front of their door on Baker Street. As he watched, the beggar stood up straight, and taking out keys opened the door to 221 B. Watson laughed to himself – it was of course Holmes. He walked over to the door to the rooms and called down the stairs.

"Don't bother with the theatrics Holmes, I saw you come in from the window."

Holmes came up the stairs taking off pieces of his disguise as he climbed the steps. As he entered his rooms, Watson stood there laughing.

"Never take away an artist's opportunity to perform, dear Watson." Holmes began to laugh as well.

"Where have you been dressed like that Holmes?"

"Give me a few minutes to get cleaned up and I'll tell you all about it," Holmes went straight to his bedroom and Watson could hear the sounds of water being poured into the basin and of Holmes cleaning up. A few minutes later and Holmes entered the room dressed as usual and in his mouse-colored dressing gown. Watson was by this time sitting at the table waiting for dinner.

"Have you asked Mrs. Hudson to bring dinner, Watson? I am very hungry."

"Yes, old man. Sit down and tell me all about it."

Holmes walked over to the mantel and chose his long-stemmed cherrywood pipe, filled it, lit it, and stood looking at Watson.

"Well, where to begin? After you left Mrs. McKinnon and I together, and after she left, I sat here playing my violin and thinking about the case. I decided to go to the Gemini Club in the guise of a beggar and keep the area under surveillance. It was a fruitful afternoon. I got to know the area in some detail and after speaking with a fellow beggar or two learned that the establishment is managed by a woman. She has turned the heads of every man in the area, but is infrequently seen, except when she comes and goes at all hours of the day and night.

"The club is mostly busy in the evening and appears to be a very popular establishment. When I sat in the alley way, appearing to be much the worst for drink, I observed several young ladies enter the club through a back entrance. All well-dressed and of several different types, shapes, and hair colors. These were followed by young men and boys of all stripes and sizes as well.

"Just before leaving to come back, I approached the front door of the establishment seeking to use their facilities, and was almost assaulted by two men, identical twins, who physically threw me into the street and ordered me never to return."

Watson laughed, "You are lucky they did not call the local constable to arrest you for trespassing. But not so fast, Holmes. What did Mrs. McKinnon wish to speak with you about?"

Holmes sat in his wicker chair and turned his left side to Watson looking directly in front of himself. "That was very much a private matter, Watson. As a gentleman, I am not at liberty to discuss it."

Watson scoffed and then fell silent. Holmes was serious. His silence told him so. Watson sat and thought for a few minutes in silence and then a smile spread across his face.

"My dear fellow, are you insinuating what I think you are?"

"I am unaware of insinuating anything, Watson. I simply am not at liberty to discuss it."

"Holmes, you are not the only one that can read what is meant but left unsaid. Applying your own methods, I would venture to guess that Mrs. McKinnon expressed an interest in seeing you socially. It was clear to me that she found you fascinating. From the first, her eyes practically shined when she met you. And this afternoon, she hardly acknowledged my presence except to ask me to leave. Have I hit upon it, Holmes?"

"My dear Watson, women are your area of expertise, not mine. I can really say no more."

Mrs. Hudson knocked quietly on the door and entered with dinner, interrupting the conversation. "Should I set a place for you as well, Mr. Holmes?"

"Perhaps for three...hey Holmes," Watson said laughing.

"Yes, Mrs. Hudson, and dinner for two please. Now stop your nonsense, Watson."

Mrs. Hudson looked at both men with confusion, set a place for Holmes, and while waving her hands above her head, left the two of them alone for dinner. As she walked down the stairs, she could hear Watson laughing.

Chapter 5

Rodrick Hudson was not the man he used to be. His shoulders were rounded and bent forward. His eyes were sunken in his head surrounded by dark circles. He was rail thin and breathed with short bursts of wheezing. He was a wreck of a man. Those who knew or worked with him believed him to be suffering from an illness or disease. His body was wracked with pains and his arms were scarred from injecting heroine. He had gradually moved, over the past two years, from the cocktail of laudanum and absinthe he drank at the Gemini Club to injecting heroine into his veins.

He woke this morning in a bed wet with sweat and stinking of body odor. He shook as he got up and walked to the basin for his morning routine. Having shaved with shaking hands and dressed, he looked at himself in the mirror. His heart banged inside his chest, his breathing was irregular, and he frequently had sharp chest pains that made him dizzy and short of breath. He knew that this must stop, but Becca had him in her embrace, and he did not know how to escape. He called her Becca now; such was the nature of their "relationship." She supplied him with his needs and wants, and he did what she required. Appearing to be working at his lab on some obscure research, but in the end, providing her with what she wished. He was an obscure entomologist, in an obscure lab, in London's natural museum. Lost in research, so far as the world knew, and it didn't care or know.

He turned away from the mirror and looked about his rooms, meager as they were. A small bedroom and small sitting room were all he had on the near West End of London.

A single window overlooking the alley behind his building was his view. He rolled up his sleeve and patted the inside of his elbow. He tied a belt around his arm and looked for a vein that wasn't already collapsed from misuse. Taking the syringe, he plunged the needle deep into his vein and injected the liquid that was his life. A much larger amount than usual.

"Ahh, Rodrick my friend, that is what you need. Escape this life. Escape the witch." He shook in involuntary spasm at the mention of "the witch." "What can she do to you now? What can she demand? That witch. The very embodiment of seduction, desire, and death." He put on his jacket and nearly swooned as the drug began to take effect.

He walked out of his building and into the bright sunlight of a warm summer morning, and yet he shivered. He hailed a hansom and getting in told the driver to take him to the natural museum where he worked, but immediately changed his mind.

"Driver, take me to 221b Baker Street, to the home of Mrs. Martha Hudson."

He fell back into the cushioned seat and closed his eyes. He hadn't seen his mother in years, not since their falling out and his blaming her for the death of his father, some twenty-years ago. Would she even see him after all this time? He closed his eyes as the hansom made its way through London and there was the face of the witch looking back at him.

Holmes was in one of his dark moods, still in his bed clothes and dressing gown, hair uncombed, and his chin unshaven; smoking a cigarette while Watson finished his breakfast.

"Do have something to eat Holmes. The cold beef and eggs are particularly good this morning."

Holmes stared down at his bare feet and simply grumbled in reply. "I am not hungry, Watson."

"What has put you in this dark mood?"

"This infernal case is not revealing anything useful to me, Watson. We need to go to the Gemini Club this evening, but I hardly have the energy for it." Holmes looked over at the desk between the two windows facing Baker Street with a longing expression.

Watson immediately noticed and putting down his cup of tea and clearing his throat said, "You will find no stimulation there, Holmes. You have a case, work it, but do not go to that drawer. I will not allow it." Watson was standing now and threw his napkin to the table.

"Not to worry, Watson. It was just a fleeting thought. Perhaps I will take some coffee."

Their interaction was interrupted by the bell ringing and hard knocking on the front door below.

"Watson, I will see no one this morning!"

Watson walked to the landing just as Mrs. Hudson opened the door and let out a cry of surprise.

"Rodrick, my God, what has happened to you. You look awful." Mrs. Hudson had both hands over her heart and was staring at a shaking, sweaty man in business clothes at the front door.

"Mrs. Hudson, is everything alright?" Watson was at the first step looking down at Mrs. Hudson with concern. As he watched the young man fell forward into Mrs. Hudson's arms grumbling something incoherent. Watson immediately went down the steps as fast as he could and held the young man up by one arm.

"Mrs. Hudson, do you know this man?"

"Yes! Yes, he is my son!"

———————————

It was late afternoon and Watson and Mrs. Hudson were busy trying to ease the pain of Rodrick Hudson who was laying covered in blankets on the settee in Holmes's sitting room. Holmes was dressed and sitting in his chair, leaning forward watching the scene play out in front of him. Holmes had already examined Rodrick's body. He immediately noticed the needle marks on his arms and knew that it meant this man was an addict. He stood and walked over to one of the windows overlooking Baker Street and breathed in the air blowing in from the open windows.

"Mrs. Hudson, I was not aware that you had a son. Do you know how he came to be in this condition?"

"Oh, Mr. Holmes, I haven't any idea. We haven't spoken in several years. After his father, my dear husband, passed he was much changed. He was at university when his father died and coming home afterward, he was much shaken. It was like he was lost deep within himself. He seemed to close out the world and that included me. After university, we had a terrible falling out. He blamed me for his father's death.

I remember him saying, 'Why couldn't it be you, mother? Why did father have to die?' And now he comes home, after all these years, stricken with some terrible illness."

Holmes winced at these last words. He and Watson exchanged glances. "I am sorry, Mrs. Hudson. Very sorry indeed. I must tell you, and it is painful to do so, that Rodrick is not suffering from an illness, but from addiction. The marks on his arms are proof that he has been injecting a drug, likely cocaine or heroin, and is in the throes of a horrible reaction. I would venture to say that his body has had all that it can take of the drug, and he is in his last hours."

Watson took Mrs. Hudson's hand as her other went to her face and she began to cry. "I am afraid that Holmes is right. I must tell you that it doesn't look good for Rodrick. I have never seen such an advanced case. His heart and his body are giving out. I can give him something to ease his pain and suffering and to keep him asleep through the worst of it, but given his physical condition, I am not sure he has the strength to make it through."

Holmes walked to the desk and taking the key at the end of his watch chain, unlocked it and handed Watson his syringe and bottle of cocaine. Watson looked at Holmes as if to reject the notion, but Holmes nodded resignedly.

"Injecting him, Watson, may help his symptoms."

Mrs. Hudson looked on while Watson removed the blankets and bared Rodrick's arm. He administered the cocaine and almost immediately his patient's shaking stopped, and his breathing became more regular. After a few minutes, his eye lids began to flutter.

"He appears to be coming out of it a bit." Watson put the covers back over Rodrick and felt his pulse along his neck. "Heart rate is rapid, but not shallow as before."

"Oh Rodrick. Rodrick. I forgive you son. Please come back to us!" Mrs. Hudson was on her knees beside the settee, her hands clasped in front of her face, and weeping.

Rodrick stirred and opened his eyes in terror. "The witch! The witch! She has me!"

Watson held him down as Rodrick went into a convulsion of delusional yelling and fighting. "Holmes, help me keep him down!"

It took both Watson and Holmes to keep Rodrick down as he shook and yelled out, foaming at the mouth. Mrs. Hudson simply sat on the floor and cried, between bouts of praying. It seemed like hours as Watson and Holmes worked to control Rodrick's fits while Mrs. Hudson cried.

The end came, mercifully, after a quarter hour of fits and incoherent yelling about "The witch." He was suddenly still. His breathing shallow and irregular. Then finally, one last deep breath, and Rodrick breathed no more. Watson felt for a pulse at his neck and finding none looked up at Holmes and shook his head. Mrs. Hudson clung to his limp body as Watson fought back tears. Holmes had moved back to the window and was himself shaken with sadness and grief.

"Watson, we need to make the arrangements. Mrs. Hudson is in no condition to do so. As the physician on scene, will you do the necessaries?"

Watson was sitting on the edge of his usual chair with his head in his hands. By the motion of his shoulders, it was clear that he was crying. He lifted his head to look at Holmes, his face tear-stained and said, "Yes, Holmes, I will contact the coroner. In the meantime, Mrs. Hudson, allow me to cover his face. It is time to say, 'goodbye.'"

Mrs. Hudson gave Rodrick one last hug, a kiss on his forehead, and stood. "I am very grateful to you both. I do not know what I would have done today, without you. He was always a troubled man, after the death of his father. I expected to simply to be informed of his death. I never thought that I would be present. That is a kind of grace is it not? That he came back to me so as not to die alone. I am at least grateful for that."

Watson hugged Mrs. Hudson as she wept into his shoulder. Holmes continued to stand near the window his face drawn and dark with sadness. Mrs. Hudson released her grip on Watson and turned toward Holmes. Holmes stiffened, but Mrs. Hudson's eyes and posture of supplication at last overwhelmed him. He reached out for her, and Mrs. Hudson walked forward and leaned into his arms. Holmes held her without saying a word until she moved away, and with an air of self-control, left their rooms.

"Watson, attend to Mrs. Hudson. I will send a telegram for the coroner. Go now. See that she is comfortable."

Watson acquiesced and left Holmes alone with the body. Holmes stood with his hands shaking and worked to regain control of himself. He turned to his desk and taking pen and telegram form, he wrote a telegram to call the coroner. He stood with the form in his hand and turning looked at the man's clothes lying in a heap on the floor. He walked over and began to go through the pockets as Watson returned.

"She wants to be alone. I have given her a light sedative to help her rest and hopefully to sleep. What are you doing?"

Holmes had pulled out a match box. It was white and there was an intricate design on the cover in black ink. Holmes stopped and looked up at Watson. "The Gemini Club."

Watson stepped forward in disbelief and taking the match box from Holmes looked at the ornate cover. It was two female faces facing each other within an ornate decoration in black ink.

"But, Holmes, how?"

Holmes was standing, his eyes aflame with renewed energy and excitement. "I do not know how, Watson. But I know where I must go. Here is the completed telegram form. Please see to the arrangements. I must be elsewhere at present."

"Yes, of course," said the dumbfounded Watson.

Holmes grabbed his walking stick and hat and left Watson standing staring at the matchbox in one hand and holding the telegram form in the other, not knowing what to make of the situation before him.

Chapter 6

It was a busy evening at the Gemini Club. The gambling room was crowded with patrons drinking, smoking, gambling, and flirting. It was clear to the Sobotta twins that Miss St. John's strategy of feeding information to Persano, albeit through intermediaries, was working. His series of exposes on the other clubs was having the effect of members leaving and joining other clubs, including the Gemini Club. The ladies on the top floor were busy, the lounge was busy, and the gambling was going strong.

Steven and Scott were both working this evening, busy meeting the needs of the rich and powerful of London and making sure no one not a member, was allowed to enter. Membership was of course obtained by invitation only and then only after an interview with Miss St. John. Interviews usually occurred during the day and each new member was given an ornate Gemini medallion to prove membership. But the medallions were unnecessary after The Twins became familiar with the new members. Guests were allowed but only when accompanied by a member, and then only a trusted member. The Gemini Club was exclusive.

Holmes had been standing across the street from the club for the better part of two hours, watching the comings and goings. He stood in the shadows cast by one of the streetlamps as the light struck the corner of a building. He had put aside the horrible events of the late afternoon and was focused on the task before him. It was now evening and there was a near continuous stream of hansoms and private carriages bringing men to the Gemini Club. Holmes decided it was time to make his appearance.

Holmes watched as a carriage came down the street and as the streetlamps lit the interior, he could see that there was only one passenger, male from the silhouette of the hat through the carriage window. As the carriage approached, Holmes made for it with a quick stride arriving at the left-side door almost before the carriage came to a stop. He quickly opened the door and entered, alarming the sole occupant.

"Please forgive this intrusion, my Lord. I am Inspector Lestrade of Scottland Yard, and I must warn you against visiting this establishment this evening. We have a suspect under surveillance, and we may need to enter the club to make an arrest. It wouldn't do to have Your Lordship there while that happens." Holmes was of course prevaricating.

"Well, what?" was the only response from the startled aristocrat.

"Please, it would be an enormous help and cause less chaos if you were to tell me your password."

"I haven't a password," said the man. "Only this medallion for entry." The man took a medallion from his waistcoat and Holmes quickly took it.

"Thank you for you cooperation my Lord," and with that Holmes left the way he came. The carriage quickly moving forward and down the street.

Holmes chuckled to himself and going back to his hiding place, awaited another carriage. He didn't have to wait long; he could see another carriage coming down the street. Again, he quickly walked up to the carriage, but this time waited for the occupant to open the right door and begin his exit, he quickly opened the left door, entered the carriage, and followed the confused man out the other side.

"Good evening, sir. Thank you for the ride," was all Holmes said as he hurriedly approached the doors to the Club, the man standing in disbelief about to protest.

As Holmes approached the doors they were opened by a large man with a smile on his face that quickly turned stern. "Who might you be?"

"Good evening. I am sorry, but we haven't met. I am a new member, only interviewed yesterday. Here is my medallion."

Steven Sobotta stiffened. "I don't remember you, sir. My brother and I arrange all the interviews. I have a very good memory for faces, and I don't recognize yours." Sobotta put a heavy hand against Holmes's chest and looking behind himself said, "Scott? Damn he's about. You there, boy, yes you. Go and find Scott." Looking back at Holmes, Sobotta lifted his hand from his chest. "I'm sorry, sir, but I will need to confirm that you are a member before you are allowed entry. We are blocking the entrance at present, so please step inside and stand here."

Holmes laughed, "Well, is this how you treat all the new members?"

"I am sorry, but this club, as you are no doubt aware, is very exclusive. Members and their guests only. Scott and I are good at remembering, and I don't remember you. Consequently, you will stand here until my brother comes. Understood?"

"Quite." Holmes stood looking about the hall and the closed doors around it. His gaze brought him to the door marked, "Gemini Management."

"I am very much displeased, sir. I wish to speak with the management. Immediately!"

Steven looked at Holmes with disdain, "I am sorry, but Miss St. John is otherwise occupied and cannot possibly be disturbed."

"Miss St. John will recognize me. I dare say you will likely be redundant to requirements unless you allow me to see her and clear-up this misunderstanding." Holmes raised his voice. "I demand to see her immediately. This instant."

As Holmes continued to demand entrance, in a loud voice, the door to management opened to reveal an annoyed but beautiful woman. "Is there an issue, Steven?"

Steven stood at attention and leaned toward the woman to whisper in her ear.

"I see, and your name, sir, is?" Becca looked at Holmes with an inviting and polite smile.

"I am Sherlock Holmes, perhaps you have heard of me, Miss St. John?"

Becca's face immediately changed from smile to shock. Holmes observed from her reaction that she knew his name. He also observed how quickly the woman regained control of her features and the friendly, inviting smile returned to her face.

"Mr. Holmes, of course. I am sorry for this inconvenience. May I make it up to you by inviting you into my office for a drink? Please, I won't take 'no' for an answer. Please, this way."

Steven moved aside as Holmes joined Becca, stopping at the threshold of her door, he turned and tossed the medallion to Steven and followed Becca inside. As the door closed behind them Holmes stopped to look at the room, taking in every detail. Becca walked past her desk to a fine liquor table and turning looked at Holmes with an inviting smile and tilt of her head.

"Scotch, Mr. Holmes?"

"Thank you, yes. Scotch and soda if you please. What a wonderful portrait, Miss St. John. The resemblance is rather striking."

"Thank you, Mr. Holmes. I commissioned it myself from a painter on the Continent. I could give you his name if you wish to make a commission of your own?"

"I am afraid I have no need for self-portraits. I can see the real thing each morning in my shaving mirror."

Becca walked over to Holmes carrying two drinks and handed him one. "Please do have a seat, Mr. Holmes. To what do I owe the distinct pleasure of your company this evening? Are you perhaps interested in joining our club? I am happy to take your application, but usually we require a member's reference. But, for one such as yourself, we may be able to come to an understanding eliminating such a requirement." She looked at Holmes with seductive eyes as her free hand caressed her thigh.

"No, it is not membership that brings me here this evening, Miss St. John, it is a case."

Becca feigned a dainty pout and took a sip from her drink. "Such a shame, Mr. Holmes. Any club would be privileged to have you as a member. A case, you say? Involving one of my members?"

"That is what I am here to learn. Miss St. John, it is clear to me that you are an educated woman, from the upper classes. You are used to dealing with ordinary men who fall prey to your obvious charms. You have likely had a falling out with your family and have been cut off. You have made your way up the social ladder by sheer will and determination. How you came to own this club, I can only guess. Yes, own I say, for your bearing is that of someone who owns, not someone who is employed. You are the mistress of all you survey and are quite used to getting what you want, no matter what it may take. You have learned your trade from a master and whom that might be would require me to speculate. You appear to me to be far more than merely the owner of this establishment, for the managing of it would simply bore a woman like you. No, unless I am very much mistaken, you are quite a formidable woman."

Becca laughed, "Ahh, the famous Sherlock Holmesian penchant for observation. I am very privileged to be the inspiration for such. How wonderful it is to make your acquaintance, Mr. Holmes. I am indeed the owner of this Club and other businesses as well. But I am sure that you will learn that for yourself very quickly after you leave me this evening. How can I help your investigation?"

"Two men have died recently, and it seems both or at least one, was a member of your club."

"Oh my, how very dreadful. We do have many members Mr. Holmes, but two deaths and recent, is indeed troubling. Can you share their names with me?"

"The one that I am sure was a member was named Robert Holcomb, a solicitor. The second man, who died only this afternoon, was named Rodrick Hudson. Are these names familiar to you?" Holmes looked at Becca with hard eyes. "Oh, I see that they are familiar to you. Both or just one?"

Becca was shocked at hearing the name, Rodrick Hudson. She blanched but regained her composure. "Mr. Holmes, my reaction is simply that of a concerned woman of society. It pains me any time that someone dies. I am aware of the name, Hudson, but not the first name. As you will no doubt learn on your own, he was a frequent member of the club. I know of him only because of his deterioration over the past few months. One of our girls, whom he was fond of keeping company, made me aware of his declining health. I offered to refer him to a doctor, but he refused. I am afraid that is all I know about Mr. Hudson."

Holmes smiled, "Of course, and Mr. Holcomb?"

"I am afraid that name is unfamiliar to me. We have many members Mr. Holmes, and I cannot be expected to know them all by name. I am also not accustomed to revealing the names of our members. I made an exception for Mr. Hudson, in order to be accommodating to you and your investigation, but I am afraid I cannot confirm whether this Mr. Holcomb was a member."

"Do you not have books? Membership lists, Miss St. John? Books that you might refer to, to help me with my investigation?"

Becca smiled in return and took another sip of her drink. "I see that you have not tried your drink Mr. Holmes. Is it not to your liking? May I offer you something else?"

Holmes stood. "I am a very busy man Miss St. John; and I assume that you are very busy as well. I have taken up enough of your time this evening. It has been a pleasure to make your acquaintance." Holmes took a large swallow of his drink. "As for the Scotch, it is very fine. Thirty years old, I venture. Thank you for the drink and your company." Holmes moved towards the door to leave.

"Leaving already, Mr. Holmes? What a shame. We were only just getting to know one another. Good luck in your investigation. Please extend my condolences to the bereaved. Perhaps we shall meet again. Good night."

Holmes stopped at the half-opened door and looked back on Miss St. John. "I have the distinct feeling, Miss St. John, that we shall meet again. Good night." Holmes shut the door behind him and made for the entrance to the club. The Twins were both present, two large men, identical to each other. "Good evening, gentlemen," Holmes said as he exited the club and called for a hansom.

It was past three o'clock in the morning and there were very few patrons left at the Gemini Club. While Scott was at his place at the door, Steven Sobotta was meeting with Becca in her offices.

"Do you have any idea how Mr. Holmes found his way to this club this evening?"

"No. I am sorry for that Miss St. John. I have no idea."

"He came here and asked me about Hudson and Holcomb. He was casting his net in hopes of finding something. I, of course, gave him nothing but an admission that Hudson had been a frequent guest. I couldn't very well deny that. But I gave him nothing on Holcomb. That degenerate solicitor. Nothing."

"What do you want us to do, Miss St. John?"

"That will require some thought. Holmes is not an ordinary man and certainly a very worthy adversary, should it come to that. I will need some time to think this over." Becca looked down at her desk with a feeling of foreboding. There must be something that could be done, but her usual use of seduction and blackmail would not work with Holmes. She was, for the moment at least, beyond her depth.

Chapter 7

Holmes had returned to Baker Street to find Rodrick's body gone and a grieving Mrs. Hudson. It was late, almost half pass ten when Holmes returned. Watson was speaking with Mrs. Hudson in their sitting room when Holmes arrived. She was dabbing at her eyes but seemed otherwise to be taking the death of her son in her stride. Holmes hung his hat and put away his walking stick as he entered the room.

"Mrs. Hudson how are you feeling after this very difficult day?" he asked.

"I am as well as I can be after today. Dr. Watson has been a wonderful support. We were just discussing the arrangements for Rodrick's funeral. I don't want anything elaborate. He was a lonely and solitary man and should be remembered as such. There is no family left to me now. We will bury him next to my husband. With foresight we purchased two additional plots next to his. We will be buried as a family when my time comes."

"And we pray that that time will not come for a very long time," Watson said in a soothing and comforting tone.

"Mrs. Hudson, please allow Dr. Watson and I to purchase the headstone."

Mrs. Hudson's hands both went to her heart, and she said, "Oh thank you Mr. Holmes, Dr. Watson. How very kind of you."

"I need to ask you some questions, Mrs. Hudson. It may be important to one of my cases. I must ask you these things even during this sad time. Please forgive me. Do you know where your son lived?"

"No I do not, Mr. Holmes. He never told me. I am afraid I know nothing of his life after his university years when we had our falling out."

"What did Roderick study at university and what was his profession?"

"He studied bugs, Mr. Holmes. He was always interested in beetles and moths, worms, butterflies. He kept a menagerie of bugs in his room when he was just a boy. Running about looking under rocks and in crevices for bugs. It was harmless enough, so I abided his interest though I never understood it."

"You mean he studied entomology, Mrs. Hudson?" asked Watson.

"If that is what it is called, then yes. He studied bugs. After university he was hired by the natural history museum and worked there continuing his studies I suppose and managing the exhibits. That's all I know about his professional life, Mr. Holmes."

"Thank you, Mrs. Hudson." Holmes walked over to his desk and sat as he began to write.

"Well, I have imposed on you gentlemen enough for one day. Thank you both again." Mrs. Hudson gave Watson's hand a squeeze and turning went downstairs to her rooms.

"What are you writing Holmes?"

"An advertisement for the papers. We need to find out where Mr. Hudson lived. Here it is, what do think?"

Watson took the paper from Holmes and read the following advertisement:

REWARD. Due to the unexpected death of Mr. Rodrick Hudson, inquiry is being made as to the location of his lodgings. A reward of two pounds will be given to the deceased's landlord upon answering this advertisement by coming to 221b Baker Street between the hours of four and seven in the evening. Time is of the essence.

"Two pounds? Really Holmes. Rather extravagant. That should bring out the landlord without delay. And as to the natural history museum?"

"We will make our visit there tomorrow morning on our way to getting this into the afternoon papers."

"And this evening? What happened at the club this evening?"

"Nothing of very much consequence. I have confirmed that Hudson was a member of the club, and I met a very remarkable woman who is the owner of the establishment. Nothing more."

"What about Holcomb? Did you confirm his membership?"

"I hardly needed to, Watson. We know that from Mr. Gruel. But I am satisfied that he was a member as well."

"Come now Holmes, your eyes tell of more adventures than that. What else happened? What of this 'remarkable woman'?"

Holmes looked at Watson and yawned. "I am afraid that the emotions of the day have me quite tired." Holmes walked towards his bedroom. "Good night, Watson. Please turn down the gas when you decide to go to bed." With that Holmes closed the door to his bedroom, leaving Watson without answers.

The next morning, Holmes and Watson took a hansom to the British Museum of Natural History, stopping on the way to get Holmes's ad posted in the afternoon papers. They arrived at the museum, its imposing twin towers and immense size dwarfing its patrons as they entered, never ceased to amaze Watson, despite the number of times he had visited. Its cavernous halls were filled with all forms of life from around Her Majesty's kingdom. A place one could easily get lost in both figuratively and literally.

Holmes approached one of the many people who assisted visitors in finding their way. "Can you tell me how to get to the entomology department?"

The nice young man, likely a student, described the way and Holmes and Watson walked hurriedly in the direction the young man had described. Upon arriving, Holmes looked about for an official door and found one marked, "Private," and knocked quietly and then entered as Watson followed.

"I am sorry, gentlemen, but this is a private office very much off-limits to the public." The warning came from a short, round man with bushy lambchop side whiskers, white with age. He could barely be seen from behind the magnifying lenses perched like reading glasses on his long-curved nose. He had on a long-brimmed crownless cap revealing a balding head. Only his head was visible from behind the crates, sawdust, packing paper, and trays of assorted insects. The room was not well lit, and only a gas light hanging over the table where the man stood illuminated the room.

"I am sorry to disturb your studies. I am Sherlock Holmes, and this is my friend and colleague, Dr. Watson. I am here to make some inquiries relative to one of my cases. Whom do I have the pleasure of addressing?"

The short man's eyes grew large, and his mouth was agape. His head disappeared behind one of the boxes, only to reappear again as if to confirm that he was not hallucinating. He stared at Holmes for several seconds before disappearing behind the boxes again. Holmes looked at Watson who was near breaking out in laughter. Holmes made a dramatic facial expression meant to communicate the need for decorum, which only made Watson want to laugh the harder.

The little man appeared in full body from behind his boxes with a smile on his face and outstretched hand. "Mr. Sherlock Holmes! Wait until the missis hears about this. She won't believe me." The man had taken ahold of Holmes's hand and was shaking it vigorously while looking first at Holmes and then at Watson and back again. "The missis and I read of your exploits in *The Strand* we do. Of a Sunday afternoon, after our lunch. It is indeed a pleasure to meet you Mr. Holmes!"

"Yes, it is a pleasure to meet you as well. I am afraid that I am going to need my hand back, if you do not mind."

"Oh, sorry Mr. Holmes. I am most excited. I get no visitors here. Just me and my insects. I don't think I've had a visitor in three years. No, I am a liar. I had a visitor, a lady who was lost in the museum, just two weeks ago. She was a beautiful dainty thing. Fainted and fell right to the floor she did, at her first sight of my beetles. She laid there and I went off into the museum to get some help and some water. When I came back, she was gone. Couldn't have been five or six minutes I was out and about, but when I returned, she was gone. Embarrassed I should suspect. Oh, but no visitors like you Mr. Holmes. You say you are here on a case? How may I help you?"

Holmes, who had maintained a disinterested and aloof look as the short little man spoke, suddenly seemed to gain some interest in the man's story. Watson could see the sudden keen interest in his eyes, and the way his face took on a more interested and concentrated appearance. Watson could think of no reason for Holmes's sudden interest in such a common anecdote. An unrelated trifle in an otherwise irrelevant story. Watson was about to ask Holmes when he was interrupted by the man himself.

"Well, you can start by giving us your name, sir."

"Sorry, sorry. I forget my manners. I am Dr. Daniel Philbin."

"Well fine. Dr. Philbin do you know Rodrick Hudson, an entomologist who worked here at the museum?"

"Well of course I do. He works just in the adjoining room through the door in the back of my room. He has an office back there and a small lab that he keeps locked. He comes in later in the day he does. But we can have a look and see if he is here now, just the same."

"Dr. Philbin, I am afraid that I am the bearer of some bad news. Mr. Hudson is dead, and I am inquiring into a matter that may be related to his death."

Dr. Philbin went pale and reached for a box to steady himself. "You say he has died?"

Watson looked at Holmes with an exasperated expression, "Yes, I am afraid so, Dr. Philbin. We are sorry to give you such a shock. He died only yesterday. We were hoping to talk with one of his colleagues and learn more about the man."

Dr. Philbin took a handkerchief from his back pocket, wiped his forehead under the brim of his cap, blew his nose loudly, and then stopped and took a deep breath as if the effort of blowing his nose had taken his breath away.

"I am very sorry to hear about Mr. Hudson. I didn't know him well mind you. He kept very much to himself. Though we are only separated by this wall, we rarely spoke to each other. You see my specialty is beetles, in particular a type of beetle that lives in the north of England, *Cicindela Campestris*, commonly known as the Green Tiger beetle. I'm not capable of going out and finding them anymore, but I have students and understudies who do the field work for me. They are the fastest beetle in England.

"Mr. Hudson's specialty is worms, and so we have infrequent opportunities to talk or to share our research. Not to mention my beetles eat his worms, so there is that conflict as well. I would see him sometimes when he arrived in the morning, at times at lunch, but not much after that. I leave before he does in the evening, and his habit is to stay very late and work. At least that is my understanding as I was never here of an evening to see him. Would you care to see some of my beetles?"

"Thank you, Dr. Philbin. Would you be so kind as to show us his office?"

"Oh yes, Mr. Holmes. Right this way. Mind you watch out for the boxes. I am in the middle of unpacking the latest collections from my students in the field. Fascinating work it is. You never know when the box you open will reveal a new species. Unpacking time is like Christmas. So full of surprises. Perhaps I will show you some beetles a little later?"

They had arrived at the door behind the doctor's table and Holmes moved to stop Dr. Philbin from opening it. "Please allow me to make my examinations before you step into the room, Dr. Philbin."

"Of course, Mr. Holmes!" Dr. Philbin took a step back as Holmes stepped forward. Looking over at Watson, Philbin said, "This is such an honor. The missis will not believe it."

Holmes knelt in front of the door and began a brief examination of the keyhole and doorknob, but abruptly stopped and stood with impatience.

"Do you have a lamp Dr. Philbin? I cannot see anything in this poorly lit room."

"Yes, one moment please Mr. Holmes." Dr. Philbin having gone back into his office returned with a lit lantern. "Hudson's room has more gas lighting Mr. Holmes, but you can use this to examine the door."

Holmes took the lamp from the doctor and resumed his examination of the keyhole. He took out his magnifying glass and carefully examined the keyhole again.

"Watson, look here. There are relatively fresh scratches where someone used lock-picking tools to open this door. Here, use my glass."

"Yes, Holmes. I can just see scratches, two or three, in the brass. The brass stripped by the scratches is not as tarnished as the surrounding brass. But what does it mean?"

Holmes took his magnifying glass and handing Watson the lamp, slowly opened the door to Hudson's office. He turned immediately toward the wall to his right. "Watson, remove the lamps chimney glass and hand me the lamp." Holmes used the flame from the lamp to light the gas lamp on the wall as he turned the valve to release the gas.

"Is there another lamp in this room Dr. Philbin?"

"Yes, on the wall to the left."

Holmes repeated his efforts with the lamp on the left wall and the room was well lit with light. "Please stay back Dr. Philbin. Look Watson, the floor is dusty." Holmes went to his hands and knees and began to examine the floor, letting out little mumbles of glee as he appeared to find something interesting.

The desk in the middle of the room was a mess of papers and there were stacks of papers about the room. Articles from academic journals and pages of notes and scribbles that appeared to have been stacked for some time, as they too were dusty. Holmes made his way to another door in the back of the room and tried to open it, but it was locked.

"Is this Hudson's lab, Dr. Philbin?"

"Yes, Mr. Holmes, but the door is always locked and only Mr. Hudson has a key."

"Well, that shouldn't be an obstacle." Holmes knelt in front of the door and examined its knob and keyhole. "Bring the lamp over here Watson, if you please." Watson complied and Holmes examined the keyhole with his magnifying glass. "Ahh, the same as the other door Watson. Someone has used lock-picking tools here as well."

Holmes reached in his jacket pocket and pulled out a small bundle, wrapped in leather, and rolled it open – revealing lock-pick tools. He carefully selected two tools and began to work on the lock. In just a very brief time, there was an audible click and Holmes stood and opened the door.

"Watson, the lamp." Holmes took the lamp and began to examine the floor, again letting out little sounds of pleasure as he moved about the floor on his knees. The lab was small and each of the four walls were fronted by lab tables, except for the space required by the door. There was a lab stool at each of the four tables. The far wall had two shelves above the lab table, full of lab books neatly arranged in chronological order, with dates on the spines of each lab book.

"Look Watson, four lab books are missing. November through December of 1895, January through February of 1896, March through April of 1896, and finally May through June of 1896."

Holmes looked at each lab table carefully and having satisfied himself that he had seen what there was to see, relaxed and walked back into Hudson's small office.

"Dr. Philbin, there is evidence that someone has been in this office and this lab in the recent past. I would say, in the past two to three weeks, and that four lab books, several rectangular trays, and two glass jars have been taken. Are you aware of anyone breaking into this room?"

"Of course not, Mr. Holmes. As I said before, no one visits us in these rooms. We are free to conduct our research in peace. But how do you know that the rooms were broken into during the last two or three weeks?"

Holmes looked absently at the doctor, "From the amount of dust that has accumulated in the space where the missing lab books were and where the trays and jars were. It is only an estimate but judging from the dust in the rest of the room, I think it is fair to say that the lab was broken into two to three weeks ago. Also, from the amount of tarnish on the brass exposed to the air, by the scratches made by the lock-picking tools. Have you any idea what Mr. Hudson was researching?"

Dr. Philbin was looking at Holmes as a man might a magician. "No, no Mr. Holmes. I have no idea. But how wonderfully you work, sir. I have a story to tell my grandchildren. The missis will simply not believe it."

"Thank you, Dr. Philbin. Watson, will you spend some time both in the office and this lab looking over the papers and lab books for anything of interest to the case? You're a medical man and more used to deciphering lab notes and the scribbles of researchers."

"Of course, Holmes. If you think it will help. What do you expect me to find?"

"Unfortunately, I expect you to find almost nothing relevant to the case. But all the same, it is worth the effort to be sure."

"And as for you? What will you be doing while I spend the day in this dusty, gloomy room looking over old papers, notes, and lab books?"

"I will be at Baker Street awaiting a response to my advertisement and then a visit to Hudson's rooms. Thank you, Dr. Philbin. This has been a most enlightening visit. I cannot say that this is not the most illuminating visit I have ever experienced at the Museum of Natural History."

With that, Holmes walked out of Hudson's office and toward the door back into the museum, but he stopped and turning asked Dr. Philbin, "The dainty lady who fainted and was gone when you returned, did she have a large carpet bag with her?"

Dr. Philbin blinked and looked toward Watson with some confusion and disbelief. "Well, yes, she did. I remember commenting to the missis as I told her the story, that the woman had the most remarkable red-carpet bag with her. Unusual I thought for such a well-dressed lady. But, how did you know?"

Holmes smiled and turning said, "Hah! Thank you Dr. Philbin and please give my regards to the missis."

Watson was back at Baker Street before Holmes, having arrived at a quarter to six in the evening. He was tired and felt dusty and grimy from his inspection of Hudson's notes and lab books. He went immediately to his bedroom and washed himself, brushing the dust from his clothing. He came back downstairs to the sitting room, feeling much better after his quick bath, and found Holmes sitting in his chair smoking a pipe.

"Ahh, Holmes. You have returned."

Holmes looked up at Watson and nodded. "Anything of interest at the laboratory?"

"Well, if you discount the hour-long introduction to the Green Tiger beetle that I received from Dr. Philbin, no not much of interest. Hudson's research was very academic. He did have some interesting ideas about cross-breeding different worm species but nothing more. I will say that his handwriting grew worse over the course of the past few months. Many of the notes on his desk were nearly illegible in the past few weeks. Clearly a sign of his declining health."

"Watson, that is excellent. Well done. I was paid a visit by the landlord and visited Hudson's rooms. Nothing of significance there either. He was very untidy in his habits and the rooms were, frankly, a sad sight. Poor as they were. He appears to have been a very lonely, sad, and unaccomplished man. The death of a father can sometimes do that to a sensitive person."

Watson bowed his head in sadness.

"Have you asked Mrs. Hudson to bring up dinner? I must admit to being very hungry at present."

"No, Holmes, I have not. I was concerned whether we should make such a request given her state of nerves."

"Nonsense. Work is what she needs, a welcome distraction. Ah, I hear her coming up the steps now."

"Mr. Holmes, Dr. Watson, I hope you are both hungry. I am roasting game hens, and they should be ready shortly."

"Mrs. Hudson, you have outdone yourself. Yes, that will be very welcome." Watson's eyes shined and his smile filled his face, as he rubbed his hands together.

"Good. Will you eat as well, Mr. Holmes?"

"Yes, thank you."

"Very well, I will bring dinner up shortly." With that Mrs. Hudson went downstairs, mumbling to herself.

Holmes was deep in thought as he smoked one of his oily clay pipes. Watson turned to look at him and said, "This morning, as Dr. Philbin talked about the lost young lady who fainted and was gone when he returned, you seemed very interested in that part of his tale."

Holmes merely grunted in response.

"Well, Holmes? Why would such a trifle interest you?"

Holmes took the pipe from his mouth. "The trifles, Watson. There is nothing more important than trifles." He then went back to his brown study and smoking his oily pipe.

Watson let out a loud sigh and sat in his usual chair convinced that he would get no more from Holmes this evening. "Holmes, you are at times a very frustrating man."

Chapter 8

It was mid-afternoon and Holmes was pulling his bow across his violin strings in a dissonant and irregular fashion and had been doing so for more than an hour. Watson, trying to read a book, had endured this without comment, but not without looking at Holmes several times to communicate his irritation at the practice. Holmes finally stopped and standing, dropped his violin and bow in his chair.

"Holmes as you said this morning there is nothing we can do on the case until tonight. Please, relax."

Holmes paced up and down the room behind the settee. "I know, Watson. But I am full of nervous energy and have nothing to expend it on."

"Let's take a walk, Holmes. That will surely help. It's a mostly sunny day, the rains of this morning are gone, and we could use the fresh air."

Holmes acquiesced and having retrieved their hats and walking sticks, the two stepped out onto Baker Street. Almost immediately a hansom stopped in front of their door, and Inspector MacDonald exited.

"Holmes, Dr. Watson, are you late for an appointment or do you have time for a visit?" MacDonald had a swagger and a big smile on his face. It was clear to Holmes that he had something he wanted to brag about.

"No, not at all. Just going out for a walk. The interruption is much appreciated, Inspector. Come inside."

Holmes, Watson, and the inspector retreated to the comforts of the sitting room. "So, Inspector, you seem quite pleased with yourself. Tell us all about it."

"Well, we have solved the little mystery surrounding the death of Mr. Holcomb. Appears it was murder as you suspected, Mr. Holmes."

Watson looked at Holmes and then at the Inspector who was sitting on the settee. "Solved it? How?"

"We had a woman come into the Yard this morning and confess to the entire affair. It appears she poisoned the unfortunate Mr. Holcomb and rather than kill him outright, the poison made him lose his faculties and run out into the street." MacDonald looked at Holmes who was smiling and lost a great deal of his bravado. "What are you smiling about, Holmes?"

Holmes cleared his throat, "Congratulations, Inspector. Very accommodating for the murderer to turn herself in and give a full confession. Have you verified her account with any other witnesses?"

"I have constables out looking for the street vendor who sold the pie at this very moment and interviewing the tenants again. We will get collaboration. Of that, I am sure."

"And what is this woman's name and occupation?"

"She is one of the surviving working women who was friends with the unfortunate Mary Kelly, one of the Ripper's victims. Her name is Lizzie Albrook, and she is mad as a hatter, she is. We had reason to speak with her during the murders, and she was very much affected by her friend's death, and the horrific nature of it."

Watson looked concerned, "One of the women associated with the Ripper murders and insane. That is very disturbing. Did she say how she killed Holcomb?"

"Yes, she admits to putting strychnine, a very large amount, in a kidney pie he ordered from a street vendor."

"Holmes, strychnine, especially in a large dose, will begin to affect the mind and body within a quarter of an hour after it is ingested. It will cause extreme agitation, apprehension, fear, and eventually stiffened muscles, respiratory failure, and death. It was used as a medicine in pill form not very long ago and is easily available at most apothecary shops.

"In some people it could cause a temporary mental instability motivated by fear and paranoia. It could explain why Holcomb suddenly became insane and ran into the street."

Holmes looked at the inspector with a wry smile. "And what was the motive for this alleged murder, Inspector?"

"No motive at all. She dislikes men. Hates them in fact. I would guess she has felt this way since the Ripper murders and the way she is treated by her clients as she plies her trade. Mr. Holcomb was the unfortunate victim of a simple random act of hatred by this mad woman." The inspector looked confident again. "Well, Holmes?"

"And how did this mad woman gain access to the pie to insert the poison?"

"She says that she sometimes helps the pie vendor make the pies for some extra change. I am sure that's how it happened here."

"Oh I see. And when did Mr. Holcomb purchase this pie? The evidence is that after dropping Mrs. Snyder at her aunt's, he went home."

"We don't know where he went, Mr. Holmes. He may have gotten a taste for a pie and took the hansom to his usual street vendor; or maybe the street vendor happened along and he bought it on a whim."

"There was no evidence of a kidney pie at his apartment."

"Perhaps he ate it on the street or in the hansom on his way home. Listen Mr. Holmes, we could speculate all day. The fact is I have her, a full confession. Hey, Mr. Holmes?"

Holmes stood and chose a pipe from amongst the many on the mantel, filled it, and made a show of lighting it. He sat back down and blowing a large cloud of blue smoke into the air said, "It is indeed very convenient, is it not, that this woman appears and makes a full confession? How do you account for the evidence at the scene? The boot and shoe marks in the carpet and in the soil outside the building?"

"Obviously unrelated, Mr. Holmes. Could have been anybody and could have happened at any time before the murder. No, I think you put too much stock in those boot marks. She did it. You must admit it, Holmes, the Yard beat you to prize this time."

"Well congratulations, Inspector. You go in your direction, and I in mine. But allow me to give you some advice. I would not rest my case for murder on the word of a mad woman. I would be suspicious of anyone coming forward to admit killing a man there is no evidence she even knew. I would not ignore the evidence at the scene of the crime nor the questions that I have just asked you."

"And if my constables find collaborating evidence that puts her at the street vendor's cart at or around the time that Holcomb purchased his pie? What then Mr. Holmes?"

"I would not be at all surprised if the food vendor collaborates this woman's story and puts her in the area very near the time of the crime. I suspect he has been well-paid to do so. As for this unfortunate woman, it wouldn't take much to convince a mad person that she committed an act she knows nothing of. I am certain she is very convincing in her telling."

"It sounds to me, Holmes, that you have information unavailable to the Yard that causes you to doubt this new evidence. If so, it is your duty to tell me before an innocent person is tried for capital murder."

"I have no information or evidence to share with you. Only my own conclusions based on what I have seen and what I have inferred from the evidence. Nothing that would support charges, let alone be admissible in a court of law. As I said, you work the case your way, and I will work it mine. Anything else, Inspector?"

MacDonald looked at Holmes carefully, stood, and said, "Very well, Mr. Holmes, but if you develop evidence that might lead to a different theory of the case or point to another as the murderer, I will expect you to make that evidence available to the Yard."

"Of course, Inspector. Have I ever done less?" Holmes stood and walked toward the open window facing Baker Street as Watson choked a laugh. "I may have an opportunity in the not-too-distant future to call upon you for help in arresting the true murderer of Mr. Holcomb. But that time has not yet arrived. In the meantime, Inspector, I would not risk my professional reputation on the word of this mad woman, or the accounts given by collaborating witnesses on the street. Tread carefully."

"Thank you, Mr. Holmes. I always do."

With that the inspector said his goodbyes and left, leaving Holmes and Watson alone in their rooms. His affect upon leaving showing a bit less confidence in his case than he had when he arrived.

"What do you make of these new developments, Holmes?"

"I make nothing of them, because they are irrelevant to the case, except to confirm some of my suspicions."

"Come, Holmes. I am in the dark and admit that I see nothing we have learned during the past few days contributing in any manner to the resolution of this case. At least the inspector has a bird in hand."

"Watson, I mean really. Do you not find it rather coincidental that less than two days after I visited the Gemini Club a person comes forward admitting to Holcomb's murder? And a mad street woman at that. No, this is a ruse designed to put us off the scent and to provide the police with an easy resolution. Nothing more. It means that we are getting close to the solution and have forced our adversary to act. Tonight's vigil may prove very enlightening indeed. I feel it in my bones, Watson."

That afternoon Holmes left Baker Street and ran some errands, leaving Watson to think about the case and to read the late afternoon paper. It was full of the arrest of the mad woman for the unfortunate death of Mr. Robert Holcomb, Esq. As Watson sat, smoking a cigar, and thinking about the case, the bell rang, and Mrs. Hudson brought up their client, Mrs. Brenda Snyder, and her aunt, Mrs. McKinnon.

"Ladies, so good to see you. I am afraid that Holmes is not here at present. How may I help you?"

"Have you read the newspapers, Dr. Watson?" The aunt spoke first.

"Yes, and I can assure you that Mr. Holmes is certain that this entire affair with the police is a ruse meant to stop our investigation and put the police on the wrong scent. Mr. Holmes told the Yard as much earlier today."

"But it all seems so certain, Dr. Watson. The police are convinced that my Robby was murdered by this poor, unfortunate and insane woman. They have her in custody and the inquest is only days away. What makes Mr. Holmes think that she isn't the right person?" Mrs. Snyder was crying as her aunt sought to comfort her.

"Because I know things that the police do not, Mrs. Snyder." All three turned at once to see Holmes standing at the door. "I am certain that this mad woman is not responsible for your fiancé's death. Of that you can be assured."

"Thank you, Mr. Holmes. Can you please explain what makes you so certain?" asked Mrs. McKinnon.

"I am not at liberty to explain my thinking now. Suffice it to say that my inquiries into the case and the evidence that I have seen, not to mention a second death of which you are unaware, all point to something more complex. Ladies, you will simply have to trust me. I am on top of the facts and Dr. Watson, and I, are taking steps to ensure the real killer is brought to justice. In the meantime, I recommend that you do not trouble yourselves with what you may read in the papers."

Both ladies appeared satisfied by Holmes's assurances and stood to leave. "I appreciate you so much Mr. Holmes, thank you." Mrs. Snyder was smiling through her tears as her aunt lead her to the landing to leave.

"Mr. Holmes, I trust that you were not put off by our private conversation earlier. I appreciate what you are doing for us, and I trust you implicitly." With that the two ladies left Baker Street.

"Well you returned at just the right time, Holmes. Not knowing what you know, or not seeing all that you have seen, I am at a bit of a disadvantage in dealing with our clients on my own."

"All will become clear, I promise Watson. My arrangements are in place for this evening. In the meantime, there is nothing more to do and speculation will only cloud the issue."

"And what do you expect to happen this evening?"

"I do not expect anything specifically. Our evening vigil may be for naught. But, better to be prepared and not avail ourselves of our preparations than to experience the need and fail for want of them. Have you your revolver?"

"Yes, I believe it is in my bedroom side table. Do you anticipate violence this evening?"

"If things are as I suspect, we may indeed confront violence this evening." Holmes was himself retrieving his own revolver and checking it. "Watson, I believe that we have stumbled upon the beginnings of a new crime organization. Not nearly as complex as that of the Professor, nor as widespread, as it is still in its infancy. If we can stop it now, before it grows more complex, we will have done Her Majesty a great service."

"Really, Holmes? I have seen nothing of the kind."

"I have developed a kind of natural intuition for these things, Watson. They leave their mark on certain crimes. I have learned how to identify those characteristic scents, and look for other marks of the professional, the intelligent, the creative, and the complex. Those characteristics are present here. You will remember the affair of "The Red-Headed League," and *The Green Dragon*, to name but two. They too shared certain characteristics in common with this case."

"I must confess that I see nothing of those two cases in this one. *The Green Dragon* affair nearly cost us both our lives and led to your final confrontation with Moriarty himself. Are you saying this case shares those dangers?"

"No, not quite. But our present case shares certain qualities with those two cases and some similar dangers. Be careful tonight, Watson. Do not hesitate to fire your pistol should the need arise. They will not hesitate. There is a bigger game at play here. I am sure of that, even if I am not at all aware of what the end game is. I am in hopes that tonight's developments will enlighten us further so that we know more about what game we are playing at."

Chapter 9

Lady Tabitha was a bit distracted during the evening's séance. She had been upset at the boys in the basement who operated the apparatus that made her effects work. There had been a slight hesitation in the rocking of the table during the last séance and despite her efforts to confront the boys and ensure that it didn't happen again, she was concerned. The timing had to be perfect. Attention to the details of the loose script were vital. The two boys assisting her in making the "show" believable had to be in top form this evening, and if not, she knew that Becca would dispatch them, and that would cause a disruption in her business. She needed to focus and forget her worry.

"The spirits are here," she said in a low voice, almost a whisper. "They want to commune with us. They seek out the living, the powerful, those with the bright light of life. Come to us!"

The lone woman at the table, her eyes closed and holding Lilith's hands, began to shake with fear as the table jumped perceptibly and hit the floor hard. She was trying to contact her mother, who had only recently died. She was desperate with grief and guilt and wanted to contact her mother to alleviate both. She was, of course, very wealthy and would pay almost anything to reach into the nether world and communicate with her dead mother.

"We want to speak with Lady Whimscourt. Come Lady Whimscourt. Come to the light of the candle. Feel the bright warmth of the living. Come to us!" Lilith fell silent, her head on her bosom.

Her client opened one eye to look at why everything was quiet. She could just see Lilith in the light of the single candle in the otherwise darkened room. She was breathing hard, her head down and her arms limp.

"Come to us mother! Oh come!" she almost shouted in a pleading and crying voice.

"Silence!" Lilith shouted and her entire body stiffened. Her head now up and her eyes wide. "She is here. She is here with me. She is in pain. Oh, the pain of sorrow, of regret, of desire. She suffers."

"No, no. Mother, I am so sorry. Do not be in pain." The client's eyes were open, and she looked desperately into Lilith eyes. "Please Lady Tabitha. What is the cause of my mother's pain?"

"She is in pain because of you, my dear. Because of you." Lilith collapsed onto the table letting go of her client's hands.

"No! Not because of me." The client began to sob heavily and laid her head upon her arms resting on the table.

A drumming roar began, first softly and then louder and louder as the table shook again and then, the sound and the table's shaking stopped in unison. The room was quiet again, except for the client's weeping. Lilith slowly raised herself up, as if exhausted.

"I am afraid, my dear, that the bond has been broken. The spirits are gone. Your mother is gone. I can do no more tonight."

Holmes and Watson were in a dark alley, the same one Holmes had used before, watching the comings and goings at the Gemini Club. It was dark and a light rain had begun to fall. Watson was not happy. He was wet, he was tired, and he longed for his rooms on Baker Street. Holmes was alert, his attention focused on the club.

"Holmes, is there no opportunity to surveil the club from the pub just down the street?"

Holmes hushed Watson with a wave of his hand. "We must be here, Watson. Ready at a moment's notice. I have made arrangements. There are two hired hansoms just down the street awaiting my signal. John Clayton has proved his worth again. His acquaintance has served me well. One of the little benefits of my chosen line of work. We must be quiet and vigilant."

"But Holmes, why can't we make our vigil inside the hansoms?"

"Hush, Watson. We mustn't give our presence away. What time is it?"

Watson struggled to see his watch in the dark alley, moving forward a bit to catch some of the light emitted by the streetlamps. Holmes grabbed his arm as he did. "It's half pass one, Holmes. I had to move forward to see my watch. Blazes!" Watson limped slightly as he moved back into position. The old army wound in his left leg was beginning to throb.

"Will your leg withstand the rigors of the evening, Watson?"

"Yes, yes."

"Good. You may have need of it before this evening is done. Look!"

Watson leaned forward just enough to see two men exit the Gemini Club. Both were remarkably similar in appearance. As they came down the steps two small carriages came down the street and each man went into a separate carriage. Holmes moved from the darkness of the alley as the two carriages passed, stood under a streetlamp, and gave a wave in the rain to the two hansoms further down the street.

"I'll take the first hansom, Watson. You take the second. You follow the second carriage, and I will follow the first. Come, quick! The game's afoot! Be careful, Watson. Remember, do not hesitate to use your revolver. We will meet up at Baker Street when the job is done."

Watson nodded and immediately climbed into the second carriage as Holmes got in the first.

"Quickly, John! Follow those two carriages and when they split up follow the first. Go man! Go!"

The two hansoms took off with a jerk. The two carriages were just visible as the hansoms began to catch-up. Clayton stayed a good distance behind the two carriages to reduce the chances of being found out. Holmes was glad that this evening there was little fog. Though depending on where the carriages went, that could change. And so went the chase through the streets of London toward the West End. Holmes watched and memorized the route as the streetlamps moved past him in the dark of night.

It was clear to Holmes by the many turns and changes of direction that the carriage drivers were being careful not to be followed. He knocked on the roof of the hansom and John opened the trap door.

"Stay back a bit, John. Stay within visual sight, but do not get too close."

"Yes, Mr. Holmes."

As Holmes said this the second carriage turned abruptly to the right as the first carriage carried on. Watson was fifty feet behind as Holmes watched his carriage make the right turn in pursuit of the second carriage. "Not too close, Watson," Holmes said aloud to himself.

It wasn't clear to Holmes where the carriage he followed was going. He began to think that perhaps the whole chase was a ruse. He decided he would follow the carriage for only another hour and then return to Baker Street. The carriage meandered through the streets of London in no apparent direction or visible purpose. Holmes began to feel dejected. Had he been fooled?

The carriage suddenly stopped in front of a local pub and one of the twins, Holmes could not tell which, descended from the carriage and entered the pub. Holmes struck the side of the hansom with disgust. He was being led on a wild goose chase, as probably was Watson. There was no point in stepping into the pub, but Holmes did so anyway.

He looked around the pub till he found one of the twins at a small table in a darker part of the pub, already enjoying an ale. The twin noticed Holmes, showed a large toothy grin, lifted his glass as if in salute, and took a long drink of the ale. Holmes had been bested. He shook the rain from his jacket and hat, turned and exited the pub. He sat in the hansom and said, "Baker Street, John," and then took out his pipe and began to smoke.

Watson arrived back at Baker Street at half past three in the morning. He entered the sitting room half expecting to be alone. He was tired, still wet from the evening's adventures, and in a bad mood. As he entered, he saw Holmes sitting in his usual place, smoking and in deep thought.

"Holmes! Damnation! What are you doing back here and comfortable?"

"My dear Watson. Take off your wet jacket and shoes. I'll start a fire and you can dry yourself in its warmth. I, as you can see, changed my clothes and am much more comfortable than you."

Watson complied and threw himself in his chair, after taking a cigar and lighting it.

"Watson, we were temporarily bested by those two twins and their rather intelligent leader. I am afraid I owe you an apology, old man. Our vigil was for naught."

Watson took a long drag from his cigar and blew a large cloud of blue smoke into the air. "Well…anyone who can best Sherlock Holmes is a formidable opponent indeed. Not to worry, Holmes, apology accepted." Watson leaned forward and gave Holmes a forgiving smile.

"I said 'bested' Watson, but perhaps that is still to be determined."

"What do you mean, man? We chased a wild goose through the streets of London for half the night with nothing to show for it!"

"Morning may bring fresh news and a far different conclusion. I confess, I am spent, dear Watson. As limp as a wet rag. I am off to bed, old fellow, and I suggest you do the same." With that Holmes rose and made his way to his bedroom, while Watson stared, baffled by Holmes's statement.

"You needn't keep me in suspense," he said loud enough for Holmes to hear. There was no reply.

———————————

Watson awoke at half past nine in the morning. Still feeling tired though he had slept soundly, just not long enough. He rubbed the sleep from his eyes, stood, and began his morning routine. Dressed, Watson went downstairs to find the sitting room empty. He called out for Holmes, but there was no reply. Breakfast was on the table, covered with a silver cloche. There was a note slightly under the plate. It read:

> My dear Watson, I trust that you have rested sufficiently to recover from our wanderings through London last night. I have some things to take care of this morning. Don't expect me back until mid-afternoon. I've asked Mrs. Hudson to prepare your breakfast.
> Holmes

Watson let out a sigh of exasperation, lifted the dish cover and began to eat. He realized he was half-starved and ate with less manners than was his custom. He heard Mrs. Hutson coming up the stairs.

"Dr. Watson! You look tired despite your late rising. This hot tea should help."

"Thank you, Mrs. Hudson. It was a very late night. Holmes insisted on standing in a cold, dark alley in the rain."

"It is a miracle you didn't both catch your death of cold. This tea will warm you up. Now, mind you rest this morning. No more running about today."

"A wiser woman was never born. That is precisely what I intend to do. Do you have any idea where Holmes is off to this morning?"

"Not the faintest idea. One of those street urchins came pounding on the door at half pass seven this morning. No sooner had the young lad gone upstairs to see Holmes then they both came hurriedly down the stairs and left together. I have no clue where they got off to. Mr. Holmes stopped long enough to ask me to provide you with breakfast at a little past nine, gave me a note to put under your plate, and then was out the door calling for a hansom."

"One of the Irregulars you say? Well, we will know more when he returns. Thank you, Mrs. Hudson."

Mrs. Hudson left the way she came, mumbling to herself as she closed the door to the sitting room. It was at almost the same moment that the bell rang downstairs, and Watson heard the door open and muffled conversation between Mrs. Hudson and a man, followed by Mrs. Hudson's steps coming up the stairs. The door opened and Mrs. Hudson's frustrated form reentered the sitting room.

"I am getting too old to be going up and down stairs all day, Dr. Watson. A telegram for Mr. Holmes." Mrs. Hudson laid the telegram on the table and rubbing her right hip, exited the room in disgust.

Chapter 10

Persano arrived at the Gemini Club just past noon to practice his fencing and to check on the preparations for that afternoon's match with Sir Lyle. He carried a satchel and a long, flat case where he kept his two swords – foil and saber. Though it was still early, by club standards, one of the twins was at his post as Persano walked in.

"I am not a member. I believe that Sir Lyle Hammersmith may be a member and he has arranged for us to engage in some repartee this afternoon. Are you aware?"

"Yes, Mr. Persano. I am Scott Sobotta, one of the two house managers. The arrangements are unfinished but underway. Would you care to lunch with us today?"

"No. I have come to practice. Have you a fencing second, with whom I could spar?"

"I am sure that we could meet your needs. Allow me to show you to the dressing room."

Persano motioned with his head for Sobotta to lead the way. Sobotta took the satchel from Persano and left the case of swords under Persano's control.

Watson was fidgeting in his chair by the unlit fire. The windows to 221B were open and the ~~fresh~~ breeze coming through the windows provided the sitting room with much needed fresh air. Watson had been reading but had given up on that, dropping his book to the floor beside his chair. He looked over at the table and the unread telegram with barely contained curiosity. He puffed on his mid-afternoon cigar and waited impatiently for Holmes to return. Just then he heard a hansom come to a stop in front of their rooms and he quickly stood and walked briskly to the window. Holmes was fetching his keys and in the process of unlocking the door. Watson walked quietly back to his chair, picked up his book, and feigned reading as he awaited Holmes's arrival. Holmes stopped just outside the closed door to put away his hat and stick and opened the door with a flourish.

"Ahh, Watson, I see you are awaiting my return with some curiosity and not a little trepidation."

"Oh, hello, Holmes. I am afraid I didn't anticipate your arrival. Just enjoying a book and resting after our late night." Watson looked a bit sheepish. "Oh, by the way, a telegram arrived for you earlier."

Holmes smiled to himself and gave Watson a wink. "And since when have you taken up the habit of reading books upside down, old man?"

"Confound you Holmes. There is no fooling you. Yes, I am eager to hear of your adventures and to learn what is in that telegram." Watson laughed, smiled, and gave up all pretense of reading his book.

Holmes made a show of stretching as he walked to his bedroom. He quickly returned in his dressing gown and made straight for the mantle and his pipes. Taking great pains in choosing the pipe he wanted and filling it with shag tobacco from the Persian slipper. Sitting cross-legged in his chair and lighting his pipe with a vesper. Closing his eyes and taking in the strong tobacco with delight.

"Holmes! Get on with it, man."

Holmes chuckled. "I couldn't resist, Watson. You know how I love a touch of the dramatic. It was an interesting day."

"Well, come out with it. And what about the telegram that still lies on the table?"

"Which first, Watson? The tale of the day or the contents of the telegram?"

Watson let out an exasperated breath. "If I must choose, the tale of the day."

"As you no doubt vividly remember, the fruits of our labors last night, or more accurately early this morning, were much less than anticipated or hoped for. I am afraid that we were somewhat bested."

"Somewhat? We were led on a wild goose chase through the streets of London with nothing to show for it but a cold, wet evening, and a late night."

"I say 'somewhat,' Watson, because I had another person in my employ who kept watch over the Gemini Club after our departure."

"That street urchin of yours, hey?"

"Yes, Wiggins. After we were gone, the estimable Miss St. John exited, entered a hansom, and took off in a completely different direction from us. Wiggins is a slight young man, but he has stamina and is fast on his feet. Her route was more direct, and his chase was but for twenty to thirty minutes, he reported. She alighted in a somewhat darker and older side of the city with rows of similar, older housing. It was to one of these homes that she entered, while the hansom waited for her return.

"All this I learned from Wiggins when he came to get me at about half pass seven this morning. Wiggins waited for her to come back out and when she did, she was carrying a large packet or box. It was large enough that she gave it to the hansom driver to carry for her during her return to the club."

"A large packet from an old house. Hardly incriminating, Holmes."

"Oh, I agree of course. But, worthy of inspection, nevertheless. Wiggins and I traveled by hansom to the general neighborhood and made our way to the house, carefully, by foot. We were of course hampered by the daylight, and I dared not approach the house in the light of day."

"Then what did you do half the day?"

"I watched, Watson. Wiggins went on his way, and I sat in a small, weed-infested park with a good view of the front and one side of the house and smoked. A large flat tram drove up after a few hours of watching, and men began to load the tram with boxes of what looked to be scientific equipment. When they were finished, they drove off. It was nearly impossible to hail a hansom in that part of the City, but I eventually got one and caught-up with the tram in time to follow it to a much nicer side of town and a well-established home on a very nice street, Kensington Court, where the men unloaded boxes and odds and ends through an entrance to the cellar of the house.

"I walked by the house after the men had left and looking up, I read a nice brass plaque on the front door."

"What did it say?"

"It read, 'The Gemini Society / Private / By Appointment Only.'"

"Well, what do you suppose it all means…if anything, Holmes?"

"I am not completely sure, as yet, Watson. But it is a safe bet that the Gemini Society and the Gemini Club are related in some way. After leaving the house, I went to the records office and found that the ownership of both the club and the house are listed as the same company, which is itself owned by several other companies and no investors or persons were named. A good piece of legal work…" Holmes fell silent and stared down at his feet.

Watson waited a few minutes and then asked, "Anything else, Holmes?"

"No, no Watson that was it. I returned to Baker Street after that." Holmes looked distracted and sat sullen, as he smoked at his pipe in rapid inhalations for several minutes. "Well, let's see what this telegram is all about."

Holmes arose from his chair and walked over to the table and retrieved the telegram. He tore it open, read it quickly, and handed it to Watson.

"Well, what could my brother, Mycroft, want?"

"The telegram says he wishes to consult with you about a delicate matter."

"Yes, but a delicate matter for Mycroft could be the slightest and most uninteresting of things that loom large in his world but count for almost nothing outside of it."

Holmes had moved to his desk in front of the windows and taking a telegram form began to compose a response.

"Mrs. Hudson! Mrs. Hudson, I have a telegram that needs to be sent. Watson, can you please open the door and call for Mrs. Hudson?"

Sir Lyle Hammersmith arrived at the club late, at a quarter to four, rather than the three o'clock time the duel was scheduled to begin. He came with his second. Persano was not at all happy and in his waiting for the man had become quite angry and frustrated. He looked up from his pacing in his fencing uniform, and shouted, "Well it is about time you grace us with your presence Sir Lyle. I was beginning to think you did not have the courage nor honor to see the thing through." Persano wiped his brow with a towel and turned to face in the direction of his rival.

"We will see who takes the honor from this room when I have bested you!" Sir Lyle was livid, and appeared to be a little worse for having drank too much at lunch. "I see you have no second, as is customary."

"I have no need of a second in dealing with the likes of you, Sir Lyle. The whole thing will hardly raise a sweat on my brow." Persano walked toward the center of the room and the *piste*, retrieving his glove as he did.

"Gentlemen, please. Let's save the energy for the *piste* and not waste it throwing senseless jibes at each other." Scott Sobotta was acting as referee. Both men took different sides of the *piste* and began their preparations, with Sir Lyle dismissing his second.

"Have we decided on foils or sabers, Gentlemen?"

Both men looked at each other and then back at Scott. "May I suggest foils? The chance of serious injury is significantly reduced with foils and the match more challenging. Foils then?"

Both men nodded. Each was dressed in the traditional white, tight-fitting uniforms of the fencer. Neither had brought face and eye protection in the form of headgear, but had on the white breeches, jacket, and a single white glove on their right fencing hands. Each took his position on either side of the long *piste* and glared at each other.

"Gentlemen, I understand that you are both entering this duel of your own free will. The purpose is to settle a matter of honor and the traditional rules apply. Will first blood satisfy honor?" As he said this his twin, Steven, entered the room along with another gentleman neither dueler was familiar with.

"Who the blazes are they?" asked Sir Lyle.

"This is my brother, as the acting club manager during the duel, he will be a witness as will the gentleman standing with him. His name is of little consequence, but if you insist, with his permission, I will tell you."

"I insist!" said Hammersmith.

"Very well, he is one of our solicitors and is present to ensure that the matter is managed as gentlemen and to provide testimony, should either of you be mortally wounded during the process. His name is Mr. Samuel Gurel, Esq. He is an esteemed member of our club, a solicitor, and a respected member of the London Bar. We do not have a doctor here, but one is available quickly if we send for him. Any questions?"

Both men shook their heads in the negative.

"Now, as I was saying, I need to hear each of you affirmatively state that you are entering this duel of your own free will, to settle a matter of honor, and that honor will be satisfied upon first blood. Gentlemen?"

"Yes, of course. Let us get on with it!"

Persano, more calmly and confidently said, "Yes, Mr. Sabato. All is in accord with tradition and the rules governing such things."

"And may I ask who the wronged man is and who the challenged?"

"I am the challenged, and Sir Lyle Hammersmith here is the allegedly wronged man." Persano gave Hammersmith a mock bow.

"Allegedly! When we are finished here today, there will be no doubt about either the wronged or who is responsible. You have revealed the private matters and affairs of a gentlemen of the realm and have ruined my reputation. You shall pay for it, Persano." Hammersmith waved his foil in a flourish and stared coldly at Persano who merely chuckled and waved his own foil in an exaggerated flurry of his own.

"I remind both of you that you are dueling to first blood. That is all that is permitted here today. First blood will satisfy honor. We will have no more here today. Do you both understand?" Both men answered with a nod. "I am afraid that I must insist on a verbal acknowledgement, Gentlemen." Both men replied verbally, "Yes."

"Are both of you ready to proceed?" Both men nodded in the affirmative. "Very well. The challenged man shall proceed on the attack and the wronged man shall begin on defense. Please take a few minutes and alert me when you are set."

Both men stretched their legs in mock thrusts and parries. Both lunged several times and bounced on their feet. Then they each assumed their positions, with Sir Lyle on parry and Persano on attack.

"Very well. *En Garde. Prets...Allez!*" Scott stood to the side of the *piste* toward the middle, where he anticipated the two men would meet. Steven and Gurel stood on the other side of the *piste* and watched with interest.

Holmes and Watson were in a hansom on their way to the Diogenes Club to meet Mycroft Holmes, per the arrangement made between the two brothers via telegrams.

"What do you think this meeting is about, Holmes?"

"I do not know, and it is a mistake to speculate. We will learn the reason soon enough, Watson."

Watson fidgeted in his seat. "You can be most annoying at times, Holmes." Watson crossed his arms and looked away from Holmes at the street scenes as the hansom made its way to the club.

Upon arrival, Holmes stepped off the hansom and asked Watson to pay the cabby. Holmes rang the bell and the door opened revealing a short, very stern looking older, balding man dressed in formal evening wear.

"How may I help you gentlemen?"

"I am Sherlock Holmes, and this is my friend and colleague Dr. Watson. We have an appointment to meet my brother, Mycroft Holmes. He is a member." Holmes stepped past the doorman and into the formal entrance to the Diogenes Club, taking off his hat and making an effort to hand his hat and walking stick to the doorman.

"I see. I will take you to the Strangers Room where talking is allowed. As we make our way there, gentlemen, I must insist that you remain completely quiet. No talking of any kind and please make every effort to make no noise as you walk. This way gentlemen."

Holmes and Watson followed the little man through a large sitting room where gentlemen were seated in well-stuffed chairs arranged in the room to face away from each other. Each chair had its own small table to one side and a lamp on the other. The men were reading newspapers, books, pamphlets, and some read official looking papers. But none of the men paid the least attention to the others or to the doorman as he led Holmes and Watson in a direct path across the room to an adjoining hallway. The room had a haze of tobacco smoke as some men smoked cigars, cigarettes, and other men pipes. The room was very finely but conservatively decorated and had a stuffy, unloved feeling about it; as if the walls had never experienced the sound of laughter. Watson felt the silence like a heavy blanket or the darkness of a cloudy, moonless night, and walked uneasily behind Holmes, who seemed to take no notice. They arrived at a finely decorated meeting room and the doorman left without making a sound.

"Is this not the second or third time that we have been here, and each time I am shaken, yes shaken, by the atmosphere of this place. What a strange and unfriendly feeling one gets in this place. How could any man pay to be a member of such a club?" Watson shivered as he walked over to a small table to pour himself a drink.

"Ahh, Watson. That is the nature of the Diogenes Club. A club for men who do not seek the company of others, who are some of the unfriendliest men in London. I dare say many of the members have not the slightest care regarding the names or backgrounds of the other members. Except, I suppose, when one member recommends the admission of a new member. After that, not a word is spoken between them. It is a rather exclusive and reclusive group."

"What is the point, Holmes? Why get together at all?"

"I suppose to have a place to escape the drudgery of home and wife. A place to escape the noise and chaos of London. A place to find the peace of silence and the serenity of being alone, as it were. Ahh, here comes my brother now."

Persano, left arm behind his back, quickly moved forward toward Hammersmith, in the awkward sideways fashion of the trained fencer, his foil out front, its tip raised at a forty-five-degree angle pointing upward. Hammersmith stepped forward two steps and prepared to parry any lunge made by his opponent. His gait, slightly off balance and a bit unsure. Persano's foil moved quickly first to his right, then toward the front and lowered, and then quickly in a lunge toward Hammersmith's chest. Hammersmith parried and his foil led Persano's to his right, just missing his right shoulder. Hammersmith took the advantage and lunged forward aiming for Persano's chest, but the quick Persano simply parried and moved to his left avoiding Hammersmith's foil entirely.

"You are not in your best form, Sir Lyle. Perhaps you should have delayed our match."

"Nonsense! I am in good enough form to best you any day."

The two men moved back to their starting positions and Hammersmith took his turn on the attack while Persano defended. And so it went for several minutes. Each man taking turns on attack or defense. Neither scoring a touch. Hammersmith was sweating profusely and wiped his forehead with his free hand, while Persano seemed barely winded by the match.

"A break then, gentlemen. Each man to his own side." Scott, noticing Hammersmith's condition, called for the break in action. Both men walked to their side of the *piste*. Hammersmith used a towel the dry his face, and to wipe the sweat from his eyes.

"Can I get some damn water here!" Hammersmith was out of breath and drank lustily from the glass that was brought to him by Steven. "Let's get on with it!"

"Oh please, Sir Lyle, please take your time. I am in no hurry and the excitement of the match is very enjoyable. Please, rest." Persano's smiled as he sarcastically provoked Hammersmith with his words.

"Damn you to hell. I need no more rest. Let's get on with it, I say!" Hammersmith walked swiftly back to his position on the *piste* as he again waived his foil in a dramatic flourish.

"As you wish," Persano made his way back to his position, stopping to bounce on the balls of his feet and making his own movements with his foil.

"We begin again, gentlemen," Scott said. "I believe Sir Lyle has the honors and you, Mr. Persano, are *en garde*."

Persano looked at Hammersmith, his heavy breathing, and his profuse sweating, and decided to keep his position, requiring Hammersmith to cross the length of the *piste* to attack him. He stood straight, his left arm behind his back, his foil pointing downward in front of him.

Hammersmith was infuriated by Persano's apparent ease and failure to move forward and filled with that rage, ignoring form, ran forward to meet Persano's foil. As he did so, chest open and exposed, his foil above him in the air, he growled with rage. As he approached Persano, his opponent let a smile cross his face. A petulant, arrogant, dismissive smile that stoked Hammersmith's rage the more. He cried in his rage as his foil came down.

Persano blocked his foil, using Hammersmith's own momentum against him, and as Hammersmith stumbled slightly, Persano drove his foil home, piercing Hammersmith's chest just below his heart, as he, in a low, tucked position, attacked from below, his foil piercing flesh and driving through Hammersmith's heart and out his back. Hammersmith stumbled forward, falling on his face, driving the foil further through his body and with a large exhalation of air collapsed and breathed no more.

Persano had gracefully moved to his left, avoiding the falling body of his opponent, standing just to the side and slightly behind Hammersmith with a look of satisfaction upon his face.

"Damn you, Mr. Persano! The fight was to first blood, not death! You have done him in." Scott ran quickly to Hammersmith's side and felt for a pulse, and finding none, stood exasperated looking directly at Persano.

"It was quite by accident, gentlemen, I assure you. You saw him run at me and his momentum and lack of balance caused him to fall into my foil. I meant only to take him in the shoulder, but his lack of fitness, imbalance, rage, and poor technique are what did him in. Not me." Persano strutted like a proud fighting cock looking at his dead opponent.

Chapter 11

"Sherlock! Dr. Watson! How good to see you. Thank you for agreeing to meet with me. I see that you are helping yourself to a drink, Dr. Watson. Please make yourselves comfortable." The rather large Mycroft Holmes walked into the room with the flourish of a man who is confident and powerful. His movements expansive, his expressions full, and his voice deep and resonant.

"Mycroft, you know how busy I am. I have little time to give to you this afternoon. I am in the middle of a case that demands my full attention. Please, come to the point. Why have you summoned me here?"

Mycroft looked at Watson and let out a chuckle, "One of your little problems, hey, Sherlock? What is it this time? A missing tea set? A lost pocket watch? A purloined letter of passion?"

Holmes scoffed turning his back to his brother. "Yes, of course that is what I spend my time doing, Mycroft. It has been years since such cases took up my time. I am afraid that more interesting and complex matters take my time and effort now. Now, please, can we get to the matter at hand? Why have you summoned me here?"

Watson moved and sat in one of the comfortable chairs, taking a sip from his brandy and soda. Holmes turned with a flurry toward his brother, a look of impatience upon his face.

"Always in a hurry you are, dear Sherlock. Always full of energy. Even as a child you could never sit still and do nothing. Your very presence wears me thin. Yes, the telegram. I will get to it presently."

"Alas, please do!"

"There are some rumblings in our secret service. Fears that someone is blackmailing our middle management. Noise that there is an outside influence, still in its infancy, but troubling nonetheless. There is no clue as to the motive, or what information this clandestine outside person or persons is attempting to get. But it concerns us none the less. I was asked to speak with you, engage you, to get to the bottom of it."

"Is that it then? You can tell me no more?"

"Only that certain of our men, in important but hardly significant positions, have been caught sniffing about at matters above their station and when questioned at length, and when followed to certain clubs, they finally and simply admit to certain dalliances. You know the kind. A gambling debt, a night spent with a professional lady, experiences with stimulants. The odd favor asked, the information requested seemingly unobtrusive, and there you have it. Probes by someone outside the family of government. Beginnings of something, we fear. Checking our controls. Nothing to worry about, yet. Given what you did for us in that affair of the Green Dragon, your name came up as someone who could discreetly make inquiries and tell us if something larger is amiss."

"Clubs? What clubs?"

"Sherlock, I am not in possession of all the details. Clubs, that is all I know. You are wearing me out already with your questions. If I had your energy, I would look into it myself, but I haven't the time nor the energy to do so."

Mycroft walked over to a desk and wrote on a piece of paper. "Here is the name and office of the gentleman in the secret service who can shed more light on the situation. Will you make inquiries for us? Will you look into the matter?"

Holmes took the paper from Mycroft with resignation and a sigh. "Yes, Mycroft, I will try to find some time to investigate the matter, but I can promise nothing at present. Anything else?"

"No Sherlock, nothing else. Her Majesty's government thanks you. Are you off already? Stay for a late tea?"

"I am afraid not, Mycroft." Holmes was walking out the door before Watson had the chance to stand. "Come along Watson."

"I will handle the notification to the family and the transportation of the body. I am certain the family will want to keep things quiet and handle the situation discreetly as well. A story will be manufactured for the press, and the family will save face in the process." Samuel Gurel, attorney for the Gemini Club spoke quickly and with confidence.

"Very well. I must notify the lady of the establishment and discuss what is to be done about Persano."

As Scott said this, Persano entered the room, having changed clothes and looking none the worse for wear. "I trust all is satisfactory. A simple accident during a fencing competition. No?"

"It may be more complicated than that, Mr. Persano." Steven was walking out of the room to inform Miss St. John of events.

"Why? Why must it be more complicated than that?"

"Well, because the agreement was to go to first blood, not to the death, Mr. Persano. Despite your cavalier manner, this has important implications for the club and I dare say, may have legal complications for you. We will, of course, seek to handle everything with discretion, but much depends on how Sir Hammersmith's family reacts." Scott was concerned at the indifference displayed by Persano.

"I am experienced in these matters. This isn't my first duel. All was done according to tradition and the rules that govern such matters. Accidents happen. That is part of the risk of such things. Sir Lyle publicly challenged me, made the arrangements, and failed to take proper precautions, resulting in his accidental death. Nothing more."

"We shall see if that is what comes of this. Of course, we will make every effort to influence matters in that direction."

"Very well. Now, I have matters to attend to this evening. Gentlemen, I bid you a good evening." With that Persano, taking up his case of swords, left the room and the Club.

Scott looked at Gurel, "Miss St. John will not be happy about this."

"If you need me to speak with her, I can. In the meantime, I need to make the arrangements. You know where to reach me if you need anything else." Gurel gave Scott a confident nod, and then left the club as well.

Scott looked over at Hammersmith's body and shook his head. Not out of remorse or grief, but as one who has a mess to clean up and a lack of motivation to begin. He closed and locked the door to the room and walked slowly to Miss St. John's office, where he knew his brother was already notifying the lady of the house.

Holmes was silent and morose in the hansom on the trip back to Baker Street. From long experience, Watson knew not to engage him when he was in such a mood. Instead he looked out his side of the hansom as it went through the streets of London. His mind was back on the events of the night before. He was embarrassed for Holmes, but also not surprised that Holmes had taken additional precautions and had come back to Baker Street that afternoon with more information than seemed possible from the events of the previous evening. Nothing made any sense to Watson. Nothing seemed connected. Now this distraction brought on by Mycroft. Watson finally decided to break the silence.

"Would you like for me to look into this matter that your brother Mycroft just gave us? That will let you focus on the current case. It does not sound very complicated or even very promising. I am sure that I can handle it and report back to you."

Holmes looked over at Watson and smiled. "Yes, that would be very helpful, dear Watson. Here is the note from Mycroft. Please go and speak with this gentleman, learn what you can, and report back to me. Oh, and be sure to get a list of clubs and the names and departments of the persons involved."

"Of course, Holmes. I will begin tomorrow." Watson settled into the cushioned back rest of the hansom and smiled to himself. He was glad that Holmes trusted him with this assignment and happy to take it up.

"I am afraid that we have a long evening ahead of us, Watson. I want to make a late-night excursion to the house I observed earlier today. You are not opposed to a late-night burglary are you, old man?"

Watson laughed, "How many times have you asked me that? Have I ever shirked, hesitated, or refused? All I ask is, can we please ask Mrs. Hudson for dinner before we leave Baker Street?"

"Of course, Watson. We have time before we set out. You are a faithful and welcome companion, dear Watson. I thank you."

Gurel had been true to his word. Undertakers had arrived and removed Hammersmith's body. The family had been informed of the unfortunate accident and a story for the press had been created and accepted by the family. It appeared to Gurel that the family was anxious to keep the truth out of the press and to avoid the lurid gaze of the public eye. There was almost a sense of relief that the family's prodigal son had been silenced, and the chances of more embarrassing stories in the papers eliminated.

But the Hammersmith family was only one aspect of the events that needed to be taken care of. As the twins met with Becca it became clear that Persano had to be dealt with as well. He could not be allowed to have such damaging leverage over the club and perhaps even Becca herself. It was already bad enough that Persano was a formidable adversary in the press – with his seemingly tireless crusade against London's private clubs. Beca knew that it was only a matter of time before his focus came down on the Gemini Club, its members, and even herself. Now he had knowledge of a cover-up of a death at the club and even with his involvement in that death, he had no reputation to save, he was known as a prodigious duelist and took pride in his reputation. She would need to make plans to eliminate his potential threat to her and the club.

"I am disappointed that neither of you would have foreseen the events of this afternoon and taken steps to both avoid the situation entirely and having failed in that, to better manage the duel." The Twins both bowed their heads in shame as they sat with Becca in her office at the club. "But these things are part of the risk we take when running an establishment like our club. As I said, I am disappointed, but I do not lay all the blame at your feet; I share in it as well. The person most responsible for these events, however, is Persano himself. Please look into his habits, where he lives, where he works, where he dines, and with whom he socializes. And do this quickly and discreetly. Am I understood?"

Steven and Scott almost simultaneously said, "Yes." They got up and with a small bow of their heads, left Becca's office. As they stood outside her closed door, they exchanged

142

glances. Steven was always the calmer of the two and he spoke first.

"I will arrange for the surveillance; you concentrate on running things here and keeping Madame happy. Together we will make our way back into her good graces. Stay calm. Stay focused on your work." Steven had his hand on Scott's shoulder. Scott simply nodded his head and returned to his post.

Back home, at dinner, Becca was morose and silent. She appeared to Lilith to be a seething caldron ready to erupt at any second. Lilith did not know what to say or to do. She sat eating dinner quietly as Becca barely touched her food and instead stared down at the floor.

"The workmen have finished moving the boxes into the cellar and I have ensured that everything is neatly stored. The lamps, soil, and vegetation have been left for you to arrange per your instructions. All is as you wished."

Becca simply nodded her head in response to Lilith's report.

"It seems that you had a rather trying day at the club." Lilith stood and made her way toward Becca. She stood behind her and softly caressed her hair. "I am sorry about that. Is it something you would like to discuss?"

Becca responded to Lilith's touch by relaxing her shoulders and moving her head slowly in response to her touch. "I do not wish to discuss it. A complication, nothing more."

Lilith moved her fingers deftly from Becca's hair to her shoulders slowly massaging the stress away and humming softly. She could feel Becca responding to her touch and she slowly moved from Becca's shoulders to her breast. Even through Becca's clothing she could feel her breast respond to her soothing touch. Becca slowly stood and turned to face Lilith. Becca raised her right hand toward Lilith's neck, and she held her neck firmly in her grasp, raising Lilith's face upward. Becca kissed Lilith forcefully, biting her lower lip as she did; then she stopped.

"I have no time for this now. I must change clothes and go into the basement and set things up. Perhaps later when I am finished."

Lilith gave Becca a look of exaggerated disappointment and leaned forward and kissed Becca on the tip of her nose. "You know we both need it. I will be in your room later tonight, awaiting your arrival."

Watson sat at table finishing his dinner with relish as Holmes smoked and looked out the window upon Baker Street, reading the people like pages of a book. It was dusk and the long shadows of the people, the hansoms, and the buildings gave the scene outside 221B a kind of dreamy quality. Holmes was thinking about the quality of the legal work he had seen in the hall of records surrounding both the Gemini Club and Gemini Society. That and the fact of one dead lawyer and another at the same firm who very likely was the source of the work and himself a member of the club. The pieces to the puzzle were beginning to come together in his mind, but nothing coherent enough to share.

"You obviously enjoyed your dinner, Watson. Feeling better?"

"Mrs. Hudson can do wonderous things with grouse, don't you agree?"

"I am afraid I can spare no physical energy for digestion this evening. But, yes, she cooks grouse very well indeed."

"Will you have nothing to eat this evening?"

"I finished my coffee and ate a dinner roll. I am in need of no other nourishment at this time. Ah, here she comes to clean away the detritus from your meal."

Watson looked up as Mrs. Hudson came in carrying a tray. "My, you were hungry, Dr. Watson."

"Mrs. Hudson, I was just commenting to Holmes, you do wonders with a grouse. The sauce was simply exquisite. Yes, I thoroughly enjoyed the meal you so deftly prepared." Watson was smiling and standing as Mrs. Hudson began to clear the dishes.

"I am so pleased," she said, "But as usual I see that Mr. Holmes barely touched his meal. His plate has only crumbs from a dinner roll. He drank some coffee, but that is all I can see."

"Mrs. Hudson, your observations are all correct. I ate a dinner roll and had a cup of coffee. Watson, I believe Mrs. Hudson has the makings of a detective in her."

"Oh my goodness, no!" Mrs. Hudson's face reddened with both embarrassment and appreciation. "You are detective enough for this house, Mr. Holmes."

"Do not tempt her away from her cooking, Holmes. We would both be in a sticky wicket if Mrs. Hudson were to change professions. No, I believe Mrs. Hudson that you should stick to grouse for the sake of at least my appetite, if not Holmes's."

"You two men, what will I do with you," Mrs. Hudson chuckled as Watson held the door open for her and she proceeded downstairs with her tray full.

Holmes had moved from the window over to the mantle where he took down one of his oily clay pipes and began to fill it with shag tobacco. Watson too had walked over to his place by the unlit fireplace and was in the act of selecting a cigar.

"What now, Holmes?"

"Now we wait. It is a quarter to eight and as you know it is only after midnight that one engages in burglary. Maybe we shall have a nice cover of fog by then as well. No, we wait, and we smoke."

"Well, after I smoke this cigar, I may just nap until you are ready to proceed." Watson settled into his chair having lit his cigar and the two, sitting in their chairs, smoked and watched the smoke rings slowly make a fog in 221B Baker Street.

Chapter 12

The evening was a moonless not atypical summer night in London. It was cold, and a thick, wet fog had rolled in off the Thames. Mixed with the smoke of coal fires now lit in many homes around London, the air was a thick, wet, yellow gray. Combined with the moonless sky, except for the barely visible light from a streetlight or lantern, it was very dark and very hard to see. Perfect Holmes thought for his plans for the evening.

Holmes and Watson were in a hansom on their way to the neighborhood of houses he had watched the day before. The cabby drove his horse more from memory than from sight, such was the blackness of the night and the thickness of the fog, and Holmes thrilled at the ride under such conditions. Watson, having been awakened by Holmes at just after midnight, was still not fully awake and weighed down by the carpet bag full of tools for use in their evening trade, sitting on his lap. And so it was, Holmes excited and alert, and Watson tired, sleepy, and resigned.

As they approached the general vicinity of the house, Holmes ordered the driver to stop, paid him, and leapt from the hansom onto the cobbled road. Watson was slower to step down carrying the carpet bag.

"This way Watson! Give me a dark lantern." Holmes and Watson each lit a dark lantern Watson retrieved from the carpet bag and walked slowly down the right side of the street toward the house. "This fog is perfect for concealing us, but terrible for locating the house. I can barely see the houses from the gutter. I need to get my bearings. Let's stop under that lamp."

Holmes closed his eyes and tried to picture the street from his memory of the day before, but it was no use. He instead pictured the park where he had sat smoking and the position of the house relative to the bench where he sat.

"Let us cross the road and make for the park," he said.

"In this fog we could easily be run over by an oncoming hansom or carriage, Holmes. Be careful."

Holmes grunted and made his way to the other side of the street. They walked two or three hundred feet before a space opened between the houses, signifying the location of the park. Holmes stopped.

"My bench cannot be more than twenty feet inward and in this direction." He quickly moved at an angle into the park, brushing against overgrown weeds as he did. "Ahh, here it is. The house must be in this direction." Holmes pointed his walking stick at a roughly forty-five-degree angle from the bench, slightly to the left, and proceeded – first on grass and then the cobble stones of the street and at last in front of a two-story old wooden house with a large front porch. "This is it, Watson. I am sure of it. Let us go around to the left side of the house to find the entrance into the cellar. Be careful, don't trip."

Holmes and Watson proceeded to the left side of the house and soon found the entrance to the cellar. The twin doors to the cellar were locked with a heavy metal lock.

"I need my lock-picking tools, Watson. Please retrieve them from the carpet bag."

Watson fumbled around the carpet bag more by feel than by sight and found the long rolled up leather sleeve that held Holmes's lock-picking tools. He handed the bundle to Holmes.

"Put the bag down and shine both of our dark lanterns on the lock. Hurry man!"

"I am going as fast as I can, Holmes." Watson put down the bag and taking Holmes's dark lantern shined the lantern, along with his, onto the large, heavy lock. Holmes selected his tools and had no sooner began his work, than they each heard an approaching carriage.

"Quick Watson. Close the lanterns and do not make a sound."

The carriage approached and then traveling past the house proceeded down the street and out of sight in the fog.

"Good. Let's proceed, Watson."

Holmes worked on the lock for no more than five minutes, and it soon gave way to his skills, opening with an audible click. Holmes opened the half door to the right and shining his dark lantern into the open space proceeded inside the cellar. It was dark and stuffy inside the cellar, smelling of earth, dust, and mold. Broken cobwebs hung from the ceiling revealing that the room had been recently disturbed. Holmes shined his lantern around the room, but nothing of interest was visible.

"We need to make our way to the ground floor, Watson. There is nothing of interest here." Holmes shined his lantern about and soon revealed a set of stairs and a door that presumably led to the first floor of the house. He proceeded in that direction followed closely by Watson.

The stairs creaked loudly under the combined weight of Holmes and Watson but did not give way. The door to the first floor was unlocked, and both men proceeded through it without difficulty. They entered the kitchen and Holmes proceeded into what was a large sitting room, though unfurnished. Further in the house was a large dining room, that was empty as well, except for three boxes. Holmes stopped and shined his lantern about taking in the details of the room.

"Look at the floor, Watson. The dust is thick, and one can see where there was furniture in this room and the foot marks of men. This is where the work was performed in this house." Holmes began his close inspection of the room, having handed his open lantern to Watson. "Shine both lights in front of me as I make my inspection," he said.

Holmes walked gingerly on the tip of his toes as he gazed steadily down at the two joining circles of light on the floor. He did this for several minutes and then almost fell to his face as he examined parts of the floor more carefully, letting out little sounds of satisfaction as he crawled around the floor.

"Turn the lights to each of the corners of the room, beginning with this one," Holmes said.

He examined each of the corners very carefully, even taking a lantern from Watson on occasion and using his powerful magnifying glass, looking up and down the corners and the floor. After several minutes had passed, he stopped, and arms crossed in front of him and chin on his chest, stared downward in deep thought.

"That is all I can get from this room, in this dark. Let us proceed upstairs to the bedrooms."

Holmes and Watson went up the stairs and to each of the three bedrooms. Only one had furniture. It was clearly the master bedroom and contained a four-poster bed, a chest, a small table and chair, and a window that showed the foggy street in front of the house.

"Be careful with the lights Watson. No need to announce our presence to the world; although I doubt the world can see us through the fog. Nevertheless, close the shutters most of the way on each lantern. Here let me have one."

Holmes looked around the bedroom, the bed itself, the chest, and then the small table. He looked quickly through the papers on the table and suddenly stopped, examining one paper carefully.

"It is a note, Watson. Started but not finished. The note is addressed to Mrs. Hudson…"

"What?"

Holmes handed Watson the note and he pointed his lantern at the note reading it. It looked like a note of apology and explanation addressed to a man's mother. The address on the front of the letter was 221B Baker Street.

"I don't believe it, Holmes. What could Mrs. Hudson have to do with this? What does it mean?"

"It means that her son was caught up in whatever this intrigue is. He was here. Stayed in this very room, from time to time, and likely worked downstairs in the lab. Yes, lab. For that is what it was. Not a chemical lab, mind you, but some kind of biological lab. The floor has soil and bits of leaves.

Whatever was grown in that lab needed soil and plants to survive. Given that Mrs. Hudson's son was an entomologist, I am deducing that what was grown in the lab was some kind of insect."

"What do we tell Mrs. Hudson?"

"Nothing. Absolutely nothing. When this is finished, we will discuss how to tell her the truth about her son. At present, we don't know enough to tell her anything." Holmes looked at Watson sternly. Watson nodded his head in agreement.

"Then the crates and things you saw taken from here and moved to the other house...are the experiments continuing there?"

"I should think not. It appears whatever was being grown has achieved the desired development and all that is left is to keep the results alive. That does not likely require an entomologist but may require specialized equipment. No, that is all we can glean from here. We should make our way back to Baker Street before we are found out."

Holmes sat in his chair back at Baker Street, pipe in mouth, fingers pressed against each other in front of his face, in deep thought. Even Watson had not gone to bed. He sat in his chair looking bewildered and worried. The two men had been home for more than an hour but had not said a word to one another. Each was lost in his own thoughts trying to make sense of what the evening had revealed.

"Holmes, what possible connection could Mrs. Hudson's son have had to the Gemini Club?"

Holmes's eyes fluttered as if he had been awakened from a trance-like state. "Obviously, he was a member."

Watson's eyes grew large, and his mouth was agape. "But what could he possibly have had to do with that Club?"

"Come Watson. You are a doctor. When he collapsed in this very room, you diagnosed the symptoms of withdrawal from the abuse of some drug. And where do you think a respectable man goes to feed his hunger for the drug and likely his need for female companionship, but a private club like the Gemini Club. I am afraid that...."

Holmes stopped mid-sentence and simply stared at the floor in front of him.

"Do you remember, Watson? Do you remember what Rodrick Hudson said while in the throes of his delusions?"

"I am afraid I do not, Holmes. I was focused on care and Mrs. Hudson. I do not recall."

"He went on about a witch. He said, 'the witch has me,' and some such things. He was singularly focused on 'the witch.'"

"But Holmes you can hardly build on the ravings of a man in the throes of delirium. That reference to a witch could just have easily been about the drug itself."

"You are of course correct, Watson. And I would agree under normal circumstance, but these are not normal circumstances. No! I am inclined to believe that Hudson was referring to a woman. A woman who had him under her control, under her spell. Whom he was being forced to work with..." Holmes fell silent again as Watson simply stared at him trying to make sense of so many loose threads with no seeming way to bring them together.

"I am sorry, Holmes. I simply do not see any connection."

"Watson! Come man. Roderick Hudson is an entomologist. He comes to these very rooms suffering from terrible withdrawal. He dies on that rug shouting about a witch. We know the Gemini Club is managed by a woman, Miss Rebecca St. John. The Club was frequented by our client's *par amour* and his legal partner. We know that she went to the empty house and retrieved a crate or parcel of some sort. We know that men came the next day and cleared out the house, taking the contents to the address on Kensington Court. And now we know that Roderick Hudson spent time at the same house and that there was a biological lab set-up in the dining room. The connections are certain. The train of deductions are clear."

Watson swallowed. He looked down at the floor and then back at Holmes. "Holmes, everything you say is true, but what does it all mean? What does all this have to do with Mr. Holcomb's death; or for that matter, the death of Roderick Hudson?"

"I do not know, Watson. That is the maddening aspect of it all. I do not know."

Chapter 13

The next morning Watson was up early, before nine, and dispatched a telegram. He was waiting for the answer and drinking his coffee when Holmes came into the room, still in his night clothes and dressing gown. Holmes walked over to the table and poured himself a cup of coffee and proceeded to the window to look out at Baker Street.

"You are up early after a very late night, Watson."

"Yes. I sent a telegram to the gentleman your brother, Mycroft, recommended, and I am awaiting an answer before I make my visit. There is still some toast and some cold eggs if you are hungry."

"Thank you, Watson. No, I think the coffee and a cigarette are all I need this morning. I have much thinking to do."

Watson finished his coffee and stood to stretch. "I must say, I could use some more sleep, but I have my assignment and I mean to see it through."

Holmes chuckled, "Very well, Watson. I could do well with some silence."

Holmes walked over to his chair, lit a cigarette, and sat down. Watson followed and brought the newspaper with him. They each sat in silence as Watson read the paper. After twenty minutes they each heard the bell ring, and the familiar steps of Mrs. Hudson came up the stairs.

"Dr. Watson, a telegram for you."

Watson stood and took the telegram from Mrs. Hudson and read it. "Ahh, the gentleman can meet with me in one hour. I have written some questions in my notebook, and

I am prepared for the interview. I will leave shortly and report back to you, Holmes. Satisfactory?"

"Yes, Watson. Very satisfactory."

Mrs. Hudson looked about the room and the table, "If you want nothing to eat, Mr. Holmes, I will come back up in a few minutes to clear the table."

Holmes nodded and Mrs. Hudson sighed and left the room. Watson paced and fidgeted with his watch. He was clearly nervous.

"Would you like me to join you, Watson?"

"Absolutely not, Holmes." Watson retrieved his hat and walking stick and turning to Holmes as he walked out the door said, "The game is afoot!" He could hear Holmes's laughter as he closed the door.

Holmes was leaning against a tree watching the house on Kensington Court. He was dressed as an out of work groom, chewing on a long piece of grass and drinking from a bottle he would retrieve out of a pocket in his torn and worn jacket. He was unrecognizable. What had remained of the morning as he stood at his post, brought no new information. It was now early afternoon, and he was beginning to think that his vigil would yield no promising results. As he continued to watch, a carriage pulled up to the house and soon thereafter Miss St. John exited the front door and into the carriage. Standing at the door as she left was another woman. This woman quickly closed the door. Holmes now knew that there were at least two women in the house.

He watched as the carriage took Miss St. John away. Holmes stood and slowly ambled to the side and then to the back of the house where two more horses were kept in the mews. He approached, drunkenly, and leaned against a fence.

"What are the likes of you doing here?" asked one of the workers.

"Whawt? Me?"

"Yeah you."

"Just looking for an odd job. I'm a first-class groom, I am. Out of work."

"Really? You?" the man said chuckling.

"I don't need to take this abuse…"

"No don't go. There're some brushes. Give those two a go and I'll take care of you alright."

Holmes spent the afternoon caring for the horses, cleaning tack, washing down the mews with buckets of water, and learning everything he could about the household, without seeming a bit interested. It was close to dark before he was paid off with a few shillings, some tobacco, and half a bottle of gin. Holmes decided to make his way back to Baker Street. As he was leaving, the back door to the house opened and there stood the same petite woman he had seen earlier in the day when Miss St. John had left.

"Excuse me, sir. Yes, you sir. Are you a strong lad?"

Holmes lifted his knuckle to his forehead and tipped his hat. "Yes, mum."

"Could you help my men move some boxes about in the cellar?"

"Well yes, mum. I could."

Lilith motioned for Holmes to follow her into the house. Holmes did so reticently and shyly as was appropriate to his station as a vagrant and a groom. He came into the house through the kitchen and immediately down a set of narrow stairs and into a dark cellar illuminated in the distance by several bright lights. As he and Lilith approached the lights, Holmes could see that the area where the lights were shining was surrounded by a curtained "wall." He could not clearly see what was on the other side, but in the slight spaces between the curtains he would make out two long, wood, lab tables. The lamps were bright gas lamps meant, Holmes thought, more for heat than light. On the tables were opened boxes, but Holmes could see no more.

Holmes helped move several heavy boxes away from the lighted area of the cellar and back toward the walls in an organized stack. Some boxes were labeled, but he couldn't make out most of the writing in the darker corners of the cellar. Some of the boxes were labeled in German and clearly contained sophisticated lab equipment, as the men were constantly warned by Lilith to be very careful with the boxes.

After the men had finished, they left with Holmes lagging. As Holmes approached the kitchen door, the petite woman smiled.

"It was very kind of you to help us this evening. Here is a sovereign for your troubles."

"No trouble, mum. I don't need no tip, mum. Your men took care of me earlier. I appreciate the work, what, given the price of the gin."

"No, I insist. Thank you very much."

Holmes took the sovereign, raised his knuckle to his forehead, and left the house through the kitchen door. As he walked down the street, Holmes chuckled to himself. Whoever the petite young lady was, she was kind and he appreciated that.

Watson had returned to Baker Street anxious to complete his assignment and report back to Holmes, but when he arrived, Holmes was nowhere to be found. Watson looked for a note, but Holmes had left none. Watson was frustrated and disappointed. He sat in his chair and smoked a pipe, reading the afternoon newspaper. In the paper was an obituary regarding the unexpected death of Sir Lyle Hammersmith. Apparently, Hammersmith had suffered an unexpected and massive heart attack, leaving him dead on the spot. The family was of course devastated by the events. Burial services had been arranged.

Watson left for a late lunch of fish-and-chips and a pint and returned late afternoon to find that Holmes was still absent. He stopped and spoke with Mrs. Hudson, who knew nothing of Holmes's whereabouts. Exasperated, Watson went up to his rooms and took a nap.

When he awakened it was dusk and the light from the sun was slowly fading. He went downstairs to the sitting room, finding that Mrs. Hudson had been busy tidying up the area. Holmes was still not present. Watson retrieved a cigar and sat in front of the now lit fireplace, for it was another cold evening, and he smoked and had a scotch and soda. Just as evening was setting in, the bell rang below, and Watson could hear the rough sounds of a man speaking with Mrs. Hudson.

Watson walked out the door and onto the landing and looking down saw a drunk, out of work, groom pointing to something on a dirty paper and saying he needed to speak with Mr. Sherlock Holmes.

"But I am telling you, sir, he is not here." Mrs. Hudson was pleading with the man to return later when Holmes was in.

"What is the trouble, Mrs. Hudson?"

"Dr. Watson, this man will simply not listen to me that Mr. Holmes is not in. He is quite insistent that he see Mr. Holmes immediately."

"Oh, uh, sir. Mr. Holmes is not here at present. Perhaps I can help you? I am his colleague, Dr. Watson."

The man looked up at Watson, "It's regarding this advertisement in the paper, sir. A job. Now I'm here first and the job should rightly go to me. I am here to see Mr. Holmes about this job..." The man left Mrs. Hudson and began to climb the stairs to the landing, stumbling several times along the way.

"I am afraid that I know nothing about a job that Mr. Holmes advertised in the paper, sir. Nothing at all. You will need to come back when Mr. Holmes has returned." But the man kept coming up the stairs. "Now listen here, sir, Mr. Holmes is not here, there is nothing that I can help you with regarding a job."

The man stopped at the landing just in front of Watson. He suddenly stood fully erect and in Holmes's voice said, "Well, my dear Watson, I am sure you could help me with a glass of brandy and a nice cigar. And as for you Mrs. Hudson, dinner in an hour, if you please."

Both Watson and Mrs. Hudson below began to laugh heartily, and Mrs. Hudson, shooing Holmes away with her arms said, "Dinner in an hour Mr. Holmes. No matter how many times you do this, it never fails to surprise me."

Watson and Holmes walked into their sitting room, as Holmes began to remove parts of his disguise.

"Holmes, I have said it before, but it bears repeating, you are a prodigious actor. How in heaven's name have you been engaged all day?"

Holmes sat at his desk between the two windows and began to clean the makeup and other paraphernalia of his character from his face.

"I had a most interesting day, Watson. But first I want to hear about your day and what you learned from our man in Her Majesty's security service."

Watson was very pleased that Holmes had asked to hear his report first. He retrieved his pipe from the small table beside the fireplace, lit it, and began to tell his story while Holmes finished his cleaning and went between his room and the sitting room as Watson talked.

"There are three young men, all from excellent families, with seemingly good careers ahead of them who have been affected by these attempts at influence and even blackmail. All three were caught because they were off their stations and speaking with colleagues in other departments. Each of the departments had business with the development of naval armament. But the kinds of questions these three young men were asking were all very naïve and ill informed.

Simple questions about the length of the Mark IV torpedo, its weight, its width, but nothing more serious than superficial questions. If it weren't for their repeated attempts at questioning, no one would have taken notice.

"When individually questioned about what they were up to, each admitted to being besotted by a woman at a private club. Each knew her by a different name, but all described a similarly built woman at the same club."

"And the club, Watson. What was the name of the club?"

Watson stood up straight and proudly said, "The Gemini Club, Holmes. The Gemini Club."

Holmes let out a little whistle. "And there is little doubt that the woman they were each besotted with is the same woman?"

"Holmes, they each described a very similar woman in figure, but with different colored hair, and different accents. One was English, the other French, and still another was Scottish."

"Very interesting, indeed. Did your man have any suspicion at all regarding what the lady or ladies was looking for? What she wanted to know?"

"That is the puzzle, Holmes. The questions were so innocuous and so inconsequential, that the government has all but concluded it was not so much an attempt to get information, as it was a test of the government's controls over the information it has and the ease, or lack thereof, of getting to information within the government."

"I must say, Watson, well done. You have opened a new avenue of inquiry into this damnable problem we have been attempting to decipher."

Watson beamed at Holmes's praise and nodded in return. "Do you really think this matter is related to our case?"

Holmes looked at Watson with amusement but said nothing.

"Now, Holmes, where did you get off to today, and what have you found out?"

"I left Baker Street soon after you, in the guise of an out-of-work groom, very much as you saw me just now. I spent an uneventful late morning observing the house but was there long enough to observe Miss St. John leave the house in a carriage and at the door as she left was another woman. I eventually made my way around to the mews behind the house, and after a day of grooming and working, I learned something of the household.

"The two women of the house have all the men in that part of the city enamored and bewitched. There are but two women in the house with four servants and a cook, and three men outside who take care of the horses and the carriage. Strange meetings take place deep into the night where the one woman, whom they call Lilith, takes in paying customers for seances. It is not known what the other woman, Miss St. John, does when she leaves at all times of the day and night, but the driver usually drops her off in the same area of town, where Miss St. John proceeds on foot, unescorted and seemingly very unafraid. An area of town just a few blocks from the Gemini Club.

"They also observed the delivery of several boxes to the cellar earlier but have had little to do with them since… at least before this evening. As I was about to leave, having earned my pay for the day, the woman they call Lilith came to the kitchen door and asked me to help move some heavy boxes in the cellar. I hesitated but eventually agreed.

"The cellar was dark, but there was a ten-foot by ten-foot area, surrounded by curtains, that contained bright warming lights, two lab tables, and boxes without lids on top of the lab tables. I confess to seeing nothing more. There was a smell of earth and plants, and a peculiar smell I could not identify. I wasn't in the cellar for long, moved some boxes, some marked with German words describing what I took to be sensitive scientific equipment.

"After our work was completed, we were led back into the mews, and I was paid a sovereign by the lady who had invited us in. That, my dear Watson, is what I learned today and what happened."

At that moment Mrs. Hudson could be heard struggling up the stairs and Watson opened the door for her as she brought in dinner.

"Will you eat tonight, Mr. Holmes?"

"Mrs. Hudson, I will indeed. My day in the outdoors doing physical labor has whetted my appetite. Come Watson and bring the bottle of sherry with you."

Chapter 14

Lilith sat alone in the sitting room, site of her regular seances, and wrung her hands together in worry. Becca had not been herself. She seemed preoccupied and uninterested in conversation or companionship. She had barely touched her dinner and was downstairs in the cellar working on one of her projects. Lilith decided that she must approach Becca and learn what was occupying her mind so completely.

As Lilith came down the steps to the cellar, the space was dark except for the rectangle of light behind the curtains. She approached quietly and looking through a small space between two curtains saw Becca, sitting on a stool beside one of the lab tables, her head in her hands as she leaned on the table.

"Becca, what is the matter?"

Becca looked up with a jerk and a hard, cold stare. "You shouldn't be down here, Lilith. There is nothing you can do here. Go back upstairs. I will join you in a few minutes."

Lilith hesitated but nodded her head and reluctantly returned to the sitting room. Her seances had returned a good profit, but little valuable information for blackmail. The profits were made in the seances themselves, not in the information that she learned. She wondered why Becca kept her around. She was barely a companion to Becca. Their relationship was superficial and except for the rare occasion when Becca seemed to want her physical attention, there was little conversation or intimacy between them. Lilith felt that she was little more to Becca than she had been to the Professor. She felt alone and unloved. When she allowed herself to think about it, as she did tonight, she admitted to herself that she was desperately unhappy. It was in moments like this that she reminded herself that she lived better than she ever could without Becca. She had servants, she had nice clothes, she had a business of sorts, the respect of her clients, and the ability to enjoy a night out from time to time. All this was true, but it wasn't enough. She wanted to be loved.

Her thinking was interrupted when Becca came into the room. She looked tired and frustrated. "Things are not moving forward as quickly as I had hoped. I have invested a great deal in this plan, and it must work, or I am never going to achieve the level of power and success that I so crave."

Lilith looked at Becca as though she were a stranger. "I wish that I could help you, Becca, but you don't share your plans with me. I don't know what you are talking about nor how I can help."

Becca laughed, approached Lilith, and took her face in her right hand. "You are very beautiful, but you are so very fragile. You need someone to support and care for you; you cannot survive in this world alone. I suppose that's why I keep you here. It pleases me to have someone to care for, who needs me to live." Becca leaned forward and kissed Lilith on the forehead. "Please, go to bed. I am going to the club and will not be back until morning. Good night."

With that Becca walked away toward the back of the house to ring the external bell notifying her driver that she wanted the carriage. It was late, and it would take the driver a few minutes to awaken and get the horses and carriage ready. Becca walked toward her study and poured herself a drink. She wanted so badly to be as successful as the Professor. But she was only a woman in a world very much controlled by men. She was limited in what she could achieve through seduction and blackmail. She wanted more. To be a serious player in the criminal world on a grander scale. Her plan must work. It simply must.

It had been several days since the fatal duel at the Gemini Club and Persano was feeling confident and cheerful. It was late as he left his office to return home for the evening. As he had expected the family had covered up the true story of Sir Lyle's death.

As he arrived at his home via hansom, he approached the door and taking out his key, he began to unlock the door when a large man appeared seemingly from nowhere, causing him to drop his keys.

"Mr. Persano, I am sorry to have frightened you. You will remember me from the club. I am one of the Twins. May I speak with you?"

"What the devil? How do you know where I live and what are you doing here?'

"As I said, I have come to speak with you. May I come in with you for a short conversation and then I will disturb you no more?"

Persano had retrieved his keys from the landing and placing them in his jacket pocket said, "Not here. There is a pub down the street, let us walk there and we can talk."

Steven nodded in agreement and the men proceeded down the street to the crowded pub. Neither spoke to the other as they walked. Persano was troubled by this visit and couldn't understand what this man wanted to speak with him about. There didn't seem to be any purpose in further conversation.

As the men sat down at an open booth in the back of the pub, each looked at the other as if to get a measure of the man. Persano spoke first, "What is it that you wish to speak with me about…Mr.?"

"Mr. Sobotta. You may address me as Mr. Sobotta. The lady of the establishment wishes to get assurances from you that you will not turn your gaze upon the club as you continue your public exposure of the members and happenings of London's private clubs through your stories in your newspaper."

Persano smiled and sat back in the booth. An arrogant smirk crossed his face. "I make no exceptions and I make no promises, Mr. Sobotta. You have wasted your trip."

The landlord approached the booth and both men ordered a pint. The conversation ceased while each waited for the landlord to return with their drinks. Persano felt the rush of power through his chest. He began to think about ways that he could assert that power against the Gemini Club and its many members. The landlord returned with their pints and the two men reengaged.

"You are not as untouchable and aloof as you pretend, Mr. Persano. There are ways to get to you. We prefer to deal in business and not in threats. We can provide you with information about the private membership of other clubs and even direct you to the appropriate times when a story may be taken. The arrangement could benefit us both."

Persano sat and thought about Steven's proposition. "And why would you do this? For what purpose?"

"I would have thought that our purpose was plain. As more and more clubs are exposed, our club becomes the dominant player. We benefit from new membership, and you benefit from the pleasure of exposing society for what it is. Is that not why you write your stories?"

Persano laughed, "Well, I suppose that is one of the reasons. It sells newspapers and makes me happy." Persano suddenly grew serious and lowering his voice to a low whisper, said, "I do not make deals. My gaze is mine. Should I decide to turn that gaze to the Gemini Club, you will feel the heat that comes from living off the weaknesses and debauchery of others. Your members will be exposed to society for what they are, filthy, selfish, weak, immoral, persons of low character but with the money and position in life to live otherwise."

Steven sat in silence looking into the eyes of Persano. Arrogant eyes. Eyes that were jealous of the power and position of others. Heartless eyes. A face empty of empathy. "I am sorry to hear that you are unwilling to enter into a business arrangement. My Lady will need to hear your decision promptly. Is this your final word on the matter?"

"Yes."

"Very well. Allow me to pay the landlord. Good evening, Mr. Persano."

Holmes was up before Watson, which was not unusual. He was dressed and, in his mouse grey dressing gown, sitting before the unlit fireplace smoking. He was thinking about the connections between his case, the Gemini Club, the house on Kensington Court, the empty house where the boxes had been, and now the connection to these low-level clerks in government, brought to him by his brother, Mycroft. Everything revolved around one central point – the Gemini Club. There was the added fact of Mrs. Hudson's son and what his involvement was in these affairs.

He began to tic down the salient facts as he knew them:

- ☐ A seemingly respectable solicitor with a penchant for alcohol and women, drawn to the Gemini Club by his partner at the firm, goes mad and runs into the street only to be run over by a horse and carriage.

- ☐ The partner, Mr. Gurel, obviously both club member and solicitor to the club is hesitant about discussing the club and his partner's unfortunate death.

- ☐ The Gemini Club itself, is seemingly no different from the many such clubs in London catering to the lusts and tastes of its rich clientele.

- ☐ Miss Rebecca St. John, certainly an unusual owner and manager of such an establishment. Intelligent, seductive, secretive, and engaged in activities she wishes to keep from the eyes of the public.

- ☐ A biological laboratory kept secretly at a house in an obscure part of London.

- ☐ The house on Kensington Street, now the location of the biology lab where something was being grown.

- Roderick Hudson, entomologist, addict, member of the Gemini Club and now deceased from overuse. A man seemingly more accustomed to the laboratory than the club, but at home in both.
- And now, these clerks – also members of the Gemini Club – being manipulated into making clandestine inquiries into government affairs of a simple and unproductive nature.

Holmes smoked and thought, his legs stretched out in front of him, and his chin buried in his chest. He stayed liked this until Watson came downstairs for his breakfast.

"Holmes. How long have you been up?"

"Almost two hours before you, dear fellow."

"Have you seen Mrs. Hudson? Has she the paper and our breakfast?"

Holmes shrugged. Watson, looking a bit exasperated at Holmes, went to the door and called downstairs for Mrs. Hudson.

The morning proceeded much as could be expected with Holmes sitting in his chair smoking and Watson eating his breakfast and reading the morning newspaper. No words were spoken between the two and none were necessary.

Holmes suddenly stood and stretched. "Watson, this case is not clear to me. I must confess that I am at a bit at a loss for what to do next."

"I am not surprised, Holmes. The case presents nothing from which a theory could be postulated."

Holmes walked over to the desk between the windows and began to complete a telegram form. Having finished the first, he sat and thought for several minutes and then began to complete another.

"With whom are you corresponding?"

"My brother, Mycroft. Simply to tell him to tighten their seals and keep a watch over anyone who might be frequenting the Gemini Club."

"And the second?"

"I would rather not say, Watson. Just a bit of a whim, really. Not certain anything will come of it."

Holmes retreated to the fireplace and was in the act of filling his pipe. "What do you know of entomology?"

"Very little, Holmes. Beyond the fact that I do not like spiders, I haven't made a study of the matter."

"Hmm. I know a great deal about bees, but I have not had any reason to make a general study of insects. Of course, in my line of work, a working knowledge of plants and their uses in poisons and medicines is invaluable. The history of crime is replete with criminals using plants to poison their victims. I cannot say that I know of any use of insects in that regard."

"I had a college chum who if stung by a bee would swell up and have difficulty breathing. Are you referring to something like that?"

"I am not sure, Watson..." Holmes suddenly grew very quiet and stared down at the rug in front of the fireplace. He walked quickly over to the desk and looking at the two completed telegram forms, tore one in two and began to feverishly complete another form.

"Mrs. Hudson!" Holmes called just as she entered the room to clean the table of breakfast. "Oh, there you are. Will you please have these two telegrams sent at once? Thank you."

Part Two

Chapter 15

Holmes had gone out for the day and Watson sat smoking having just finished his lunch. As he sat, he heard Mrs. Hudson coming up the stairs. He stood and walked toward to the door in time to open it just as she arrived.

"The afternoon newspaper, Dr. Watson. I will be up shortly to clear the table of lunch dishes."

"Thank you, Mrs. Hudson."

Watson walked back to his chair and taking a long drag from his cigar, opened the paper to discover the following headline, "**First Lord of the Admiralty Suffers the Death of His Eldest Son**". The subscript read, "Duke of Foxborough Dead at Twenty-five from Cardiac Failure." Watson immediately began to read the article with interest.

It was a familiar story. The Duke was found dead in his bed. No signs of foul play. The family was devastated. The Duke had shown no signs of disease and had been an active man, a highly ranked polo player, hunter, and sailor. Services would be at Westminster and the Queen was expected to be in attendance.

Watson sat silently looking at the headline and wondering to himself what had really happened. He caught himself in disgust and said aloud, "I have been with Holmes for too long." Watson had taken on Holmes's habit of seeing intrigue even in the most innocent of circumstances. He remembered being on a train with Holmes looking out the window at the bucolic scenes that passed; only to have Holmes ruin the image by talking of the crimes that could occur in such isolated places. Watson laughed to himself and decided to accept the story as written. The unfortunate Duke had died in his sleep of apparent heart failure and nothing more.

It was late afternoon before Holmes returned to Baker Street. He was in a contemplative mood and said little as he sat in his chair smoking one of his oily clay pipes. After a while he seemed to awaken from some deep train of thought.

"I have spent a very interesting day in the study of insects, Watson. Most fascinating creatures. The study of insects is an ancient one going back to Egypt and the Far East. Many undergo the most amazing metamorphosis and though their lives are generally short, they certainly live extraordinarily. From flightless maggot to winged adult."

"And whatever inspired you to make a study of such a subject, Holmes?"

"Ahh, the answer to my telegram that arrived this morning. I can recommend you to the Rev. William Kirby and his colleague, William Spence, and their fine introductory book on the subject. The Reverend was kind enough to answer my telegram and point me in the right direction.

"It seems that not unlike plants, a wide variety of insects use chemicals to inflict death upon their adversaries and for many more uses as well. We are only just gaining an understanding of the chemical side of insect life. The field is quite exciting and both entomologist and chemist are engaged in the study. We know so very little at present about the chemicals insects use and why.

"Mr. Spence's work is quite scientific and though the Reverend's work falls on the more biblical side of things, insects being evidence of God's personal involvement in the world, his insights into insects are very interesting and very learned. When I get the time, I may add the study of insects to my chemical experiments. Adding to what I already know about bees."

"Very good, I suppose. Interesting way to spend a day, I should think. Have you seen the afternoon newspaper?"

"No, Watson. Anything of interest?"

"Not for you, I imagine, but the paper is full of news of the untimely death of the Duke of Foxborough, eldest son to one of the First Lord of the Admiralty."

"Let me venture a guess, the Duke was found dead in his bed having died of heart failure?"

"Well, yes. You have seen it then?"

Holmes laughed, "No, I haven't seen this afternoon's paper. But such is always the case is it not? Powerful young man in his prime, sportsman, full of promise, is cut down by heart failure while he slept. The truth is usually suicide."

"Well, Holmes! Suicide! I mean really."

"Watson, it was not widely known, but the Duke had a penchant for young men, nothing forced mind you and no children. There were several close calls with the press that the First Lord was able to hush up before publication. I would not be surprised if the Duke met his end via a self-inflicted gunshot wound to the heart, rather than living as he did in the shadows, ashamed of who he was. It is a pity that our society shuns such as he and forces men like him to live double lives. Always at the mercy of public gossip, the newspaper reporter, and the judgment of supposed decent society. Hey, Watson?"

"I suppose so." Watson looked at Holmes with confusion but decided not to pursue the subject further. His own reputation as a ladies' man being a bit of a sensitive topic itself. He simply cleared his throat and made much of focusing on the rest of the newspaper.

It was late afternoon and Becca and the Twins were having a pre-evening meeting. Steven had told Becca about his meeting with Persano, and she was not happy, but also was not surprised.

"Do you believe we should spend any more of our time and efforts in convincing Persano or is it a lost cause?" Becca was sitting at her desk in her office at the club with the twins sitting in their usual places in front of her.

Steven looked down at his lap and then back up into Becca's eyes, "Yes, Madam, I believe it to be a lost cause. He seemed very confident in his position. Any further attempts on our part to win him over or placate him, will only result in his focusing his attention and writing about this club, which I believe to be inevitable. No one seems capable or desirous of stopping him."

Becca stopped the conversation with a nod of her head and a wave of her hand and began to think. Both twins sat quietly and waited for her to decide on the next steps. Becca was frustrated that she had to deal with these issues rather than manage the club and push her plans forward. It was a waste of time and put her at risk of discovery.

"First, we had to deal with that curious solicitor looking into things that were none of his business, and now this damned newspaper reporter. Where did a drunken philanderer get a conscious about his law partner's legal dealings and a newspaper reporter become a one-man moral crusader?

Scott, there is nothing else for it. Make the arrangements. We will deal with Persano. I will not be there this time; you and another trusted agent will handle it. My plans are too important to put at risk for one like Persano. You know the protocol. In the meantime, cover for each other at the club and make this a priority."

Scott nodded his head and he and Steven prepared to leave before Becca stopped them with her upheld hand.

"I need you to provide me with as much information on the First Lord of the Admiralty and the death of this son of his. There may be an opportunity to exploit the situation and further our goals. I do not need to tell you that I want this information as soon as possible. Talk to current and past servants, jealous business associates, gossips, you know the game. Use our third-party sources and pay them well. I want all the family secrets."

"Yes, Madam." Steven knew the assignment was for him without asking. It was his specialty. A few crowns thrown in the right direction at the right pubs could get a person almost any kind of information about the lives of London's rich and powerful. It might not all be true, some of it exaggerated, but a professional using multiple sources could usually get at the truth of the matter. He knew he would have everything he needed within forty-eight hours of his request. He simply had to shake the bushes, pay the right people, and see what fell out.

"That's all gentlemen. Tell the girls to let me be this evening. I have much to think about."

Holmes was pacing back and forth in front of the fireplace smoking cigarette after cigarette. Watson had eaten dinner, but Holmes's dishes were left on the table untouched. Watson was standing by the window overlooking Baker Street to stay out of the way of Holmes's incessant pacing. Mrs. Hudson was in the act of clearing the table and looking worriedly at Watson.

"Mrs. Hudson, how are you getting on?"

"Oh, I suppose I am fine, Dr. Watson. I am sad for my poor Roderick, but he had made himself so scarce to me over these past few years, that though his death is sad, it hasn't made that much of a difference in my daily routine. I admit to allowing myself a good cry, now and then, but otherwise, my life is very much as it was."

"I am glad to hear that you are getting on." Watson smiled as he looked at Mrs. Hudson.

"It's strange, but now that I can visit his grave when I stop to see his father, I will actually spend more time with him in his death than I ever did in his life as a man."

Holmes had stopped pacing, "I trust the head stone will be completed and in place soon, Mrs. Hudson?"

"Yes, Mr. Holmes and thank you again for purchasing it."

Holmes threw himself into his chair full of nervous energy and nothing to do about it. Mrs. Hudson left with the dishes and Watson walked slowly to his place before the fireplace.

"Watson, there is nothing to be done with this case at present. There are obvious connections to the Gemini Club and the deaths of two men, but nothing that makes a connection that will hold up to scrutiny. I have theories, but nothing substantial. I am afraid that more evidence is needed and perhaps the death of another man before I can make any progress."

"You could alert Scotland Yard and have them make a visit to the club."

"And what would I tell Scotland Yard? That two unrelated men, one a solicitor and another an entomologist, who both happen to be members of the same club, have died and that I suspect a connection but cannot prove one? No, Watson, that will not do.

"Will I tell them that I suspect a woman, the owner of the club, in the deaths of both men, without anything to prove it? That it may be related to boxes moved to a cellar at a house in a respectable neighborhood? They will think me mad. No, there must be something more substantial."

"What of this connection to the government and the inquiries made by these clerks? Is that not worth looking into?"

"Mycroft would be incensed if I engaged Scotland Yard. I have already addressed those issues. No, there is simply nothing to be done. There is no thread to follow. Everything has come to a standstill until another move is made by our adversaries. Despite what your readers may think, I am not clairvoyant, Watson. I cannot predict the future and foretell who will die next and how."

"At the risk of driving you off entirely, have you considered spending some time in the company of our client's aunt?"

Holmes stared at Watson across the space between them.

"As I said, at the risk of driving you off entirely. Just a thought, old man."

Chapter 16

It had been two days and Holmes was no better for the waiting. One or two little problems had come in from new clients that took up some little of his time to resolve, but nothing that deserved his prodigious talents. A lost daughter found, and a bride – stood-up at the altar – placated by an innocent explanation and a rather sick fiancé; that was all that Holmes had to show for his time.

Watson had run out of things to say to Holmes and so said nothing. His presence was not helping but he dared not leave for fear Holmes would take to cocaine to relieve his shattered nerves and boundless energy. At these times Holmes was indeed like a great machine tearing itself to pieces left to run wild with nothing to focus on.

He sat at this chemistry table working on some formula and creating an awful stench that even the open windows could not dispel. Watson sat reading a book and smoking a cigar. And so the hours of the late morning and early afternoon went. No conversation and little to do but wait for a new development.

It was a cold and rainy summer evening in London. Not yet dark but becoming slowly so as each minute went by. A thick fog was just starting to roll in and everything in the weather foretold a cold, wet, clammy, foggy night. Persano had returned to his home early to edit some copy and to avoid the worst of the weather. He sat in a comfortable leather chair in front of the fire with his back to the rest of the sitting room and the front entrance.

He had a glass of sherry to his right on a small table that also held edited copy from his work during the afternoon. Red pencil marks on the latest story he was writing. This one not about the private clubs of London, but about the truth behind the death of the Duke of Foxborough. It had not been difficult bribing a low-level person working for the undertaker to tell him the man had shot himself in an act of suicide. Following the rumors about the Duke's sexual proclivities was equally straightforward. All one had to do was bribe a hotel worker, a cleaning lady, a hansom driver to tell him about liaisons between the Duke and young men.

The story would be explosive if it ever made it to print. Either way, he would profit from it. Either by way of being paid not to publish it, or by his percentage profits of the newspapers it would sell. And, of course, his personal pleasure in seeing another member of the establishment brought to ruin, and one as high as the First Lord of the Admiralty.

He had finished his editing and was looking into the fire, somewhat sleepily; he was feeling the effects of the sherry, his warm dressing gown, the fire, and the lazy feeling the weather gave him. He felt comfortable, safe, warm, and satisfied. His eyelids begin to feel heavy, and his breathing started to become sonorous. The room became shadowy and out of focus. His head fell back to rest against the cushion of his chair. He was just drifting off...

He felt a sharp pressure against his throat as a garrote held his neck firmly against the back of the chair like a vice.

His arms flayed outward in a failed attempt to grab onto whatever was choking him. His head and neck were held so firmly to the back of the chair, that the movement of his arms and now his legs were useless to release the grip of whatever held him in place. He couldn't yell out for want of air to breathe and he felt himself slowly losing consciousness. He couldn't think of anything else but breathing – which he was completely incapable of doing.

His hands found their way to his throat where he could just feel the garrote tight against his neck, and the huge, strong hands that held it in place. He could feel it cutting into his neck and, in what seemed like a last attempt to free himself, his body jumped, his legs kicked, and his hands flayed in the air as the darkness took over.

He awakened to the sharp sting of slaps to his face and a deep, hot pain in his neck. He was blindfolded and tied to a chair. He could barely breathe, the swelling and pain in his throat making inhaling very difficult. He tried to speak, but the sound he emitted was simply coughs and guttural groans. There was someone to his right and someone to his left. He could not see through the blindfold. His throat ached and throbbed, while the cuts made to his neck by the garrote stung and bled.

He was fully awake now and the terror of his situation began to set in. He could hear his heart pounding in his chest and the rapid staccato of his breathing. He was covered in sweat and by the smell and feel of it, he knew he had soiled himself. He tried to move but realized he was tied at his legs, arms, and chest to the chair. It was one of the chairs of his dining table. The wood felt cold and hard. His legs and arms were tied so tight that he had lost the feeling in all four. He ached all over.

A quiet voice to his left, almost a whisper in his ear, said, "It would have been better had you accepted our business proposition, Mr. Persano. Much better."

Persano tried to move but succeeded only in making the chair jump and strike the wood floor. He kept at it. He thought if only his neighbor would hear and come to his rescue. He was not well-liked by his neighbors. He knew they considered him arrogant and vindictive. He had once kicked a neighbor's dog for doing nothing more than coming to him for attention. He was known to berate neighbors for the smallest of offenses. But still he had to try.

"You won't get loose, Persano. You are well-tied. Save your energy for breathing and living." The voice would move from his left ear to his right ear and back again. "Hold his head back!"

Someone grabbed Persano's chin from behind and forced his head back. His throat ached and he could feel the blood go down his chest.

"Allow me to introduce you to one of our little pets. You may not wish to meet it, but it is so very happy to meet you. Hold him tight. Don't let him move his head."

Persano felt two fingers pull his nose up and felt something wet and cool fall inside his left nostril. As he struggled to move, he could hear the chair banging against the wood floor. He tried to see but he could not see anything under or around the blindfold. He stopped moving suddenly as he felt the cool, wet thing begin to move inside his nostril. It moved around at first and then began to move up his nostril toward his head. He could feel it move. The tickling wetness as it made its way up. It moved up, up, and kept moving. He panicked and began to shake and jump as the chair hammered into the wood floor.

A loud knocking. Voices. Bodies moving. The grip was released from his face. He and the chair turned over and he hit the floor hard. Blackness.

Holmes and Watson had finished dinner; or rather Watson had eaten, and Holmes had smoked. The sun had set, and the streetlights were being lit by the lamplighter as he whistled a jaunty tune. Holmes was standing looking out the window at the scene as the lamplighter made his way down Baker Street. The windows were closed, the night was cold and wet, and the fireplace at 221B Baker Street was roaring. Holmes closed the blind and looked over at Watson as he stood from the table.

"Will you eat nothing, Holmes?"

"I cannot spare nerve energy for digestion, Watson. If something is going to happen in our case, this evening is certainly the perfect setting. Cold, wet, the fog blowing in off the Thames, and the darkness of a cloudy night are perfect for the criminal to take advantage of the innocent and the foolish who are about on such an evening.

"No, it is on evenings such as this that I am most grateful for our little rooms, the warmth of our fire, and the company of my biographer, doctor, and friend."

"Well, thank you, Holmes. Not at all. I am grateful for staying in this evening. There is nothing out there for us but to catch our death of cold."

"I think I shall sit by the fire, let it warm my bones, and smoke this evening, Watson."

"As shall I, dear Holmes."

Holmes and Watson sat in their usual places. Holmes smoked his long cherrywood pipe and Watson a cigar. Both gazed at the fire and let the dancing flames take away the tediousness of the day. Holmes keen-eyed, ever the thinking machine; and Watson, glassy-eyed and beginning to feel the drowsiness brought on by food and warmth.

Both sat like this for some time when their reverie was interrupted by the bell ringing at the front door.

"Who could that be on a night like this?" Watson was roused from a dreamy state and sat up in his chair.

Holmes listened keenly as Mrs. Hudson answered the bell and began her slow walk up the seventeen stairs to the landing.

"It is a development. I would bet my soul on it, Watson." Holmes was up and having leapt over the settee was at the door to their rooms as Mrs. Hudson arrived.

"Mr. Holmes, a message and the boy waits."

Holmes tore open the message and flung it to the floor as he went to his room for his coat. Saying as he went, "Tell the boy we are on way. Watson, come!"

Watson walked toward the door and picking up the message read, "An intriguing case that has all the hallmarks that usually interest you. I invite you to the scene. MacDonald."

Holmes put on his coat and hat as Watson fumbled for his own. Holmes checked his pockets to be sure he had his magnifying glass, measuring tape, chalk, and other paraphernalia of his trade. He handed Watson his walking stick then both went down the stairs – Holmes at almost a run and Watson a bit more slowly. The boy was at the door and just beyond him on Baker Street was a carriage.

"You both take care to stay dry. You will catch your death of cold." Mrs. Hudson was standing to the side as the two men joined the boy and got into the carriage.

"It did not go smoothly, Madam." Scott was back at the club and explaining the afternoon's activities to Becca. "He struggled greatly, even when tied down. There was a lot of noise. The chair banging against the floor. I tried to hurry, but we were interrupted by a neighbor at the door. My man and I jumped the man before he could do anything and were out the back door quickly. My man going one way, and I the other. I don't think the man saw much and with the rush we put on him, he is likely confused and unable to give a good description of either of us."

Becca sat at her desk; her hands clasped in front of her face. She stared at Scott with barely concealed fury. "And what was the effect on Persano?"

Scott looked down at the floor and did not immediately answer.

"Well?"

"I don't know, Madam. We left before we could take any notice of the effect."

"Damn it, Scott. That is wasted then, isn't it?"

"Yes, mum. I am sorry."

"Anything else to report?"

"No, mum."

"And the spare?"

"Lost in the rush, mum. I don't know where." Scott stood and turned to leave the office but stopped and faced Becca again. "I almost forgot, Madam, I recovered these papers at Persano's home while my man was tying Persano to his chair. He was apparently working on a story about the death of Duke Foxborough. I thought these more salient papers might interest you." Scott handed Becca the papers.

Becca began to read and as she read her interest was piqued.

"These are indeed useful, Scott. Thank you. But rest assured, this does not act as recompence for your failures this evening. That will be all."

Chapter 17

The carriage ride did not take more than twenty minutes and during that time Holmes said nothing to Watson. His nervous energy and anticipation kept him sitting straight and stiffly looking out the carriage window, as Watson hugged himself to get warm.

"Holmes, this crime scene may have nothing to do with our case. You should prepare yourself for disappointment."

Holmes nodded, "Over the years, Watson, I have developed a kind of clairvoyance about these things. I sense that the game is afoot and that this matter is indeed related to our case. It is certainly not logical, Watson, but I seem to know that it is."

Watson grunted, "Really, Holmes. Clairvoyance…you? I am surprised at you."

"Then call it what you will. Intuition. A Freudian subconscious reading of barely noticeable signs. Whatever it is, I am experiencing it tonight. It may simply be the result of years of experience and hundreds of cases. But, nevertheless, I am certain that this little trip of ours will end in another piece to our puzzle."

The carriage arrived at a respectable neighborhood and stopped in front of a row house. Holmes immediately leapt from the carriage and began to examine the sidewalk and street. Watson noticed another police carriage that was barred and clearly meant for prisoner transport. As Holmes examined the street, Watson walked over to one of the barred windows of the police carriage and looked in. Inside were two constables seated on the left side and a man in a straitjacket. The constrained man was seated on a bench on the right side of the carriage and was bending at the waist, rocking back and forth, incessantly. As he did, he was mumbling incoherently to himself. When the man noticed Watson looking in, he stopped his bending back and forth and stared at him with large, mad, eyes and a face convulsed into a mask of sheer terror.

"It won't do you know. The trees know we are here. As does the grass. They plot. They make plans between them. I have heard them, you know. The insects are in on it too. Moving about unnoticed spying on us, they are. Yes, I have seen it and I have heard their whispers in the wind. You will see." Then he continued his rocking back and forth.

Holmes was done examining the street and sidewalk.

"Find anything, Holmes?"

"There is no telling what I have found given the comings and goings of hansoms, carriages, horses and police officers. Any signs that may have been helpful have been obscured by the riot of activity since."

Watson walked up to Holmes and in almost a whisper said, "There is a mad man in that police carriage, Holmes. Whatever happened inside that house has driven one man out of his mind."

"Well, indeed. Let us not waste any more time outside then."

As Holmes and Watson approached the door to the house, they were met on the landing by Inspector MacDonald.

"Ahh, very good! You accepted my invitation then. Come inside, gentlemen."

But Holmes was on his knees examining the door handle and the lock. "Have you a torch handy, MacDonald?"

"Yes, you there. Constable, get a dark lantern from the carriage and bring it over here. Quickly man."

Holmes took the lit dark lantern from the constable and shining it on the door handle and lock continued his examination.

"Hold this, Watson and shine the light on the lock mechanism in particular."

Watson complied and Holmes took out his magnifying glass and looked carefully at the lock. "This lock has not been picked."

Holmes took the dark lantern from Watson and began to look at the landing. "Again, too much traffic to make any examination on my part useful. Inspector MacDonald, good to see you. I surmise that there is more to see inside?"

"Yes, indeed there is. Including a witness." MacDonald led Holmes and Watson through the entrance to the home and into an oval-shaped sitting room with a fireplace to the far right. The overstuffed leather chair in front of the fireplace was overturned, as was a small table beside it.

"Have you examined this room carefully, Inspector?"

"Given what the witness has told us, no, I saw no real point. The rooms on the ground floor are composed of his sitting room, an office behind the stairs, a small dining room, and a small kitchen with a back door leading to the alley. The stairs you see to the left lead to the sole bedroom and the water closet.

"This apartment shares a wall with the one next door which is the same but a mirrored version. There is a door that opens to the other apartment in the dining room. Probably left from when the two apartments were one house. It is from that door that the witness gained access to this apartment. He has a key to the lock. Both tenants have keys, being single gentlemen, in case the other was ever in need of assistance, I suppose.

"The perpetrators left using the backdoor and alley. There was a scuffle, and our witness came out of it much the worse. He is laying down on a settee in his rooms with a wet towel on his head. But of course if you wish to examine the sitting room, please, help yourself." The inspector looked at Watson with an expression of doubt on his face.

The gas was on in the house and the room was well-lit. There was a large Persian rug in front of the fireplace where the overturned chair and table had sat. Holmes was on his hands and knees examining the rug and despite the well-lit room was using the dark lantern to provide more light for his examination. He crawled about making little humming sounds as he did. Twice he used his chalk to circle spots on the carpet. He used his measuring tape to take measurements and made notes on a small notepad he kept in his vest pocket.

He picked up the chair and placed it in its usual spot, using the impressions in the rug from the chair's legs to do so. He examined the leather chair in detail being careful to cover all parts of the chair, front and back. He stood and examined the fireplace mantel and using the poker, fished around the grate disturbing the coals and nearly putting out the fire itself.

Next, he turned his attention to the overturned accent table. He placed it upright and conducted a similar examination of it. Holmes dropped again to his knees and standing he held a sherry glass and placed it on the table. He then bent over and picked up several pieces of paper that he made a quick examination of, dropping the papers in the chair.

"I would like to examine the dining room, if you please, Inspector."

"Of course. That is where we found Mr. Isadora Persano when we arrived. He was tied to one of the chairs and laying on his side. Just there. That chair is the one he was tied to and that rope on the table is what was used to tie him. He was a raving lunatic when we arrived. I had to send for a special carriage and straight jacket so we could conduct our investigation. A simple case of interrupted burglary if you ask me, except for Persano's madness and that matchbox on the table. That's why I sent for you Mr. Holmes. You will never guess what is inside that matchbox."

"An insect. Very probably a small worm."

MacDonald's jaw dropped and he looked over at Watson in astonishment. "Mr. Holmes, how did you guess that?"

"I never guess, MacDonald. I saw from the papers on the floor in front of the fire, that the man who lives here is Isadora Persano, the journalist. It appears that he was in the process of editing a story about the recent death of the Duke of Foxborough. There are several pages missing from his draft."

Holmes began examining the knots on the ropes and the chair. "These knots are peculiar. What do you make of them, Inspector?"

"Except for cutting them off Mr. Persano, I made no particular examination of the knots, Mr. Holmes."

"Of course you didn't. Watson, look at these knots. They were tied by a sailor. You see the curious figure eight pattern and this square shaped knot; each is typical of knots used by sailors. Though Mr. Persano was tied from foot to chest, as well as his arms, a single long piece of rope was used, and these sailor's knots were used to secure him in place. The man who tied these knots is either a sailor or works amongst rigging. Judging by his size and obvious strength, I would say a sailor."

"Size and strength? How the devil do you know that?" MacDonald was scribbling notes in his own notepad and starring at Holmes with disbelief.

"If you would have taken the time and effort to examine the sitting room, you might have noticed the boot marks in the rug. They were made by a wet and slightly muddy round-toed boot. I have circled those boot marks with my chalk. It is not difficult to estimate a man's size and weight by the size of his shoe and the deepness of the impression he leaves in a rug. The man was large, I would say over six feet tall, and weighed seventeen or eighteen stone.

"I conclude that he was strong because he managed to pick-up Persano and carry him into this room and into that chair without dragging him across the wood floor, which would have left scuff marks had he been dragged. He then tied him to the chair using the rope you cut and tied the unusual knots doing so. Have you examined Mr. Persano for marks on his body?"

"No, but there was no need to examine him when I could clearly see ligature marks in bright red around his neck. He had clearly been garroted, probably while tied to this chair when the men were questioning him trying to get some information. Likely about where he kept the valuables."

"The evidence is more consistent with him having been garroted while he sat in the leather chair before the fireplace. That would explain the turned over table and chair. He was then carried into this room while unconscious – because there are no signs of a struggle – and tied to the chair.

"Now let us turn our attention to the matchbox." Holmes examined the matchbox carefully. "A commonplace matchbox that could be obtained at any tobacconist anywhere in London. Let's see the worm inside."

Holmes carefully opened the matchbox and inside the box was almost filled with dirt. Holmes used his lead pencil to move a small amount of dirt and revealed a small, white worm.

"Look at this, Watson. We will learn soon enough, but I would wager that this worm is unknown to science. It is likely a new species of worm, bred for a very singular purpose."

"The worm? The worm has nothing to do with anything, Mr. Holmes." MacDonald looked at Holmes as if he too had gone mad.

"Then how do you explain its presence on this table in the midst of this crime scene?"

"It's a complete coincidence. It has nothing to do with the case. Neither you nor I can say how long that matchbox has been there. The worm may have simply climbed into the box, when it was left open, having come from a bad piece of meat, cheese, or bread. It's nothing, Mr. Holmes."

"And Mr. Persano so kindly prepared the matchbox with dirt for the worm to enjoy? No, Inspector. Look at this dirt. This dirt is not from the streets of London. I am familiar with the dirt and mud around London, this dirt is fine grained and clean. There is nothing in the dirt. No twigs, pebbles, mud, etc. It has been sifted and any debris removed. You do not find dirt like this in nature. Care has been taken in making this dirt, Inspector."

"Then where in blazes did the matchbox come from, Mr. Holmes?"

"It could only have come with the two men who came into this house. It was deliberately brought with a specific purpose in mind. May I keep this worm and box, Inspector?"

"If it makes you happy Mr. Holmes."

Holmes closed the matchbox containing the worm and put it in the pocket of his coat. He then walked toward the back of the house and began to examine the back doorknob and lock. He dropped to his knees and examined the lock carefully, using the dark lantern he retrieved from the table where he had placed it while he examined the matchbox.

"This lock has been picked and the pick marks are still fresh and shiny. I can even see very small flakes of metal where the picking tools forced the mechanism. Someone has gained entry to this house without the use of a key and very recently as a key hasn't been used in the lock since, and removed or disturbed the metal flakes."

"But Holmes, backdoors are infrequently used. That evidence may be weeks or months old." Watson was standing by the table watching Holmes as he worked.

"No Watson, the metal has not changed color and is still shiny. This happened very recently, and it is safe to say, reveals how the two men gained entry to these rooms."

"At last you say something that makes sense, Mr. Holmes. I agree that the men likely gained entry to the house through the backdoor. The alley would have been darker than the street in front making it easier for them." MacDonald continued to scribble on his notepad.

"I would like to speak with the witness now, Inspector."

"Of course, through this door."

The inspector led Holmes and Watson through the door and into the dining room of the adjoining apartment. They went from the dining room into the adjacent sitting room where a man lay on a couch holding a damp cloth against his forehead.

"Watson, can you attend to the gentleman?"

"Certainly, Holmes. I am a doctor, sir. Please allow me to examine your head." Watson took the damp cloth away and below it was a large, purple wound swelled to the size of a goose egg. Watson felt around the man's skull and neck and finished by quickly examining the man's arms and legs.

"Except for a likely concussion from a hard blow to the head, I would say the man is fine. Sir, please stay seated or lying down. You have suffered a concussion from a hard knock to your head. You may be dizzy or lightheaded."

The man sat-up and nodded to Watson. "Thank you, Doctor. I am sure that I can sit-up and talk with the inspector."

Watson looked at Holmes who had a whimsical smile on his face. "I am not an inspector. I am not even with

Scotland Yard. I am Sherlock Holmes, a private, consulting detective, whom Scotland Yard consults from time-to-time. And you are?"

"I am Richard Banter. I own a small furniture repair business just down the street. I live a quiet and respectable life, Mr. Holmes. Nothing like this has ever happened to me. I don't know what the vestry will think of this. Not to mention our vicar. People will talk, they will." Mr. Banter was speaking quickly and was still in shock.

"Mr. Banter, I would not worry about the vestry nor your vicar, for that matter. It appears that you did nothing to be blameworthy. To the contrary, you may have saved your neighbor from death…although all signs indicate you arrived too late to really make a difference in the outcome of events. Please tell me what you saw and what you experienced and please, be precise as to details." Holmes stood looking down on the sitting Mr. Banter.

"Well, it was more about what I heard Mr. Holmes. I was sitting in that chair before the fire having a late cup of tea. We can sometimes hear sounds through the walls we can. Mr. Persano and I try not to disturb the other with noises. He can get a bit angry if he is disturbed while he is engaged in his newspaper writing, during the evening.

"Well, as I said I was sitting there having a tea in front of the fire. It's a cold and wet night and I thought a nice cup of tea before bed would be just the thing. To warm my innards as it were. At first, I heard some muffled bumps. They were irregular like and stopped after a short passage of time. Then everything was quiet. Then not two minutes later, I started hearing this loud banging on the wood floor. That was regular and louder than the sounds before. I started to wonder if something had happened to Mr. Persano; had he fallen or something, and was knocking loudly on the floor?

"So I stood up, I did. I put down me tea and I went over to that bowl on the cabinet by the door to his rooms, and I took out the key. Me and Mr. Persano both have keys to that door that joins our two places. Never to be used unless the other was in need. You see, we are both bachelors and have no family or friends to speak of, so the keys are a way for us to look after each other in case something happens. Although I always had the impression the keys were more for Mr. Persano's safety than mine. He seemed always to be worried about strangers in the area, and always was careful when he went out.

"Well, I stood by the door and the knocking kept happening. Then suddenly it stopped. I thought for a moment that everything was okay, but then suddenly it started up again and this time faster than before. So I knocked on the door, stuck in the key, and opened it up.

"What happened next, I really can't say. There was two of 'em. Both large men. They were on me quicker than you can blink. My head hit the door frame, I think, and after that it's a bit of a blur.

"I came to me senses, I can't say how long that took, and when I did, there was Mr. Persano, tied to the chair and a lying on his side on the floor. He was talking constantly, but not making any sense. I managed to get up and make my way to the same bowl inside my rooms, where I keep a police whistle. I grabbed that and went to the front door, and out on the landing. I started blowing that whistle as loudly as I could, and two constables came running toward me.

"I was so spent by my efforts that I collapsed on the settee and there I remained until you came in to question me. One of the constables was kind enough to set a towel in the basin and put it on me head.

"That's all of it, sir. I don't know nothing else."

Holmes was standing looking carefully at the man while he told his story. When he was finished, Holmes thought for a second and then said, "No, I believe you have told me everything that you know. Inspector, this man's story collaborates in every detail what the evidence here suggests. I am confident he can tell you nothing else."

"Then do you mind telling me what you think happened here this evening, Mr. Holmes?"

"All in good time, Inspector. I would like to see the unfortunate Mr. Persano, if he is at all capable of being seen and questioned."

The inspector nodded his head and turning began to leave the apartment the way they had come. "I think out the front door, if Mr. Banter does not object, would be quicker, Inspector."

"What? Oh, of course Mr. Holmes." The inspector led Holmes and Watson out of the house and back onto the street.

Watson tugged at Holmes's sleeve and said quietly into his ear, "Mr. Persano seems to have been driven mad by this experience, Holmes. I must warn you that he is likely to make no sense at present."

"Thank you, Watson. We must try."

The inspector ordered the door to the locked carriage opened and the two constables brought out Mr. Persano. They escorted the straitjacketed man to a position under a streetlight as Holmes and Watson approached. Mr. Persano was wide-eyed and looking around him as if he did not know where he was.

"Mr. Persano. Mr. Persano. I am Inspector MacDonald of Scotland Yard. This is Sherlock Holmes. He is assisting us in this investigation. Can you understand me, Mr. Persano?"

Persano appeared to notice the Inspector and looked from him to Holmes and Watson as Inspector MacDonald spoke. "I can understand you. What has happened?" Persano had visibly changed since Watson observed him in the carriage. He appeared to be in control of his faculties, but his eyes were blank and his face emotionless except for a kind of naïve curiosity.

"You were attacked in your home, Mr. Persano. I am Sherlock Holmes and this my friend and colleague Dr. Watson. I have been retained in another matter but was asked by Scotland Yard to help in this investigation. What can you tell us about what happened to you in your home this evening?"

Persano looked at Holmes, then at Watson, and back at the Inspector. "I can tell you nothing. I am not sure where I am or who I am for that matter. You called me Persano. Is that my name?"

Holmes looked at Watson and he stepped forward. "I am a doctor, Mr. Persano. May I examine you?"

"What? Examine me?"

"Yes. You may have suffered an injury to your head. You have certainly suffered an injury to your neck. May I examine you under this streetlight?"

Mr. Persano simply stared at Watson but did not object as Watson began to inspect the wound.

"Holmes, in addition to the ligature injuries to his neck, he has a small depression on his skull. Likely when his head hit the floor while he was tied to the chair. In this light and without a more thorough examination, I can see nothing else."

Holmes looked at Persano. "Mr. Persano, lift your right arm." Mr. Persano complied. "Now put it down. Good. Now lift your left arm. Very good. You can put the arm down. Stand on your right leg only. I am sorry for asking, you are a bit off balance. Please say, 'God save the Queen.' Very good. Constables, you may put Mr. Persano back in the carriage. I suggest that you take him to a hospital and that you strictly limit his access to others. Do not allow others to speak with him except to the extent necessary to treat his head wound. Thank you."

"And what was all that about, Mr. Holmes? Do you want him to dance a jig for ye as well?" The inspector was laughing as he nodded for the constables to take charge of Mr. Persano.

"Would you join us back at Baker Street tomorrow morning, Inspector?"

"Uh, I can move some matters around and join you, yes. What, say ten in the morning then?"

"Perfect. Thank you, Inspector. Come along, Watson. We can catch a hansom just down the street, Inspector. Good night."

The inspector stood under the streetlight as Holmes walked briskly away, disappearing into the fog, followed by a confused Dr. Watson.

Chapter 18

Captain Lord John Corke of Her Majesty's Royal Navy, and his wife Lady Corke were ushered into a home on Kensington Court. Lady Corke was trembling with anxiety as she and her husband stood across from one another at Lady Tabitha's round table, in a darkened sitting room, lit only by a single candle held by an elaborate stand, in the middle of the table.

Lord Corke was there only because Lady Corke insisted on it. The family had recently lost a son at sea, and Lady Corke could not adjust to the idea that his body was "buried" at sea. That he was sewn into his hammock, two cannon balls placed at his feet, and "dumped" into the ocean, who knows where, to sink to the cold, dark, and slimy bottom of the sea. To be chewed on by who knows what. She needed assurances that his soul was at peace and that it was not trapped in a cold, dark place, where the only company was the denizens of the deep. And so, she demanded that her husband, Lord Corke, accompany her to Lady Tabitha, whom she had heard had brought great results for others.

"Thank you so much for agreeing to help us contact our son, Lady Tabitha. I so appreciate your efforts on our behalf this evening."

Lord Corke cleared his throat rather loudly and responded, "I must warn you now, Lady Tabitha, that I do not put much faith in mediums. I have seen things that I cannot explain at sea, in the dead of night, in blazing weather, in the cold, and during storms. But nothing that cannot be explained by a lack of sleep, the heat, the cold, the weather, bad cheese, or too much drink. When you are dead, that is that. You are gone, never to be seen again nor heard from again on this earth."

"John, please! We must come to Lady Tabitha with open minds and open hearts. She has been quite successful contacting the sons, daughters, and parents of many of our friends, in and out of the admiralty. Please, for my sake, give this a chance to succeed."

Lord Corke straightened his uniform jacket, looked around himself as if lost, and nodding his head said, "Very well, darling. I am here. Let's get on with it."

Lady Tabitha, sat in silence as the little discussion between the lord and lady took place. She had studied hard to be ready for this meeting. She had practiced with the assistants in the basement until their actions were almost instinctive. Everything had been choreographed perfectly. Everyone knew their parts well and timing was critical. Becca insisted that this séance was central to her plans and must go perfectly. Lilith would not let her down.

"Please be seated in the two chairs opposite each other and let us hold hands to form the sacred circle."

The lord and lady complied, the lady with enthusiasm and anticipation, the lord with doubt and acquiescence.

"Now, let us take hands and vow never to release our grip so long as I am searching the other side for your son. We must keep the circle complete. You must work with me, help me with your belief and your psychic energy. Now close your eyes, close them tight, and with me begin this sacred chant. Before we begin, what did you call your son?"

"I called him Johnny Boy when he was little and when he needed comforting when he was older," Lady Corke responded with trembling voice.

"Then that is how I shall call him from the other side. Let us begin."

Lady Tabitha lifted her face toward the ceiling and slowly closed her eyes. The room was silent. The three held tightly to each other's hands, the lord's and lady's faces down with eyes shut tight. The silence was broken by a barely audible humming coming from Lady Tabitha, the volume and the rapidity of her humming slowly increasing, until it filled the room.

"And now repeat after me, 'Come to us, Johnny boy! Come to us.'"

Lady Corke began the chant with Lady Tabitha, but the lord was slow to engage. He joined the two only at the last two words, 'to us,' and then cleared his throat and adjusted his position in his chair. He took a deep breath and then joined the other two and began to repeat the chant with them, but with little enthusiasm.

"You must join us in heart, mind, and spirit, Lord Corke, or else there is a chance that your son will not join us."

Again, Lord Corke cleared his throat and adjusted his position in his chair. He took another deep breath. "What I do this evening, I do for you, my Lady. For you and for you alone." At that his strong base voice began to join in the chant, his voice sounding as it would if he were giving orders from the quarterdeck. His voice, louder than the other two, began to echo off the walls of the sitting room as his passion for the moment grew.

Lady Tabitha was pleased. She had the two engaged and focused. The lord's grip on her right hand was strong, almost painful, as she led the two in increasing the rapidity of the chant. She tapped her foot three times on the wood floor of the sitting room and the table began to slowly move. Just a slight rocking at first, intermittent, and then slowly more frequently. The slight moving of the table turned into a rocking, a pitching, and the table rose a little higher each time the sequence repeated itself. The rocking and pitching of the table became constant and more violent as the rapidity of the chanting increased. Then, in a loud slamming the table came to rest on the wooden floor and rocked no more. Lady Tabitha's head was now against her chest and her arms had gone limp. Only the lady's and lord's grip kept her arms outstretched.

"Someone is here. Someone seeks to communicate with the living." Lady Tabitha's voice was just above a whisper and was filled with her heavy breath.

"Oh, yes, my son! Speak to us." Lady Corke was desperate.

"Quiet! The spirits answer only to my command. Are you here, Johnny Boy? Is it you who is present?" Lady Tabitha stomped her foot against the floor once – a signal to the assistants below.

Three small vents, hidden in the floor under the table opened quietly, and the assistants below began to fan a large block of ice to bring the cold air around the ice into the space under the table. Slowly in the silence, as Lady Tabitha moaned, the space under the table began to feel cold, the lace and cloth table covering that went to the flood holding in the cold air from below.

"It's getting cold, Lady Tabitha. What does that mean?" Lady Corke was trembling both from fear and from the cold under the table as it gripped her legs.

"Hush, Lady Corke. They are here. There are two. Who is this second spirit who dares to cross without being called? Who are you?" Lady Tabitha knocked her foot against the floor three times, as she let out a wail, and the table rose, hovered, and then slammed against the wooden floor.

"Now there is only one. The intruder. Who are you and what is your desire?" Lady Tabitha's head began to move in circles and her body began to shake and tremble. "It is not Johnny Boy! This spirit is troubled. This spirit is angry and tortured. This spirit wants release. Who are you angry, spirit? Who are you?" Lady Tabitha tapped her foot on the floor one time, and the table rose and shook and then slammed to the floor. The vents below were shut, and the room became suddenly still and quiet. Lady Tabitha released her grip on the lord's and lady's hands and fell forward, her head lying on the table. As she made this motion, she blew out the candle. The room was dark, except for the light of the streetlights outside. A kind of bluish, grey light from the fog of the evening.

Lord Corke was first to stir and to speak. "What the blazes just happened?"

Lady Corke followed, "Was he here? Did he come at your request? Oh, Lady Tabitha I must know."

Both the lord and lady, eyes opened and sitting upright in their chairs, bodies stiff, looked through the dark at the form of Lady Tabitha lying on the table.

"Lady Tabitha, are you all right?" The lord reached over and touched her hand.

Lady Tabitha slowly rose from the table as if every move of her muscles required great effort. She moved her hands to her face and then her hair. Her hands trembled in the dark. She reached forward and taking a box from beside the candle, lit a vesper and then the candle. She looked first at Lady Corke and then at Lord Corke, as if exhausted.

"Your son was here, but another came with him. The other is tormented, angry, and confused. It is being tortured on the other side. It seeks communion with its parents. But you are not his parents. He is angry. He needs solace. He suffers so!"

"Who, who is this tortured spirit?" Lady Corke was crying and trembling. She reached into her sleeve and drew out a lady's lace handkerchief and began to dab her eyes.

Lord Corke pushed his chair away from the table and began to stand, but Lady Corke motioned for him to stay. He hesitated in his motion and then sat back down.

"I ask you again, Lady Tabitha, what is the meaning of all this? I have never experienced anything like this, and I have no explanation for what happened this evening. What does all this mean?" The lord was shaken, but his voice was sturdy and commanding.

Lady Tabitha looked over at Lord Corke in an exaggerated slowness and with a weak voice said, "The spirit that drove your son away. The spirit that was here tonight. That poor, tortured spirit, was of a man, who in life, committed suicide. He is being tortured by the other spirits for giving up his life. For throwing away the gift of life, for giving back the light."

Lady Corke's hands went to her mouth, and she let out a muffled scream.

"The tortured soul is the son of someone you know, Lord Corke. He must be reached again. He must be released from these spirits who torture him before he can ever find release and the peace he so craves."

"What do you say? Someone I know? I know of no one who has lost a son by suicide. This is madness." Lord Corke stood as if prepared to leave.

"Wait! Who is this poor tortured spirit, Lady Tabitha?" Lady Corke reached out and held Lady Tabitha's left hand.

"It is the spirit of the Duke of Foxborough, who in life was the son of the First Lord of the Admiralty."

Chapter 19

Holmes sat in his usual chair, Watson across from him, both in front of the fire, as it was a cold morning. Inspector MacDonald sat in the settee, smoking a cigar that Watson had given him.

"What do you make of this Persano matter, Inspector?" Holmes had chosen a large, bent pipe and was making large clouds of blue smoke as he spoke.

"It's a simple matter, Mr. Holmes. Two men broke into Mr. Persano's home, no doubt planning on taking away the valuables, were surprised to find Persano home, and in the process of trying to subdue him, were interrupted by the neighbor and fled out the back door into the alley."

Holmes rolled his eyes and steepled his fingers in front of his face. "And how do you account for their decision to burgle the house when it was clear that the lights were on? Is it not usual for such men to wait until the dead of night when they are sure those in the home are in bed, asleep?"

The inspector laughed, "Not all burglars plan things out so well, Mr. Holmes. These two men are obviously new at their work or their faculties were influenced by drink, or both."

"I see. And what do you make of the fact that nothing was taken from the house?"

"They were interrupted before they could finish the job." The inspector looked as if he was speaking to a dim-witted child. "Not all cases are as complex as you want them to be, Mr. Holmes. Sometimes it's just a simple matter of stupid men and wicked chance."

Holmes laughed and taking his pipe from his mouth said, "I see. So what do you make of the worm, left at the scene? The box? The soil? Not to mention, the temporary madness and the strange condition of Persano?"

"You are going on about the worm again. It means nothing to the case, Holmes. Nothing. As for Persano, he took at least one blow to the head. He lost his faculties, by the time you spoke with him he had regained some of them. You will see, he will recover fully, in time."

Watson had been listening and watching, as he smoked his own cigar. "Holmes, I must confess that everything the inspector says makes perfect sense. But you seem to have seen more than either I or the inspector. What is your theory?"

"I doubt I saw more than either of you gentlemen, but I observed and deduced more than each of you. I am also benefited by more information than the inspector, but not more than you, Watson."

"More information? What information, Mr. Holmes?" The inspector sat forward and looked frustrated.

"Nothing directly related to last night, Inspector. Just I have one or two other matters that may or may not be related to the events of last evening. No, I will go my way and you go yours, Inspector. We will see who comes out well in the end."

"If you have information related to the events of last night, Mr. Holmes, you are duty bound to share it with me." The inspector had now clearly lost his patience with Holmes.

"I will tell you this much, Inspector, broaden your thinking. Do not be limited to the apparent facts and circumstances as presented. Foremost, do not discount the evidence that is presented. Discount nothing. Even the seemingly unrelated may be the key trifle that opens a simple case into a much more complicated scheme." With that, Holmes stood as if to show the inspector out the door.

The inspector, looking confused, stood as well. "I assure you, Mr. Holmes, that I will find the two men who burgled Mr. Persano's house last night. And when I do, you will see that this matter is a simple case of two men, probably drunk, forcing their way into a house and getting surprised by the neighbor, and fleeing the scene. Worms and schemes will have nothing whatsoever to do with it."

Holmes smiled and walked to the window overlooking Baker Street. "Have a good day, Inspector."

Watson shook hands with the inspector and walked him to the door to their rooms. "I hope it warms up today, Inspector. It is a typical London summer, is it not?"

The inspector grunted and left, going noisily down the seventeen steps and out the front door to Baker Street.

"And what was the purpose of all that, Holmes?"

"Just my feeble attempt to get the inspector to see more and to deduce more than what is presented and what is obvious. But I am afraid, to no avail."

"I must confess," Watson was back sitting in his chair and smoking his cigar, "that I have seen what you have seen, know what you know, and yet I see no connection between our case and what happened last night."

Holmes walked briskly to his chemistry table where he had placed the small matchbox and worm. "And what about this, Watson? What do you make of this?"

Watson stood and turned around to see Holmes holding up the matchbox. "I do not know what to make of it, Holmes. It is surely an unusual thing to find at the scene of a burglary. But, beyond that, I can make nothing of it. As for Persano's madness, the inspector's theory fits the facts."

"I think there is more to all of this than you or the inspector are making of it. A great deal more."

"Then enlighten me with what I am missing, Holmes."

Holmes stood looking at the worm inside the now opened matchbox. "I believe I will take our little find with me and spend the afternoon at one of the larger labs conducting some experiments into what this worm might be, and what its purpose is. For clearly, it has a purpose."

With that, Holmes closed the matchbox and pushed it into his waistcoat pocket and went into his bedroom to retrieve his jacket and hat. As he came out of the bedroom in his jacket and carrying his hat, Holmes said, "Watson, while I am at the lab, would you please find where Scotland Yard is holding the unfortunate Mr. Persano, and drop around to see him?"

"Of course, Holmes. What do you want me to do while there?"

"I want you to observe Mr. Persano. Ask him questions. See if he can maintain a conversation. Learn if his memory has returned. And most importantly, see if he is susceptible to suggestion. Learn if he will do what you ask him to do. Tell me if you could control Mr. Persano if you were so inclined."

"All right, Holmes...control him you say?"

"Yes, Watson. Control him." Holmes went out the door of their rooms, taking his coat and walking stick with him.

Watson stood as if nailed to the ground. "Control him," he whispered to himself.

Watson had learned that Scotland Yard had taken Persano to St. Mary Bethlehem mental hospital in Bromley, on the southeast side of London. Watson shuddered at the thought of spending any time at the hospital better known as Bedlam. But he had arrived and as a result of his position as a physician, and a note from Scotland Yard, he was granted permission to meet with Persano. Watson was taken to a private consulting room and waited there for the arrival of the patient.

Persano came into the room accompanied by an orderly dressed in white. He was dressed in the same clothes that he had been in the previous evening and looked a bit disheveled and unshaven. He was otherwise very compliant, followed the orderly's instructions to take a seat, and turned and looked at Watson, curiously.

"I am afraid I do not know you sir."

"I am Dr. John Watson, I am a medical doctor, and I am the friend and colleague of Sherlock Holmes. We were present last night when you were taken into custody by Scotland Yard. If you do not mind, I would like to spend some little time getting to know you better. Will that be all right?"

Persano sat straight in his chair and tried to smooth his waistcoat and arrange his shirt collar. "Yes, that would be fine."

"Do you remember the events of last evening?"

"It is all a bit of a blur, but I am slowly remembering some things as the day progresses. For instance, I remember that my name is Isadora Persano and that I am a newspaper columnist."

"Good, that is good. You are making progress then."

"Yes, it seems that I am. I remember that I was working last night editing some copy at my home when I was struck from behind. The next thing I remember is being outside, under a street light and being questioned by a man I did not know. I don't remember what we discussed. I remember waking up here in a private room this morning and what has happened since then. My memory from this morning, after waking, is much better. I am having trouble remembering much of anything of my past."

"That may come back in time. Do you remember anything of the two men who were in your home last night?"

Persano looked at Watson languidly. "Were there two then? I am afraid that I do not remember anything about them. The inspector has already asked me these things earlier this morning. I am afraid that I will be of little help. I cannot remember my address for instance, what I was writing about, or what I was editing. The doctor says that in a few days they may show me articles that I have written over the past several months to see if that helps me recover my memories."

"How do you feel? I mean what is your mood?"

"I feel calm. I feel no real urgency about anything. I do not really feel much of anything. Just normal and calm, I suppose. I am not sure what or how I felt before so I have nothing to compare it to. Though I remembered my name when I awoke this morning, and after some discussion with the doctor, I remembered my occupation, I am afraid I am a stranger to myself and oblivious to the details of my past."

"Have you had any dreams?"

"The doctor asked me that this morning. In my current state I am not quite sure what is a dream, a memory, or sometimes even what is happening now. If it was a dream, I am not sure, but I remember feeling very frightened and concerned about my nose. I am not sure why. My nose is fine, as you can see. But I have a distinct memory of being frightened half out of my wits about my nose."

"Well that certainly is unusual. Anything specific about your nose?"

"Not that I can recall. Even now as I try to remember I am feeling very anxious about it. I want to protect my nose." Persano cupped both of his hands and put them over his nose. "It is bad you know. A bad thing what they do to my nose."

Watson looked at Persano carefully. "Who is 'they'?"

"I am sorry?"

"Just now, you said, 'what they do to my nose.' Can you remember to whom you are referring and what 'they' did to your nose?"

"Did I say that just now?"

Watson nodded.

"I do not know why I said that. Like I said, I cannot tell if what I am remembering, or the images and feelings that come to me, are dreams, memories, or things that happened recently. I just cannot tell." With that Persano removed his hands from his nose.

"Do you remember Mr. Holmes speaking with you last night? Do you remember his telling you to do certain things?"

"I remember talking to a tall man, under a streetlight, in the cold and fog. I do not remember what we discussed or what he asked me to do. I am sorry."

"Mr. Persano, can you please raise your left arm, stretched out in front of you like so?"

Persano nodded and stretched his left arm straight out in front of him. "Like this?"

"Yes, that is good. Can you keep your arm in that position for me, please?"

"Yes, it is not difficult."

"Keeping your arm in that position, can you please stand very straight with your feet together beneath you?"

Persano complied, asking again if he was satisfying Watson's request. Watson asked Persano to assume several different awkward physical positions and each time Persano complied without question and inquired if he was satisfying Watson's desires. Eventually, Watson had the man sit back down in his chair and relax again.

"Tell me, Mr. Persano, would you have any difficulty if I asked you to leave this hospital, gave you specific instructions to go to a specific location, and to enter that home and to stay until called for?"

"Of course not, Dr. Watson. Would you like for me to do that now? I am happy to comply."

"No, no. Not now. Just a question. What are you thinking about right now, Mr. Persano?"

"I am not aware of thinking about anything in particular. I am enjoying answering your questions and doing the little things you ask of me. Otherwise, I just await your next question."

"Good. Let us just sit quietly for a little while. Can we do that, Mr. Persano?"

"Yes, of course."

Watson and Persano sat in the small consulting room for more than half an hour. Mr. Persano never said anything during that time. He simply sat in his chair and looked at Watson, as if waiting for another command. For his part, Watson sat and observed Persano and was amazed at the man's seeming lack of any personal will or drive to do, say, or to act in any way except what he was instructed to do. It was as if the man had given up his own will to think, to decide, to act, to speak, etc., and acquiesced completely to the will and direction of whoever was in front of him.

"Would you repeat the following limerick for me four times, 'There once was a man, Rider Haggard, who was known as a right little blackguard. King Solomon's Mines was the least of his crimes, as from barroom to barroom he staggered'?"

Persano repeated the limerick four times as instructed without any question, and without any hesitation, and when finished asked if he had done it well.

"Yes. Very good. Thank you. Well, I think that we are finished here, Mr. Persano. I have enjoyed our visit. May I come to see you again?"

"Yes."

"Good. I will get up and knock on the door for the orderly." Watson got up and walked over to the door that was behind Persano. The man did not follow Watson with his eyes or head. Watson knocked on the door and the orderly opened it and easily led Mr. Persano out of the room and presumably back to his room.

As Watson was leaving, he saw another orderly moving quickly to intercept Mr. Persano before he and the orderly got very far down the hall. He overheard the second orderly mention that Persano had another visitor this morning. Watson took no particular notice of it. Probably just another physician he assumed and he left and returned to Baker Street.

Holmes took a hansom to the British Museum of Natural History and there found Dr. Philbin very much as he had found him before. The good doctor was just as happy to see Holmes as he had been earlier. Again saying that the "misses," would simply not believe that he had had a second interview with the great detective.

"I am afraid that my visit is related to a case, Dr. Philbin, and not a social one." Dr. Philibin was delighted. "I have an insect I would like to show you and to get your opinion."

"Yes, Mr. Holmes. I would be happy to do so. A beetle, is it?"

"No, I am afraid not. A worm." Holmes took the small match box from his top left waistcoat pocket and laying it on one of the empty crates that was scattered about the room, slowly opened it to reveal the small white worm. "Can you tell me what species of worm this is, Dr. Philbin?"

The doctor looked down at the worm and back at Holmes. "I am afraid that worms are not my specialty, Mr. Holmes."

"I understand. But surely a man of your letters can give me an educated opinion about this worm?"

Dr. Philbin smiled and moving one of the magnifying glasses he wore attached to an apparatus around his face, he picked up the box and began his examination of the worm.

"This is a most unusual specimen, Mr. Holmes. I am not sure that I recognize this species. Allow me to consult a book." Dr. Philbin walked over to his desk and moving several books found the thick volume he was searching for. He spent several minutes thumbing through pages of hand drawn pictures of various worms native to England, coming back to the small match box from time-to-time.

"I cannot find any known worm that matches this specimen exactly. It appears to be a hybrid. A worm that has been bred from two different species. There are a half dozen worms that resemble this one in some capacity. It may not be native to England, of course. Where did you find this specimen, Mr. Holmes?"

"That is not important for the moment. In your opinion then, this worm is likely not native to England and is a new species, perhaps a hybrid bred for a particular purpose?"

"I think that is as likely a hypothesis as any, Mr. Holmes. If Mr. Hudson were here, he could likely do a better job of identifying this species. But alas…"

"Yes, I am very sure that Mr. Hudson would be able to shed light on this worm. Have you a chemistry lab here at the museum that I might be allowed to use for a few hours?"

"Yes, yes of course. It is a bit unorthodox to open the use of one of our labs to members of the general public. But I think we can make an exception for you Mr. Holmes. Come with me, I will take you to a lab just down the way here."

Watson had done what he could to fill the time as he sat alone at Baker Street. It was now late afternoon and Holmes had not returned. The excitement of his interview with Persano had diminished, and Watson was yawning and moving about to keep himself from falling asleep. He had eaten a late lunch and the combination of boredom and digestion had made him positively drowsy. He sat back down in his chair before the now cold fireplace and began to doze. The familiar room coming in and out of focus as he slowly drifted in and out of a light sleep.

"I am loathe to wake you Watson. You are sleeping so peacefully, but we do have our reports to make."

Watson awoke with a start to see Holmes's face just inches from his own and a hand at his shoulder gently shaking him awake.

"Holmes, you have returned."

"Obviously, dear Watson." Holmes was now in the act of taking off his coat and hat.

"Well, what have you learned?"

"You first, Watson. You start first."

Watson gave Holmes a complete report of his interview with Persano as Holmes sat across from him in his chair, eyes closed and fingers steepled in front of his face, listening intently.

"Very good, Watson. And so, as you describe it, you found Persano very calm, compliant, and very easy to control?"

"Yes, that is the gist of it."

Holmes sat and thought for several minutes. "Did Persano mention anything about being injected; or perhaps complained about pain in his ears, throat, or nose?"

"Now that you mention it, Holmes, he did say he was having dreams about something related to his nose. He even covered his nose while speaking with me and said that 'they' did something bad to his nose. I did not take that seriously as there is nothing wrong with his nose."

"Most interesting indeed."

"Really? What then?"

Holmes did not immediately answer, simply closing his eyes and thinking.

"So what did *you* learn today, Holmes?"

"I learned a great deal. I paid another visit to our Dr. Philbin at the Museum and spent the rest of the afternoon in one of the chemistry labs conducting chemical experiments on our unique little worm."

"Good. Good. What did you learn?"

"The good Dr. Philbin confirmed what I suspected. The worm is unknown to science. The rest I learned myself. Chemistry is such a pleasure, Watson. Such an exact science. Mathematical in its precision and so capable of proving or disproving a hypothesis with near certainty. I really recommend that you take it up. It does wonders for the mind and the faculties of deduction." Holmes fell silent and seemed to be contemplating some new idea.

Watson sat for several minutes waiting for Holmes to continue, but to no avail. "Well, are you going to keep me in the dark Holmes or are you going to tell me what you learned?"

"What did you say, Watson? Oh, yes. The worm excretes some very interesting chemical compounds. One could say it was bred to be a kind of living chemical factory. Some of these chemicals are quite powerful and can have very strong effects on the brain and mind.

"Have you not read, dear Watson, of aboriginal tribes in the Caribbean who perform rituals wherein they subject their unfortunate victims to certain plant extracts that transform the individual into very willing subjects? I believe they have a name for these individuals when they are under the influence of the witch doctor's spell. Zombies, yes that is it."

"What in blazes does that have to do with this case, Holmes? Aboriginal witch doctors indeed."

"Do you not see the connection? It is rather obvious to me."

Holmes arose and walked to his desk and sitting took out a telegram form and began to write.

"Who are you sending a telegram to, Holmes?"

"To my brother, Mycroft. It is time that we see him and put certain actions into motion. It is time indeed."

Chapter 20

It was early evening and Becca was in her office at the club. She was pleased with how the séance had gone and was optimistic that Lady Tabitha's performance, and more importantly, the little trap that she had baited would prove both useful and successful to her overall scheme. She was awaiting a report from one of the Twins about their afternoon work at Bedlam, when she heard a knock on the door.

"Yes, come in."

It was Scott who greeted her as he came in. She found it difficult to tell the Twins apart and so they usually began any greeting or conversation first by identifying themselves.

"Good evening, Madam. It's Scott. I have the results of our interview with Persano."

"Come in, come in. Have a seat. Can I get you anything to drink?"

"No, mum. I did as you asked, and we retained an out-of-work actor to play the part of an alienist. He went to Bedlam and gained access to Persano. He arrived just after Dr. Watson interviewed him. Persano is as we expected, tame and compliant. It appears that this generation is successful. According to our source at Scotland Yard, Persano suffered temporary madness, followed by amnesia, which is slowly resolving itself, and has remained a very compliant personality. The "alienist" had him jumping around on one foot, had him singing a song, and doing whatever else he commanded."

"That is very good news. I will separate this generation to curtail any further breeding on their part and keep what we have alive and well until we can use them. I have hopes that will be soon. Very soon." Becca drifted into thought temporarily oblivious to Scott and her surroundings. "Anything else to report?"

"No mum."

"Thank you. That is all for now."

Scott rose and left the office, in a state of confusion. He only knew bits and pieces of Becca's plan and had no idea what her ultimate purpose was. He doubted anyone but Becca knew her whole purpose. He sighed. It would all become clear soon, he thought.

Becca, for her part, was filled with impatience and anxiety. Her plan was audacious, she knew that, but the payoffs would be great. She reached down and opened one of the drawers of her desk and pulled out a book on naval armaments, opening it to the pages she had read and reread these many weeks. She reread the section on modern naval torpedoes.

"If this works," she said softly to herself. "If only this works."

Persano was trying to sleep. He was in a very small room that contained a bed, a chair, a small table and not much more. The room was dark. Bedlam was unusually quiet this evening. He could not hear the routine screaming that usually formed the background noise of the mental hospital. His door was locked, and an orderly had just opened the small viewing port built into the door, shining a torch into the room, and ensuring all was secure. The sliding of the cover as it closed made a loud enough sound, accompanied by the light, that it had awakened Persano from a shallow sleep. His hands went immediately to his nose.

"What they did was bad," he said to himself. He had faint images or vague feelings more accurately of a presence, something alien that did not belong. Not in the room, but inside of him. He was sure there was something inside his head. No, his face. He sat up in bed as if he had been called out.

"I must remember," he said to himself. But all his efforts at remembering seemed only to make the vague feeling or memory the more difficult to recall. He laid back down and tried again to go to sleep.

As he fell in and out of sleep he fell into and out of a kind of dream state. He could feel his head pulled back hard, iron-gloved fists holding his head back by his chin. He could not move. He was drowning but was not in water. In his dream state the place he was at was dark. It was earthen. He could smell wet soil and could feel the humid mustiness of a shallow cave or hole. He tried to look around himself, but his head was held in place by the iron grip and his arms and legs were held in place by forces he could not define. He suddenly realized he was in a grave. A grave dug for him.

Persano awoke from his shallow sleep covered in sweat. Was he dead? Was he in his grave? If so, what evil held him still? He could feel his rapid breathing. His heart beating fast in his chest. The cold sweat running down and pooling at the small of his back as he lay flat. The fear came back. His nose. What they did to his nose was bad. He squirmed in his bed as if trying to avoid whatever it was.

He lapsed into sleep again. Back in his grave, the iron hand was holding his head in a death grip, his body unable to move. He felt it. Wet and slimy, on his lip. Cold and alien. Moving slowly toward his nostril. He was filled with an all-consuming panic. A terrible compulsion to prevent the evil from entering his body. His heart raced. His breath was so rapid his stomach began to ache and cramp with each intake. He couldn't move. He had to move. The wet, cold slime moved into his nose, seemed to look about, and then slowly moved forward. He could feel the horrible tickle of it as it went up his nose.

Persano could not scream. His terror had so consumed him that he had lost the ability to make a sound. He felt his bowels release. He felt his throat clinch. He could not breathe. His heart raced ever faster. He felt the room spin. The tickle of the slime as it moved. Moved toward the center of his skull; in his nose. And then at the pinnacle of the experience, a lightening flash of light in his mind and then blackness.

It was morning at Bedlam and the orderlies were making their rounds, arousing their charges from their night of sleep and nightmares. The place smelled of urine and vomit, the remains of the patients' night of dread and fear. That would need cleaning before the head maiden made her rounds. The orderly came with keys in hand to Persano's door. He knocked and called his name, but there was no response. He slid open the small door and peered into the room, only lit by the small window placed high toward the ceiling. He could see that Persano was still in bed, but nothing more.

"Time to get up Mr. Persano. It is time for breakfast." But there was no response. "Mr. Persano do not make me come in and get you up. We are having porridge this morning. It is nice and hot."

The orderly gave up and unlocked the door. Opening it slowly and entering the cell. He looked up and what he saw would haunt him for the rest of his life. Persano was lying on his back, his face a mask of blood and terror. His hands like claws had torn into his face, had ripped away parts of his nose, and he lay there dead, staring in horror at the ceiling. And as the orderly watched and wretched his own breakfast, a small white worm came crawling from what was left of the man's nose.

It was late morning and Watson had finished his breakfast and Mrs. Hudson was clearing the dishes. Holmes was playing his violin, a few of Watson's favorite pieces, as recompence for the two hours of scratching and scraping that preceded it. Holmes was in no mood for talk. He had been in deep thought all morning. Watson doubted that he had got much sleep the night before. He was still in the same clothes as the day before and in his mouse grey dressing gown. Having finished his playing, he dropped the Stradivarius and his bow to his chair and began to pace.

Watson, for his part, was still sitting at the table and reading the newspaper. He and Mrs. Hudson exchanged knowing glances but said nothing. She walked quietly out the door and down the stairs with what was left of breakfast and the dishes in a large tray she carried gingerly in front of her.

"There is a missing piece, Watson. Something that I cannot find to finish the puzzle that is this case. It is the 'why' of it. To what end does she do this?"

Watson laughed, "There remains much more than one piece for me to make any sense of this puzzle, Holmes. If you would only let me into your thoughts, I might be of some assistance."

"I am afraid that this case is not one you will bother your long-suffering readers with old man. I can feel it. Feel it in my bones as the children say. There is something much larger at stake here, and I cannot find the thread that will lead me to it."

Watson tried to take Holmes's mind off his troubles, "Have you received an answer from your telegram to Mycroft?"

Holmes looked at Watson as he paced and gave him a shrug. Watson took that as a "no." He went back to reading the paper as Holmes continued his pacing, which was finally interrupted by the sound of the bell below, followed closely by the familiar steps of Mrs. Hudson ascending the steps. She knocked twice on the closed door and opened it carrying a telegram.

Watson rose and took the telegram from Mrs. Hudson. "He is in a mood this morning!" Mrs. Hudson shook her head and left the way she had come.

"Do you want me to open and read it, Holmes?"

"Yes, please do so."

Watson opened the telegram and read it quickly. "It is from Inspector MacDonald. Persano was found dead in his room this morning. The body and the scene are being left as they were found awaiting our arrival."

Holmes quickly moved to his room to change out of his dressing gown and into his jacket.

"Holmes, listen to this, 'One of the doctors on staff retrieved a small white worm from the body.' Absolutely unbelievable!"

"It certainly has the advantage of proving me correct in the eyes of Scotland Yard, but hardly surprising. Come Watson, no need for a coat, it is nice outside."

Watson grabbed his medical bag, hat and walking stick and accompanied Holmes down the stairs to Baker Street. Holmes and Watson arrived at Bedlam via hansom and were immediately escorted to Persano's room by a waiting constable.

"Ahh, you have arrived. Good. I have kept the room as is, even the body, such as it is, hasn't been moved, Holmes. I know your little ways and thought I would oblige you this morning." MacDonald stood a few paces in front of the room looking over his notes as Holmes and Watson arrived.

"Any sign of forced entry?"

"No. The room was locked from the outside as per procedure, and the orderly had to unlock the door to gain access. I think that once you look into the room you will see that the damage to the body was self-inflicted, probably in a fit of uncontrolled madness."

Holmes walked carefully into the room taking everything in. Persano's body and the condition of his face caught Holmes's immediate attention, as did the awful smell. He looked at Watson and motioned for Watson to examine the body and Watson complied.

"The wounds on the face and especially the nose are as the Inspector described, self-inflicted. Rigor mortis has set in, and the limbs are a bit stiff. Both arms are stiff and held with the fingers clenched near the face. The fingernails are caked in blood and tissue, most likely from the act of clawing his own face and nose. Do not be fooled by the amount of blood, Inspector, terrible as these wounds are, that is not what killed the poor man."

"Can you estimate a time of death?" asked the Inspector.

"From the amount of rigor and wait a moment while I take the temperature of the body. Constable, can you help me with the body?"

Watson and the constable turned Persano's body to its left side. The back of Persano's body was a disgusting mess, having eliminated his bowels in the process of dying. Watson grimaced and in a natural reaction, backed away from the body. He used the bed sheet and blanket to clean what he could and, having retrieved a thermometer from his medical bag, took the man's temperature.

"Can you bring me some soap and water to wash my hands please? I would estimate he died ten to twelve hours ago. That would put the time of death between 10:30 P.M. last night and 12:30 A.M. this morning."

Watson moved away from the body awaiting the soap and water, as Holmes moved in to conduct his own more cursory examination of the body. It did not take long.

"I agree Watson. The poor man probably died of heart failure, or some brain fever caused by his mental state. One has to be truly mad to cause such damage to one's own face; and, very motivated by some unreal, irrational fear, or some very real fear experienced and remembered."

"Yes, sudden, acute heart failure or an extreme shock to the brain are the likely causes of death. An autopsy will settle the matter." Watson was cleaning the thermometer he had used, washing his hands, and drying each with the cloth an orderly had provided. "Thank you orderly for the soap and water."

"Can we remove the body now, Mr. Holmes?"

"Yes, Inspector there is nothing more to learn here. What of the white worm you mentioned in your telegram?"

"Yes, one of the doctors has it. The damned thing is still alive." The inspector motioned for one of the constables to retrieve the doctor and the worm.

A young doctor, probably still in residency, came down the hall holding a glass petri dish. He looked shaken by events but still very curious about the worm, carrying it with great care and looking at it through the glass lid of the dish as he walked.

"I am Sherlock Holmes, and this is my friend and colleague Dr. Watson. May I see the worm?"

"Yes, of course. You are *the* Sherlock Holmes?"

"If you are referring to the Sherlock Holmes of the many stories Dr. Watson has written about our little cases, then yes, I am he. What do you make of this worm, Doctor...?"

"Oh, where are my manners. I am Dr. Kenneth Gillett, and I am a resident here at this hospital. I do not make much of the worm. Strange thing to find in a body so immediately upon death and in a clean indoor room. One would expect to find a great many of these worms had the body been found after many hours outside, but certainly I would not expect to find it here."

Holmes took the petri dish and taking out his magnifying glass began an examination of the worm. He handed the dish and worm to Watson.

"Oh, this worm did not come from the environment, Dr. Gillett. No, it was deliberately placed in this man's body, some forty-eight hours ago, by two men who forced their way into his home. I assure you that it was the presence of this worm and the madness that followed, that caused the unfortunate Mr. Persano to inflict such horrible injuries on his own person."

"Really? Intentional you say? And to what end?" Dr. Gillett was gob smacked at the very idea of such a thing and took the petri dish Watson was handing him in a distracted way.

"Yes, intentionally done. As to what end, well that is precisely what I aim to resolve." Holmes turned to Inspector MacDonald. "And you, Inspector. I hope that you have learned your lesson and that you will not ever again ignore or brush aside evidence that is presented at a crime scene. Everything is of use at a crime scene. You must discount nothing."

"Well, I am sure…"

"As for the worm, it is the same species of worm that we found left in the match box at the crime scene. Anything else, Inspector?"

"Well no, except what does it all mean? I mean, this scene is no crime; it is a simple case of a mad man killing himself in a rather awful manner. No, what do you make of the worm and the events as we know them so far, Mr. Holmes?"

Holmes smiled at the inspector, "It means, Inspector, that you and I, we have a new and developing criminal mind to contend with. An heir as it were to the late Professor Moriarty. Yes, an heir, but a young one. Still inexperienced but eager and intelligent. It means..." Holmes stopped speaking and was staring at the worm, now being held by Dr. Gillett. "It means that I have been an imbecile and that the quicker we bring this case to a conclusion the better."

The inspector starred at Holmes bewildered and confused. "The worm means that?"

"Think, MacDonald. Think and deduce. Come Watson, we are finished here."

"But I am not finished, Holmes. Wait."

Holmes and Watson walked briskly down the hall and toward the exit, avoiding any more of the inspector's questions.

"Damn it all. How can you work with such a man!" The inspector stamped a foot to the floor and looked around him as if to seek agreement from those around him.

"Holmes you should really be more cooperative with the Inspector. We are all trying to solve the same mystery." Watson was frustrated with Holmes, both because he refused to help the Inspector and because of his own confusion about the case.

"Watson, as I have said before, I am not retained to supply Scotland Yard's deficiencies. MacDonald has seen what I have seen and if he were more imaginative and patient, he might deduce a great deal more from his cases. As for my work, it is for my client and not for Scotland Yard."

The hansom they had arrived in waited outside the hospital door. Watson entered first and then Holmes.

"221B Baker street driver." Holmes sat sullen in the hansom, disliking the rebuke from Watson. "If I keep anything from you, dear Watson, it is because I am not as yet certain of the accuracy of my deductions. Despite what you tell your readers, not everything that comes into my head is correct. No, I must work through a great deal of intellectual noise as it were, before I can hold in my hands the critical threads that solve a case. I am working through those threads now and I have come to some conclusions. But as I was saying before we left Baker Street, it is the why of this case that puzzles me.

"Before coming to the hospital, I had a whim. Ergo the telegram to Mycroft. But that whim, I think is beginning to crystalize into a theory. I need just a few more threads to make the solution to this matter complete. I am in hopes that Mycroft is willing to provide those."

Watson listened with interest to what Holmes said. He enjoyed any opportunity to look into the mind and methods of his dear friend.

"I did not mean to chastise you, Holmes. For that I am sorry. As your friend and partner in these little adventures that we engage in, it is a bit frustrating and daunting to be kept in the dark while you seem to see everything and know everything. You are correct of course; it is not for you to fill in the deficiencies of Scotland Yard. You are working your case in your own manner, and they in their manner.

"We mere mortals who are privileged to observe and to be a part of what you do are frequently left feeling the dumber and thus the more frustrated. I have seen what you have seen, heard what you have heard, and I am aware of your methods. But I simply see no way through these seemingly unrelated events to any kind of solution. While you, you are at the very cusp of a solution."

Holmes chuckled, "I am guilty sometimes of assuming that everyone around me sees what I see and deduces what I deduce. Your presence is always welcome, old man. You may not get to the matter on your own, but many times your presence, your comments, act as a kind of focused beam of light in the darkness, that leads me where I need to go."

The two men sat silent for some time as the hansom moved through London taking them back to Baker Street.

"I am still confused by what if anything that affair with the young clerks at the Admiralty has to do with any of this. That affair seems quite separate and distinct from these deaths and madness, and the white worm. I mean the Admiralty Holmes. What has that to do with this?"

Holmes was suddenly very still. His eyes had a gleam, and his body revealed a nervous energy that was barely hidden under his demeanor of calm of reason.

"Holmes, you have achieved a breakthrough. I can see it in your mannerisms."

"As I just said, Watson, sometimes the questions you ask can be very illuminating."

Chapter 21

Holmes and Watson arrived back at Baker Street and as they entered the front door, they interrupted Mrs. Hudson who was halfway up the stairs carrying a telegram.

"Oh good gracious, you startled me. But you saved me a trip up these stairs. There is a telegram for you Mr. Holmes."

Holmes bounded up the stairs to where Mrs. Hudson stood and took the telegram.

"Thank you, Mrs. Hudson. Some tea I think would be well-received if you have the time?" Holmes continued his climb up the stairs to his rooms.

"Yes, Mr. Holmes. Anything to eat with it?"

"No, no thank you. Just tea please."

Watson stopped at where Mrs. Hudson stood and said, "Yes, something to eat would be very nice, Mrs. Hudson."

Mrs. Hudson chuckled to herself and turning went down the stairs to her rooms to prepare the tea and some small sandwiches. Watson continued up and into their rooms to find Holmes tearing open the telegram, quickly reading it, and tossing it over to him.

"He is coming here, Watson. Within the hour. My, a visit from Mycroft. Only the second or third time that he has been to Baker Street. My telegram must have made an impression."

Watson read the telegram quickly. "What did you say to him?"

"I only hinted at a possible connection between my own case and that of the issue with the Admiralty clerks. As I said in the hansom, at that time it was only a whim. Now, however, it is much more." Holmes stopped and thought for a minute. "Would you be so kind as to delay our tea and sandwiches until after my brother leaves, Watson?"

"Of course, Holmes."

Holmes moved to his chair in front of the cold fireplace and taking down one of his clay pipes began the process of filling and lighting it. "I would be the better for some silence, Watson, until my brother arrives."

Watson was at the door to their rooms, on his way to inform Mrs. Hudson of the delay. He simply nodded and then made his way downstairs.

Separating the male worms from the female worms was not an easy task. It was difficult to be sure which were male and which female. The task was tedious, and it required focus and resilience. Becca had been at it for some time in the basement of her home on Kensington Court. She was tired and hadn't got any sleep since the evening before. She had spent the evening at the club, had left in the morning to come home to rest, but couldn't sleep, and so had been engaged with the worms most of the late morning and afternoon.

The cellar was dark except for the heating lamps above and around the boxes that held the worms in a soil and vegetation mix. She had to carefully dig into the loose soil to find the worms. She finally gave up on that approach, and simply dumped a third of the box of soil onto one of the flat lab tables and with tweezers and a magnifying glass, picked out the males and placed them in a box of soil that contained no worms.

As Becca was working, she did not notice that Lilith had come down to the cellar and had been observing her work for some time.

"Why are you separating the worms?" she asked.

Becca was startled and gave a start. "What?"

"Why are you separating the worms and putting them in that separate box of soil?"

"What are you doing here? I have told you not to come down here and not to ask me about this project."

"It is my house as well and I have the right to know what is going on between these walls. Why are you growing worms? Why are you separating those worms and placing them in another box of soil?"

Becca was enraged. "How long have you been watching me?"

Lilith came through the curtains separating the area where the worms were kept from the rest of the basement and approached Becca.

"I have been watching for a few minutes. I am curious. Interested in your work. We are partners after all. Aren't we?"

Becca worked to regain her composer. "Please go back upstairs. We can talk about this later. I have important work to do now that will take me another few hours, after which I will want to rest. So please leave me to my work."

Lilith cocked her head to the side and put on an exaggerated frown. "But I am bored, and I want to help. Please let me help."

"No! Lilith I am trying to be clear. You cannot help me with this project. You cannot know all my plans. We are not full partners in everything that we do. This project is very critical and confidential. Your work is the seances, not the worms and not my bigger plans. Know your place. Now, go upstairs and leave me to my work."

Lilith stared at Becca and put both her hands on her hips. "I will not go! I wish to know what you are doing with these worms."

Becca's face was a mask of rage. "You want to know what these worms are for? You want to know? Why don't I just tie you down and introduce you to one of these worms and then you will see what they are for. Care for a worm to wriggle up your noise until I can control you...if you don't go mad first. Is that what you want?"

Becca had grabbed Lilith by the arms and was shaking her as she screamed at her, Becca's face barely a few inches from Lilith's. Lilith had never seen Becca like this before. Her fear rose inside her until she almost fainted. She broke herself lose from Becca's grip and ran out of the basement, up the stairs, and to her bedroom where she fell on her bed crying.

For her part, Becca took several deep breaths and regained her composure. She returned to the task of separating the worms. As she did, and her emotions subsided, she began to think more clearly. She wondered if Lilith had become a liability. Were her naiveté, curiosity, and boredom going to be a problem for the project's success? She would need to decide what to do about Lilith soon, but not until her role in the scheme was completed. "One more séance," she said to herself, "And then your usefulness will have waned."

Holmes had spent the last quarter of an hour smoking and in deep thought as Watson sat reading a medical journal. The sound of the bell below announced that Mycroft had arrived. Holmes came out of his self-induced stupor and stood, knocking out the spent tobacco from his clay pipe. Watson stood as well, carefully marking his place in the journal, and straightening his waistcoat.

Mrs. Hudson entered first followed almost immediately by Mycroft. He was an imposing figure. Taller than Holmes and weighing much more, his every movement seemed to threaten to knock over furniture, books, and sundry items as he made his way into the room. Mrs. Hudson did not bother to make the introductions and simply turned and went back downstairs.

"Sherlock, you look fit. Dr. Watson, how are you sir? Both looking none the worse for wear."

"Mycroft, come in. Please have a seat. We have much to discuss."

"Straight to business then." Mycroft worked his way over to the settee and taking a small silver box from his waistcoat pocket, drew out some snuff, and sniffed it in with the ease of someone who has engaged in the habit for far too long.

"Cigar, Mycroft?" asked Watson.

"No, thank you, Dr. Watson."

Holmes filled one of his long-stemmed cherrywood pipes and having lit it sat and looked at Mycroft with an air of amusement.

"I am sorry not to inquire about how you are, but as you know, I can see all that I need to know just by looking at you; and of course you can do the same with me. I need for you to be very candid with me, Mycroft. None of the usual secrecy, avoidance, and empty talk. I need to ask you some few serious questions and I expect you to be candid with me."

"Well, Sherlock, I will be as candid with you as the subject matter of your inquiries allows. You keep your clients' secrets and I keep my government's. That is the way of things."

Holmes scoffed. "As you are very much aware, I have been retained on several matters for her Majesty's government and have brought those matters all to successful conclusions. At the risk of sounding boastful, had I accepted it I could be a peer of the realm. Your little government secrets are safe with me. As for Watson, well his patriotism is beyond dispute, having served the Crown with distinction and carrying the wounds to prove it. No, none of the usual nonsense, Mycroft, I need information."

"I will provide information to the extent that I can without violating my own very serious obligations and duties." Mycroft stiffened and took on an air of diffidence and caution.

"Very well. We understand each other. I will get straight to the point. Is Her Majesty's Navy engaged in developing any technology of a particularly sensitive nature?"

Mycroft chuckled. "You cannot possibly expect me to answer that question, Sherlock. First, there are any number of secret programs being developed at the same time, and I cannot possibly know to which you may be referring. Secondly, the types of programs to which you refer are particularly departmentalized and the usual seals of secrecy are doubled in their case. No, I cannot possibly provide you with any information concerning the subject of your query."

Holmes looked at Watson with an expression of amusement and frustration.

"Mycroft, it was you who consulted with me regarding the little matter of the junior clerks in the Admiralty. It happens that the party who very likely instigated those queries also features prominently in one of my little cases, as you are wont to put it. I will tell you why I need the information, and then you can judge whether the purpose of my inquiries is sufficient to give you reason to divulge what you can.

"I have reason to believe that a new and eager power in the criminal element here in London, has developed a means by which to control the brain and therefore the actions of any person whom she exposes to a specially bred worm. I do not know what her eventual plans are nor the specific purpose she has in mind. But I can deduce that her target and her attention is focused on the Admiralty. Why? Because she attempted to gather information, by manipulating those under her power, by dint of her position in the darker aspects of society, via these little inquiries she made through vulnerable junior clerks at the Admiralty. I believe that she learned more about a particular secret program than these junior clerks are disclosing; or that she learned enough to deduce the rest – she appears to be a formidable intellect.

"If she could gain access to men at the higher levels of the Admiralty, expose them to this worm, and gain access to information critical to the security of this nation, and sell such information, well she would accomplish two things. First, she would have access to much wealth, and secondly, she would have someone under her control at the highest levels of Her Majesty's Navy. The results of which could only serve to harm the nation we both love and serve in our own little ways."

Mycroft listened intently as Holmes explained himself. One hand on his knee, leaning forward and looking intently into his brother's eyes. At the end of Holmes's explanation, Mycroft sat back in the settee and thought for several minutes. The room was silent, except for the occasional sound of Holmes's inhalations as he drew from his pipe. Mycroft looked at Watson and then back at Holmes. He again took his little silver box from his waistcoat pocket and applied snuff. He sneezed and taking out a great handkerchief from his jacket pocket, blew his nose loudly.

"Very well, Sherlock. I will tell you what I can."

Holmes's shoulders relaxed and he settled more into his chair, sitting crossed legged, his face all attention. For his part, Watson sat at the edge of his chair, both feet on the floor, and looked at Mycroft intently.

"Thank you, brother Mycroft. I ask again, is Her Majesty's Navy engaged in any particularly sensitive development of technology that, if successful, would give the navy an advantage at sea?"

"You are a little familiar with the underwater apparatus known as a submarine, I believe, from the affair of the Bruce-Partington plans? Yes, good you remember. Submarines are particularly good at sneaking up on the enemy and dispatching the same by use of a torpedo. Are you familiar?"

"Yes."

"Good. This is very much state-of-the-art warfare. The powers that be are each engaged in the development of these torpedoes and with particularity, the guidance systems, to increase the accuracy and range of these very deadly weapons of war. Anyone with access to this information and a desire to turn traitor to their country, could make a king's ransom selling such information. Enough said then?"

"Quite, Mycroft. And am I correct in assuming that this kind of information is known to only a very few and only by the upper levels of Her Majesty's Navy?"

"Yes. Even the engineers and designers working on the project only know as much as they need to know to complete the designs and prototypes of the parts of the whole torpedo that they work on. A handful of men know the full design and the full purpose. Anyone wishing to gain access to this information would need to compromise one of only a small handful of men to gain access to the whole."

Holmes sat in thought and smoked his long-stemmed pipe as clouds of blue smoke circled above his head. Watson fidgeted in his chair and looked back and forth between Holmes and Mycroft.

"Are you privy to any personal information regarding the members of the Admiralty?"

Mycroft moved uncomfortably and cleared his throat, "Yes, I am aware of things that are not generally known."

Holmes smiled, "I thought as much. Any reason to believe that due to issues of a personal nature, any member of the Admiralty is particularly vulnerable at present?"

Mycroft thought for a moment. "No."

"Come Mycroft, no dalliances, no personal proclivities that would make a man more vulnerable to approach?"

"Holmes, these are men of the highest character. They live their lives above reproach. Beyond the occasional use of too much alcohol, or the infrequent wandering eye, there is simply nothing that I can point to. No, there is nothing that would make such men particularly vulnerable, as you put it."

Holmes sat in thought. "Has there been a recent personal loss that has impacted one of the Admiralty or his spouse that might be used to gain access to the man and win influence over him?"

Mycroft hesitated, thought again, and then finally seemed to acquiesce. "The First Lord of the Admiralty has recently lost his son. It is a great loss to the family, a great tragedy, and I understand that his wife is particularly affected by the loss. But I cannot see that the tragedy of the loss of a son could possibly compromise the First Lord or make him vulnerable to treason."

Holmes was lost in thought again. He stared down at the floor, puffing on his pipe. "No, I suppose not." The room was silent.

"Well, I am sure that you have other matters to attend to and I certainly have mine, Sherlock." Mycroft stood and

Watson with him. Holmes stayed as he was, focused on the floor in front of him.

"Good evening, Mycroft. It was a pleasure to see you again." Watson shook the large man's hand.

Mycroft walked toward the door and as he opened it, he motioned with his head for Watson to come closer.

"He is a bit thin and worn. More so than usual. Attend to him." With that Mycroft exited the rooms and could be heard going down the stairs heavily and out the front door to Baker Street.

Chapter 22

After Mycroft left, Holmes sat in his chair beside the cold fireplace smoking his pipe. As the time passed, Watson did not ask for tea, and then did not ask for dinner because he could see that Holmes was engaged and he did not wish to interrupt or disturb him. It was becoming dark by the time Holmes appeared to be finished thinking and stood and stretched.

"Are you in the mood for dinner, Holmes? I certainly am."

"My long-suffering friend, yes, you may request that Mrs. Hudson bring something up for dinner. I may or may not partake." Holmes stopped and thought for a minute. "On the other hand, it is likely that she will be unhappy with me as we never sent down for the tea and sandwiches, she made for us earlier. I will oblige her by eating something for dinner. Yes, please inform her we want dinner."

"Oh good. I will go down and speak with her now." Watson went quickly downstairs and informed Mrs. Hudson that they would like dinner. She was a little out of sorts about the tea and sandwiches, but Mrs. Hudson was by now familiar with Holmes's ways. Dinner, Watson was assured, would be up shortly.

When Watson returned to their rooms, Holmes was in a more congenial mood and Watson took advantage of it.

"What are your next steps in the case, Holmes?"

"Tomorrow morning I may have to make a visit to Kensington Court."

Watson looked completely confused. "Kensington Court you say."

Holmes chuckled, "Yes. Do you not recall when I, in the guise of an out-of-work groom, was asked to help move boxes in the cellar of that home on Kensington Court? Yes? Good. You will no doubt remember that I learned one of the women in the house conducted private seances for paying customers."

Watson smiled and his eyes positively shined, "Yes, I see, Holmes. You are thinking that this woman, the one who gives seances, is in a conspiracy with Miss St. John of the Gemini Club and that she will use information obtained from one of the unlucky lords during the séance to compromise him and thus make him vulnerable to her persuasion. Have I hit upon it?"

"I am afraid that you have missed my point entirely, Watson. No, I do not believe that Miss St. John plans to use information obtained from a Lord of the Admiralty at a séance overseen by her friend and housemate.

"You know my methods, Watson. You know the facts as I know them. What do you deduce Miss St. John might use a séance to achieve? Put yourself in her position. You have absolute control of the space. You can lie in wait. You can bring in accomplices. You have access to the worms. Any lord attending a séance in the that house on Kensington Court is at grave risk."

"Holmes! We must immediately warn Her Majesty's Navy!"

"We have some time, Watson. These are busy men. However, your suggestion that we act with alacrity is a good one. I will telegram brother Mycroft and ask him to set-up a meeting with the Admiralty the day after tomorrow. I believe that will suffice."

Holmes walked to the desk between the two windows facing Baker Street and began to complete a telegraph form. "Ahh, here comes Mrs. Hudson with our dinner now. Mrs. Hudson, would you be so kind as to see that this reaches the telegraph office and is sent immediately?"

"One thing at a time, Mr. Holmes. I am setting up your dinner at present and I shall get to telegrams afterward."

Holmes held the telegram form close to his chin and looked properly chastised. "Of course, Mrs. Hudson. Thank you very much for dinner and a thousand apologies for missing the tea and sandwiches."

Mrs. Hudson scoffed. "I am used to your ways, Mr. Holmes. I drank most of the tea, and as for the sandwiches, you may just have them for breakfast in the morning."

Holmes looked at Watson, who seemed aghast by the notion of eating stale sandwiches for breakfast. Holmes began to laugh heartily at both Mrs. Hudson and Watson. He rose and handed Mrs. Hudson the telegram form and continued to laugh as he sat down at the table to eat dinner.

The next morning Holmes was up early, having slept very little during the night. He sat in front of the mirror applying make-up and prosthetics for his disguise as an older, somewhat naïve Anglican priest. The nose prosthetic made his nose longer and finished in almost a point. The false teeth gave him a pronounced overbite and the long, gray, bushy sideburns and mottled skin make him look several years older than he was. The wig he was busy placing on his head, was disheveled, a bit kinky in appearance, and mostly gray. He finished his make up making his neck appear covered in age spots.

Holmes moved to his armoire and took out the priest's traditional black clothing and collar and got dressed. He chose an old beaten walking stick, the flat brimmed black hat of the vicar, and retrieved the copy of the family Bible he kept on a shelf in the armoire. He was ready.

As Holmes exited onto Baker Street, the sun was up, and London was waking up. He had assumed a bent over position and was now walking uneasily with short steps and a frequently unbalanced gait. He hailed a hansom and ordered the driver to take him to Kensington Court. He spoke in a barely audible shaky, squeaky voice. As the hansom drove him to his destination, Holmes planned his interview with the young lady who conducted the seances and worried a bit about whether his plan of action was the right one, at the right time. Driving a wedge between the young lady and Miss St John was a risky maneuver, but it also might facilitate his plans. He could not make any definitive plans as he would need to improvise as events warranted. He planned to knock on the door and feign that he was lost and tired, out of breath, and attempt to get invited into the home and there pursue a conversation.

When the hansom arrived at Kensington Court, Holmes had it stop several houses away from the one he was looking for. He walked in his bent over and shaky gait, using an old walking stick as a cane to support his weight as he did so. He arrived at the house and crossed the street to the little park and sat on a bench as the sun filled the blue sky with its light and his body with its warmth. He feigned reading the Bible and hummed to himself.

As he sat, Miss St John exited the front door, and her carriage picked her up and drove away. He did not see the young women at the door this morning. Holmes sat wondering when he should approach the front door, but decided patience was the better part of virtue. His keen instincts honed over years of case work, cautioned that he sit and wait. He sat as the morning slowly went by and after two hours, he was surprised to see the front door to the house open and the young lady exit.

Lilith had not planned to take a walk, but the events of the evening before had upset her. She had not shared breakfast with Becca this morning and had slept in her own bedroom that evening. She looked around her neighborhood and breathed in the air of a glorious sunny morning. She thought she would go to the park and sit for a while and then perhaps take a walk to the market and buy some things for dinner. As she started to cross the street, she saw the old priest sitting on the bench and sighed to herself. He looked so peaceful sitting there alone with his Bible. She was drawn to him and made her way to the bench.

"Good morning, sir. May I join you?"

Holmes was surprised by her question and thought that perhaps she had seen through his disguise but decided to play along. Fortune, patience, and his instincts had brought her to him.

"Oh yes, little miss. Please. My name is Rev. Jonathan Beckwith, and your name, little miss?"

"My name is Lilith." She smiled as she said it and sat next to Holmes in a very feminine and girl-like way; her two gloved hands in her lap. "Are you a local vicar?"

"Alas, no miss. I am retired. Do you attend services locally?"

Lilith looked at Holmes and smiled and then looked absently at her hands in her lap as she fidgeted with her gloves. "Oh no. I do not attend. That way passed me by long ago."

"Our Lord is always available, my dear. He is ever-present, all-knowing, and welcoming to anyone at any time. You are young, your time has not passed you by. Perhaps this chance meeting is another opportunity. A door opening and the gracious Lord awaiting you with welcoming arms."

Lilith fidgeted the more with her gloves, struggling with what to say. "Well, what a wonderful image, but no, I have chosen my path, it is much too late for me. If you knew more about me, I am sure that you wouldn't be so inviting."

"Tell me about yourself then."

"Oh, I am just an ordinary person. Nothing to tell."

"Do you live in that fine house?"

"Yes. I do."

"Your husband must love you very much and must be doing very well to provide such a wonderful place to live."

Lilith looked at Holmes for a moment, staring in his eyes, and then looked up at the house. "I am not married. No man has ever asked. I live in the house with my business partner."

"Business partner?" Holmes let silence reign for a moment or two and then picked up his questioning again. "What kind of business are you and your partner engaged in?"

"My partner owns a club and I...well I am a medium."

Holmes showed surprise with his body and looked down at his feet. "Oh, little miss, a medium. But why? Why would you do such a thing?"

"I am good at it. I help people with their grief. I can do some good as a medium, and it does pay well."

Holmes sat silently as Lilith looked the more uncomfortable. Finally he said, "I suppose you can help the grieving in your profession. But the spirit world is not one to be trifled with. The Old Testament teaches us to stay away from such things. The spirit world is God's domain, young lady. Are you ever frightened?"

Lilith let out a little feminine laugh. "Only by what I am asked to do, but never by the séance itself."

"Asked to do?"

"I have said too much. I need not burden you with my little problems. It is far too nice a day."

Holmes reached over and patted Lilith's gloved hand. "I am a priest, little miss, it is my calling to listen to the problems of others. Tell me why a beautiful little thing like you should be frightened."

Lilith raised a shaking hand to her face and then back to her lap. She did not know this priest and yet she so needed to unburden herself. Her fears, her pain, her broken spirit began to well up inside her, and she found that she could not avoid telling this sweet old priest her fears.

"I am not very happy, dear sir. My partner won't share with me what she is planning, and I am afraid. She has changed so much." Lilith began to cry softly as she spoke. "Oh please do not breathe a word of this to anyone."

"We priests are accustomed to keeping our parishioner's secrets my child. You may confide in me."

"Of late she has become obsessed with these worms that she is growing in the cellar. I do not know why she grows them or what she plans to do with them. I do know that she wants me, expects me, no, has ordered me to use one of my clients in a very bad way. This frightens me."

"And what has she asked you to do that frightens you so?"

Lilith began to cry more emphatically and to shake all over. She took out a woman's handkerchief from her sleeve and began to cover her face. "She wants to put the worm in my client's nose. She wants me to offer him a drink laced with laudanum and when the man and his wife are asleep, she plans to introduce the worm into the man's nose." Lilith shook as she said the words. "I don't know why. Why would she do this? It is so grotesque." Lilith cried and shook.

Holmes put his arm around Lilith's shoulders. "There now. You feel better, yes? Telling the truth, unburdening yourself of your fears, it helps a great deal." Holmes sat with this arm around Lilith patting her back and shoulder. "And when has she asked you to do this terrible deed?"

Lilith could not immediately answer. She turned toward Holmes and rested her face on his shoulder. "In a fortnight, less now. In fact, next week. Oh I am so frightened. I have no place to go and no one to trust."

"Oh my, so soon? But you have time, my dear. You can avoid doing this. You must simply refuse. Yes, you must refuse."

Lilith lifted her face from Holmes's shoulder and sat upright. She wiped her tears and regained a semblance of self-control. "No I cannot refuse. I have given my oath to her, and she has given her oath to me. We are Gemini. The two that are one. I cannot refuse her. What am I to do with this fear? I am so anxious dear sir. I am lost."

Holmes wanted to know the exact day but was reluctant to ask so direct a question. He could learn the exact date from his visit with the lords of the Admiralty in a day's time. He must tread carefully with this young lady. He must console and ask no more.

"There now. You have stopped shaking so. You are better now."

"Yes, I do feel better, thank you, dear sir. I am resolved. I know my path."

"Allow me to absolve you of these your sins that you have confessed to me this beautiful morning." Holmes said the words and made the sign of the cross. He hugged Lilith and she stood to go.

"Where are you going, little miss?"

"I am going back to my house. It was wonderful that fate brought you here this morning when I so badly needed you, dear sir. How may I ever thank you?"

Holmes looked up at the standing Lilith and smiled. He took her gloved hand in his two as he patted her hand he said, "Go forth and sin no more."

Holmes was back at Baker Street by noon. Watson had left to run errands and he was free to take off his disguise, wash his face, and get dressed for the day. He was in the act of calling Mrs. Hudson for lunch when the bell rang. He walked to the landing and watched as Mrs. Hudson opened the door. It was the aunt, Mrs. McKinnon. Holmes quickly returned to his rooms and shut the door. He walked quickly to the cold fireplace, took one of his pipes and began to fill it.

Mrs. Hudson knocked on the closed door and then opened it. "Mrs. McKinnon has returned to see you, Mr. Holmes. She apologizes for not having an appointment."

Holmes reached for the matches and began to lite his pipe. "Show her in, Mrs. Hudson."

The stately Mrs. McKinnon entered and as she removed her gloves said, "Good morning, Mr. Holmes. I am sorry to intrude on you like this, but I was in the area and thought I would stop by and see if there are any new developments in our case."

Holmes motioned for the lady to sit but stood in front of his chair puffing at his pipe. "I am afraid I have nothing worthy of reporting at present, but I can say that I am chasing one or two loose ends. Your niece's case is a very complex and interesting one. Have you learned or remembered anything more that might be of assistance?"

Mrs. McKinnon looked at Holmes with whimsy. "You needn't be so anxious Mr. Holmes. I am here professionally." She smiled to herself knowing as a woman does that Holmes would not be acting as he did if there weren't some small spark of interest. "No, we have learned nothing more and have nothing more to add to our previous testimony, as it were."

"Very well. I am in hopes that the case should be coming to a conclusion very shortly. In the meantime, I bid you a good morning." Holmes motioned with his arm toward the door.

"Mr. Holmes, if you anticipate that the case will be coming to a close shortly, then surely you have learned more than you are telling me. Please, what have you learned?" She sat on the settee and placed her hands in her lap and looked up at Holmes as a teacher might a child.

Holmes sat in his chair and looked at Mrs. McKinnon. "The unfortunate Mr. Holcomb met his fate because he was an honest man and a good solicitor. He learned some things about a partner that put his life in jeopardy. His death was not an accident. Other than that, I can tell you no more at present."

"Then it was murder?"

"Yes."

"Have you involved the police?"

"I have."

"Will the murder or murderers be apprehended?"

"I have plans and hopes that they will."

"When?"

"I cannot possibly tell you, Mrs. McKinnon. The case is bigger than you are aware and there are other interests that I must protect."

"I see. And so you choose to keep me in the dark?"

Holmes sighed and put his pipe in his lap. "I am not intentionally prevaricating, Mrs. McKinnon. The success of the case is dependent at present on discretion. I am sure you can understand that."

Mrs. McKinnon looked around the room absently. "I see. Then that is all that you are willing to share with me at present?"

"Yes, and please, keep what I have shared with you in confidence. Do not, for instance, tell my client, your niece."

Mrs. McKinnon stood and began to put on her gloves. "I understand, Mr. Holmes. Thank you for letting me into your confidence, even if in so limited a manner. I very much appreciate your efforts and I thank you." She extended her hand to shake that of Holmes.

Holmes stood and took Mrs. McKinnon's gloved hand and gave a small bow. "Have a good morning, Madam."

With that, Mrs. McKinnon left the room and Holmes could hear her light footsteps on the stairs and the door open and close behind her. He went quickly to the window overlooking Baker Street and looked down to see her standing and motioning for a hansom. She looked up at the window and gave a little wave of her hand as the hansom pulled up. Holmes merely nodded and moved away from the window.

––––––––––––––––––––

Becca was in her office at the club and in the middle of receiving reports from Steven and Scott. It had been a very busy morning and afternoon dealing with club business and personnel matters. She was more interested in getting back to her plans and was eager for a report about Persano.

"What have you learned from your sources about Mr. Persano's condition?"

Scott cleared his throat and looked quickly at his brother who was simply looking straight ahead.

"I am afraid, Madam, that Mr. Persano is dead. He died of self-inflicted wounds of a most ghastly nature. We expect stories to appear in the newspaper today."

Becca was stunned by the news. "Dead?"

"Yes."

"But why and how?"

"As I said, Madam, he apparently mutilated his face and died of acute heart failure brought on by insanity. We know nothing more. The official cause of death is heart failure and the story that is being released to the press is that he died in his home. There is no official connection to us or the worm."

"No 'official' connection. What does that mean, Scott?"

Steven looked at Scott, nodded, and took up the briefing. "A white worm was found on the body by one of the physicians, Madam. We are to understand that the worm is a complete mystery and is not connected in any way to the cause of death.

"One more thing, Madam. Scotland Yard and Mr. Holmes were at the scene. They are both aware of the worm. Scotland Yard is making nothing of it. We do not know what Mr. Holmes has made of it."

Becca stared down at her desk in shock. The death was bad enough news, made all the worse by the presence of Holmes at the scene. She felt as if the room were spinning.

Her left hand shook as she stood and walked over to pour herself a whiskey. She drank it down in one gulp and poured herself another. She returned to her desk and sat.

"What has Holmes to do with this matter?"

"We do not know, Madam. He was investigating the death of Mr. Holcomb. We are not sure if he has made a connection between Mr. Holcomb's death and that of Mr. Persano, but his presence at the hospital would seem to indicate that he has."

"Of course he has!" Becca yelled the words as much to the universe as to Steven and Scott. "That man has become a significant nuisance. I have neither the power nor the organization in place to do anything about it." Becca stood, looked about her office, and then sat back down again.

The room was silent, absorbing as it were her rage and the words she had screamed to the walls. Steven and Scott sat silently looking at each other, then at Becca, and then at the floor.

"We must take these developments into consideration, gentlemen. The plan must move forward. We will not change the timing. In fact, the sooner we move to the next step, the better. But it is time that we hire someone to watch Mr. Holmes. I want to know what he does, where he goes and to whom he speaks." Becca had calmed herself. She no longer shook, and her eyes were cold as she stared at both Steven and Scott, who simply nodded at her commands.

"And what about Lilith? What have you learned since I ordered her surveillance?"

"We know that this morning she sat in the park and spoke with an old priest. Not for long, but the conversation seemed serious. She was emotional. Afterward, she simply returned home and has not left the house since." Steven delivered this news with almost a sense of relief.

"A priest?"

"Yes, Madam."

Becca thought about what she had been told and then said, "She was emotional? Describe for me how she was emotional."

"She was observed crying and the priest consoled her."

Becca thought it over. She remembered the conversation in the cellar the evening before. The way that she had spoken to Lilith. The way Lilith had left crying and her absence at the breakfast table this morning. She was relieved. It was about their relationship and nothing more, she thought.

"Thank you both. If there is nothing else, please leave me."

"There is nothing else, Madam." Steven stood first and then Scott and they left the room together, closing the door quietly behind them.

Becca leaned back in her chair and then forward placing her head in her hands as her elbows rested on the desk. She was not worried about Lilith; she would come around. She was worried about Holmes. What did he know? It was not clear to her that he had made a connection between the deaths of Mr. Holcomb and Mr. Persano. If the doctor had discovered the worm on Mr. Persano's body, then it was likely that Holmes knew about that as well. But no worm had been discovered on Mr. Holcomb's body, so Holmes might not put the two together.

She thought about the worm left at Mr. Persano's apartment. That mistake had concerned her, but now she thought about it more. The only connection to the club was membership. Roderick and Holcomb had been members. But Mr. Persano had not been a member and no one else knew about the duel at the club. The worm left at the apartment could not be traced back to her. As far as anyone knew, and she hoped, as far as Holmes knew, the worm was uniquely associated with Persano and his death but had nothing to do with the death of Mr. Holcomb or Mr. Hudson. Holmes might have simply been brought into the Persano case by Scotland Yard. They were simply consulting Holmes about his death. There was no connection to Holcomb's death.

Becca slowly began to feel more at ease. There was nothing to connect the club to the worms. There was nothing to connect the club to the death of Mr. Persano. Holmes's visit to the club had been about Hudson and Holcomb, and nothing else. Her plans would continue. Her timing would not be interrupted. She breathed in deeply, took up her glass of whiskey, and drank it down with satisfaction. No reason to be concerned, she thought.

Chapter 23

Watson returned to Baker Street mid-afternoon to find Holmes working at his chemistry table. "Good afternoon, Holmes. Where were you off to this morning? Any developments?"

Holmes looked up from his bubbling beakers and test tubes. "It was a revealing morning."

Watson put down the book he had purchased, still wrapped in brown paper and string, and looked at Holmes with frustration. "And?"

"I went to the house on Kensington Street and had a conversation with one of the ladies who lives there."

Watson looked surprised. "Was that a good idea, Holmes? They will know that we are engaged."

Holmes moved away from the table and chuckled. "Did I say, 'I'? No, I went in the guise of a retired Anglican rector. I sat on a park bench across from the house and observed. To my surprise the same young lady I had met before came out of the house and joined me on the bench. Her name is Lilith. She lives in the house with Miss St. John and described herself as her business partner. The conversation between us went as one would expect between a retired priest and a troubled woman. She confided in me, and I must confess she confided more than was wise. I have learned that they plan to introduce the worm to an unsuspecting member of one of the seances that Lilith performs in her role as a medium. The plan will be carried out next week. I am not sure of the exact date, but once we meet with the Admiralty, that will become evident."

"Did you get any confirmation that one of the lords of the Admiralty is their intended target?"

"No, Watson. But I hardly need it." Holmes paused, lost in thought. "She had a very vulnerable quality about her, Watson. It is always confusing to me how one such as she can get tangled in the webs spun by the more evil and plotting personalities amongst us. I would venture to say that it is highly unlikely that this young woman would intentionally cause harm to anyone; and yet, she is a willing participant, with Miss St. John, in just such a plot. The criminal mind is such a complicated mass of emotions, needs, irrationality, and motives. Who knows why some, exposed to the same experiences in life, become criminals while others become saints? Is it some deformity in the brain? Some shock early in life? An inherited predisposition from one's ancestry? Some cruelty experienced while young that drives one to cause such suffering in others?"

"You are in a rather philosophical mood this afternoon, Holmes. The study of the human mind is a rather new and undeveloped science. Though Sigmund Freud in Austria has made some strides. Though his theories are a bit too outlandish for my taste. As a doctor, I keep to the physical and the knowable. The human mind is far too intangible, erratic, and tangled a web for strict science."

Holmes stood and walked to his usual chair by the cold fireplace. "I am not so sure, Watson. There is much evidence in the inclinations, decisions, words, and actions of people from which one can deduce the causes and inclinations in the mind. I have read one or two lectures of Dr. Freud, and he has the makings of a detective of the mind. Interesting man."

As Watson was about to respond, the bell rang, and he could hear Mrs. Hudson answering the door.

"I will go see who is here to save Mrs. Hudson a walk up the steps."

Watson arrived at the landing in time to see Mrs. Hudson closing the front door and carrying a telegram.

"I am coming downstairs, Mrs. Hudson. No need for you to come up. Have we the afternoon paper?"

"Thank you, Dr. Watson. Yes, I have the afternoon paper just here in my rooms." Mrs. Hudson disappeared into her rooms and quickly returned with the paper and handed it and the telegram to Dr. Watson. "You saved me a trip up those stairs. Thank you."

"Of course Mrs. Hudson. Tea?"

"I am in the act of boiling the water as we speak. I shall bring it up shortly."

Watson returned to Holmes and said, "A telegram from your brother Mycroft."

Holmes was busy choosing a pipe and preparing it for smoking. "Would you mind reading it me, Watson?"

"Of course." Watson opened the telegram and read it to himself. "Mycroft has scheduled a meeting with the lords of the Admiralty tomorrow morning at half passed ten. He warns that the meeting will be a short one and begs that you be on your best behavior."

Holmes laughed. "Mycroft has a respect for the ruling classes that I do not share. All this bowing and titles mean nothing to me. They are accomplished men to be sure, and dedicated to Her Majesty, but kowtowing to their egos is quite beyond my sense of dignity."

Watson gave Holmes a disagreeable and correcting look. "We must all acknowledge our places in society, Holmes. Such is the way of things."

Holmes scoffed and lighting is pipe, threw himself into his chair, releasing a cloud of blue smoke as he did. "Really, Watson!"

The next morning, Watson was up early and was dressed in his finest collar, cravat, morning coat, waistcoat, pants, shoes and spats. As he came downstairs to join Holmes for breakfast, he met Mrs. Hudson leaving the rooms carrying an empty tray.

"My word, Dr. Watson, you look from top to bottom the fine English gentleman."

"Thank you, Mrs. Hudson. Am I to assume from the empty tray that breakfast is set?"

"Yes. But whether Mr. Holmes has any, well, your guess is as good as mine. He is in a dark mood."

Watson nodded and proceeded to enter the sitting room as Mrs. Hudson gingerly descended the stairs.

"Good morning, Holmes. It is half past eight and you are still in your dressing down and night shirt." Watson went immediately to the table and began to serve himself breakfast.

"We have plenty of time, Watson. I confess that a mood of lethargy has set in with me this morning. If not for this meeting, I would lay about all day."

"You must eat some breakfast, Holmes. It will serve you well and provide the energy you will need to face the Admiralty today. Come join me."

"I suppose. Some tea, a piece of toasted bread and jam is all I need this morning."

Holmes sat at the table across from Watson and poured himself a cup of tea. He was indeed in a mood this morning. His hair was unkempt, he sat with rounded shoulders in a posture of lethargy; dressed only in his night shirt and opened dressing gown, feet bare. He drank his tea in a long gulp, took a piece of toasted bread and dipping it in the jam, ate it quickly.

"I suppose I should wash and get dressed. It is on mornings like this that I am particularly thankful to have my friend and colleague with me. You know how I can get when the ennui is upon me, and this is such a morning."

Watson smiled. "Come, Holmes. You have a case. You are meeting with the lords of the Admiralty of Her Majesty's Navy. Think of the privilege and the honor to do so. That should be motivation enough."

Holmes nodded shamefully. "You are of course correct. But all the same, I would rather stay in these rooms today and do absolutely nothing." Holmes arose and walked slowly to his bedroom as Watson looked on with concern.

The hansom ride to the offices of the First Lord of the Admiralty was spent in silence. Holmes, morose, stared out of his side of the hansom as Watson nervously fidgeted with his collar and cravat. As they arrived, Watson looked at Holmes and patted him on the knee with an exaggerated smile.

"Come man, to arms!"

"I am fine now that we are here. Please pay the driver."

The imposing five buildings that made up the offices of the Admiralty near Whitehall were impressive, but conservative. There was nothing ostentatious about the buildings or their interiors. As Watson stepped from the hansom, he could see the busy naval officers and staff coming in an out and moving to-and-fro to carry out the orders and policies of the First Lord. He stood the straighter and there was a jauntiness to his gait, as he recalled his own time of service in Her Majesty's Army. Holmes was two or three steps behind as Watson eagerly approached the entrance.

There was a fine young ensign waiting their arrival and he led Watson and Holmes through the hallways to the office of the First Lord. Standing outside was Mycroft.

"Good, you are on time. You will be meeting with the First Lord; the other lords are busy elsewhere with other business. He is a very busy man, Sherlock. Do not expect the meeting to last long."

"Thank you, Mycroft. Please lead the way."

Watson shook the young ensign's hand and patted him on the back as he joined first Mycroft and then Holmes as they made their way into the First Lord's offices. Their arrival was announced by a clerk.

"My Lord, good morning. Thank you kindly for agreeing to meet with us. This is my brother, Sherlock Holmes, and his colleague Dr. John Watson. Gentlemen, the First Lord of Her Majesty's Navy."

Watson gave a bow and stood at attention. Holmes looked around the room and barely acknowledged the First

Lord. Mycroft cleared his throat, and Holmes, taking the hint turned his attention to the First Lord.

"My Lord, it is a pleasure to make your acquaintance. May we sit? I have but a few questions and should not take up a great deal of your time."

The First Lord motioned for all to be seated around a large meeting table.

"As you say, Mr. Holmes, I am a very busy man and if not for my respect and admiration for your brother, I would not have agreed to this meeting. I certainly would never have agreed to take up the time of the other Lords with the ruminations of an amateur detective. Please be brief with your questions, I have much to do this morning."

Holmes looked at Watson with a whimsical smile. "Oh I am sorry that my Lord does not see the importance of this meeting. I am merely trying to save the Lords from the embarrassment of a personal, political, and security issue of perhaps the highest order." The First Lord fidgeted uncomfortably in his chair. "I have reason to believe that there is a plot involving an attempt to gain control over one of the lords and by means of that control to obtain secrets of Her Majesty's Navy."

"I can assure you Mr. Holmes, that we are not subject to the whims and, how did you put it, the controls of the criminal class."

"I am certain that if the means of gaining control were of the usual type that my Lord would be quite right. However, the means of control that are planned by these conspirators is very unusual and you sir, and the other Lords, are very vulnerable to it."

The First Lord scoffed. "And by all means please share this unusual means of control that makes us vulnerable."

"I understand that your Lordship has recently lost a son. He died of heart failure?"

The First Lord's face grew red, but he quickly regained his composure. "Yes, that is correct and what does that have to do with this conspiracy?"

"I have been informed by those who have reason to know such things that your wife is troubled by his death and worries about the peace and repose that your son may not be enjoying as a consequence."

The First Lord cleared his throat and looked at Mycroft and then back at Holmes. "I must congratulate you, Mr. Holmes, on your intelligence regarding the private concerns and affairs of my household, Yes, my wife is very disturbed."

"I thought as much. Does your wife believe in the spirit world, Your Lordship? Does she put much faith in mediums, for instance?"

The First Lord's face again grew red, and he moved uncomfortably in his chair. "There seems no end to what you know about my private affairs, Mr. Holmes."

"It is my business to know such things, my Lord."

"Yes, my wife has recently inquired of a medium who came highly recommended from a close friend of ours. She won't be at ease until she knows that our late son is at peace. I have learned, through much experience, to indulge my wife in these little matters. It does wonders for the tranquility of our home life."

"I am sure of it, Your Lordship. Have you made arrangements to meet this medium? Say the middle of next week at a home in Kensington Court?"

The First Lord stood. "Mr. Holmes you are privy to far too much of the private affairs of my personal life. How came you to know this?"

"Please your Lordship, sit down. As I said earlier, it is my business to know such things if they are relevant to my cases. I can assure you; the security of your private life is safe with me."

The First Lord sat back down. "We have an appointment Wednesday evening next. The medium is a Lady Tabitha, and her place of business is in her home on Kensington Court. Have you come to warn me away from that meeting?"

"Oh no, Your Lordship. I wish for you to keep that appointment and to make no adjustments to your usual habits in the meantime."

"Very well. Then why are you here?"

"In the course of investigating a case, I have learned certain facts and I have very good reason to believe that an attempt will be made to introduce a chemical means by which to control your Lordship's mind; and that attempt will be made during this appointment with, what did you call her, Lady Tabitha."

"To control my mind, you say?"

"Yes."

"This is really quite fantastic, Mr. Holmes. By what means?"

"By placing a small, specially bred, white worm into your Lordship's nostril. The worm will make its way up into your forehead, implant itself there, and will begin to produce chemicals that when ingested by your blood stream will have the effect of making your Lordship very susceptible to persuasion and control."

The First Lord looked at Holmes as if he were mad. "And for what purpose would they do such a thing?"

"To gain access to certain secrets that your Lordship is aware of and to persuade you to deliver those secrets to them." Holmes paused for effect. "Is Her Majesty's Navy engaged at present in developing an improved Mark V torpedo?"

The First Lord turned pale and looked astonished. "I am not at liberty to confirm what Her Majesty's Navy is engaged in developing Mr. Holmes. However, I can say that there are several projects in development that if successful could give Her Majesty's Navy an advantage should any hostilities develop between ourselves and the navies of the rest of the world."

"Ah, I thought as much. If you will trust me, your Lordship, I may be of service in both preventing this conspiracy and bringing the conspirators to justice."

The First Lord took what Holmes said under consideration. Being accustomed as he was to making decisions, it did not take long for the First Lord to make up his mind.

"If what you say is true, Mr. Holmes, and I have not decided yet if I believe it, then you would have done the

Crown a great service by averting this conspiracy and arresting the perpetrators. What do you have in mind?"

Becca was at her home on Kensington Court busy in a meeting with Steven, Scott, and Lilith. They were planning the events that would occur during the séance the next week.

"Are we all clear as to the timeline of events?"

Everyone around the dining room table nodded in the affirmative.

"Good. Lilith, I want to see a minute-by-minute script of how you plan to proceed with the séance so that Steven will know when to make his appearance. Yes, it is you Steven who will carry this out. I want you to retain the assistance of a trusted independent contractor. Someone who is large and strong in the event we need that, but also someone who can maintain control over their aggressive proclivities.

"Scott, you will be with me at the club. We must make everything seems as ordinary and routine as possible. I want a messenger on site here, inconspicuous, who can relay a message back to me at the club. We will likewise have a messenger ready to deliver any instructions should the need arise."

Lilith looked uncomfortable. "Are you not going to be here with me when this happens, Becca?"

"No, Lilith. I will manage this from the club, and as I said, that will help to ensure that no one thinks the Club is involved. Lilith, you must think of this as no different from any other séance you perform. Your role is limited to that. Steven will handle the rest."

Lilith nodded but did not look confident. She looked at both Steven and Scott and back at Becca. "I understand my role. I am surprised that you will not be present to finish the process yourself. Especially given the important and dangerous nature of the…the…events themselves."

Becca looked Lilith in the eyes and attempted to read her demeanor. Was she strong enough to perform her role and see this to its conclusion? "Lilith, you will not be alone. You will have Steven, whomever he brings, and the young men in the basement operating your apparatus. You needn't be concerned. Our plan is good, we are well-organized, and I have full confidence in you and Steven. My presence is simply not required."

Steven spoke up, "We understand the need to protect the Club, and to maintain the semblance of routine, Madam. Lilith, I will ensure that all goes well. You needn't worry or concern yourself with anything other than the séance. We will take care of the rest."

Becca nodded to Steven in appreciation. "If there is nothing further, we are finished here until Monday next, when we meet for the last time."

No one had any further questions or comments and Becca stood and motioned for Steven and Scott to leave. As soon as the front door closed, Becca turned to Lilith.

"Should I be concerned about you, Lilith?"

"No, of course not, Becca. I am just surprised that you will not be here yourself. Although you do not confide in me, it seems to me that all of your plans depend on this going well."

"You are correct. That is why I both need and expect you to perform your part and to do so flawlessly."

Lilith nodded her head as tears welled up in her eyes. "Am I just a pawn in your larger game, Becca? Am I nothing more to you?"

Becca looked at Lilith and immediately feigned warmth. "We are Gemini, Lilith. The two that are one. You are not just a pawn, or you would not be with me here in this house. If I do not share everything with you, it is not out of distrust or coldness, but it is to spare you from worry and concern. The less you know, the safer you are, dear one."

Becca approached Lilith and took her face in her two hands. She kissed her forehead, then her nose, and then her lips. Lilith relaxed in Becca's arms as she hugged her close. Lilith felt better. Felt assured.

"Yes, we are Gemini. The two that are one..."

Chapter 24

It was late Tuesday morning, and the day crew was busy cleaning and resetting the club for the late afternoon and evening events. Bars were being restocked, tablecloths changed, beds made, and floors and rugs mopped and shaken. Brass was being polished and all surfaces dusted and buffed. Steven and Scott were busy directing the crew and working with the chefs inspecting the incoming food stock for the evening's preparations. All was an organized chaos that was the liturgy of mornings at the Gemini Club.

Becca was deep in thought, already at her offices, for work but also primarily to be away from Lilith and to have time to think without the interruption of Lilith's emotions, questions, and insecurities. The séance was the next evening, late, and she was going through every detail in her mind. She had confidence in Steven and Scott and despite issues with Lilith, she had confidence that when the time came, she would perform as expected.

She continued to be concerned about Holmes and his investigation, despite what she showed to Steven, Scott and Lilith. She saw no overt evidence that Holmes knew about the purpose and function of the worms or her larger scheme involving the First Lord of the Admiralty. Her first instinct was to dismiss the chances that Holmes was aware and would be a hindrance to her plans or worse yet, would prevent her from succeeding. But there was a deep fear behind her bravado and her public confidence that kept her concerned about what Holmes was doing.

Those concerns and fears made her instincts of self-preservation come to the fore. She had already decided that she would not be present at the house when the séance and associated events occurred. That would give her the distance to claim innocence and to lay the responsibility on Lilith and Steven. Her plan was instead to be at the Club, well away from the events of the evening and with the opportunity to escape if the need arose. She was now thinking that making more concrete plans for escape were both necessary and prudent. She arose, left her office at the club, went out onto the street, and hailed a hansom. She knew where she needed to go.

Holmes and Watson were at Baker Street as usual. Holmes had sent a telegram to Inspecter MacDonald and was expecting his arrival shortly. Mrs. Hudson was clearing away the detritus of a late morning breakfast, while Watson sat at the table reading the last of the morning newspaper. Holmes sat by the cold fireplace and smoked one of his oily clay pipes in deep thought. He seemed aroused by the noise of the plates as Mrs. Hudson worked to clear the table.

"You are a distraction, Mrs. Hudson. I would very much be the better for some silence."

"Mr. Holmes, I am almost finished clearing the table, and I am sorry if that is a distraction, but such is the way of things." Mrs. Hudson was accustomed to Holmes's moods and even harsh words. Turning to Watson she whispered, "He is in a mood this morning." Watson simply nodded as he drank down the last of his cup of tea and handed the cup to Mrs. Hudson.

"What worries you this morning, Holmes?"

Holmes grunted and said, "It is the details, Watson. The details and the fact that I must entrust others to be particular as to the details. We have two locations to be concerned with. I can only be at one. To which should I give my attention?"

"Two locations?"

"Yes, Watson. Tomorrow evening as we bring this case to a close, we have the location of the Gemini Club, and we have the house on Kensington Court. The séance will be at one, while we cannot be distracted by the possibility that the big fish may be at the other. Throw our net over one, and she might escape by being at the other. I can be at only one location. Who is to command the other?"

Watson cleared his throat and standing walked over to his chair across from Holmes. He chose a cigar, lighted it, and sat. "I would think that whichever location you chose, I would be at the other."

Holmes looked at Watson with some relief. "My dear Watson, thank you. I did not wish to speak for you, but you are of course the solution to the dilemma. The remaining question is at which location should I put myself?"

"The answer to that question of course will come from answering the other question, 'which location do you expect Miss Rebecca St. John to be at?'"

"Exactly, Watson. Let us look at this logically. If we take as a beginning axiom that the unfortunate Mr. Holcomb met his fate after a worm was administered to him, then we know from the evidence at the scene that Miss St. John was present."

"Remind me, Holmes, how do we know that?"

"The boot marks on the rug, Watson, the boot marks."

"Ahh, yes and in the dirt in the alley as well. Yes, of course."

"But if we look at the evidence at the scene of Mr. Persano's home, she was not present. So we have one example of her being present and one example of her not being present when a worm was administered to a victim. And so my question, what will she do tomorrow evening? Will she be present at the séance to administer the worm to the First Lord, or will she manage events from afar at the Club?"

"There simply is no way to be sure, Holmes."

Holmes shrugged and continued to smoke his pipe in thought.

"On the one hand, she will want to be sure that the culmination of her plans, the administering of the worm to the First Lord, goes off without any complications. On the other hand, she may want to protect herself by being at a different location during the séance. The second possibility has the advantages of putting distance between her and the events at the séance.

"I have little doubt that she is aware of our involvement both at the scene of Persano's death and at his apartment earlier. She would surely have informants who would tell her. We must assume that as a working hypothesis. There is also, of course, the additional fact that our rooms are being watched."

"What! Our rooms?"

"Yes, have you not noticed the beggar across the street? He has been sitting in the same location for the last two days. He is not usual to Baker Street, and I noticed him on Saturday afternoon. I have taken pains to confirm his presence the last two days; and he is at his post this morning as well."

Watson rose and walked to one of the windows facing Baker Street and looked out.

"Careful Watson. Do not give us away. Do you see him?"

"Yes, now that you point him out, I do see him sitting in front of the building across the street." Watson looked for a few seconds and then walked back to his usual spot and sat back down.

"We are being observed, Watson. This tells me that our Miss St. John is aware of our involvement. To what extent, I do not know. But precautions must be taken. In my telegram to the inspector, I cautioned him to come to the back of Baker Street along the alley and to leave in the same manner. We must take her awareness of our involvement into consideration when making our plans.

"She is aware that I am investigating the death of Mr. Holcomb from my visit with her at the club earlier; and she is aware that I was consulted in Persano's assault and death as well. She is no doubt aware that a worm was left at Persano's rooms and is likely aware that a worm was discovered after Persano's death at the hospital. So she will assume that I know about the two worms. She may conclude that my knowledge of the two worms does not mean that I attach significance to them or that I can trace the two worms back to her. But being intelligent, she will not want to take the chance that I have traced the worms back to her."

"Yes, that all makes sense, Holmes. But how does that help us determine where she will be tomorrow night?"

Holmes fidgeted in his chair and adjusted his sitting posture, raising both legs to sit cross-legged in his chair. He puffed on his pipe and said nothing for several minutes.

"If I were she, Watson, I would be at the Club and I would have a plan of escape. I would place couriers to deliver a message to me promptly should anything go badly at Kensington Court. I would also have watchers outside the Club to tell me of any unusual activity taking place there. No, she will be at the Club, Watson, and that is where I shall be as well.

"I will need you at Kensington Court with a contingent of police officers. Good and trustworthy men with a definite plan of attack. I will be at the Club with the inspector and some of his men to block any escape. We will have the Club surrounded by the inspector's men. Yes, I believe that is the best plan of attack."

"I agree, Holmes. Your logic is sound. I will ensure all goes as planned at the house, and you will block her escape from the Club. To borrow your metaphor, we use two nets at two locations to increase the odds that we catch both the small fish and the larger one. Excellent, Holmes."

"Well, we will see Watson. The best laid plans…"

It was at that instant that a loud knocking could be heard from downstairs and from the direction of the back door leading to the alleyway behind Baker Street. Watson stood and walked toward the landing in time to see Mrs. Hudson standing and looking down the hall toward the back door.

"I will get the back door Mrs. Hudson, it's Inspector MacDonald."

Mrs. Hudson nodded and went back into her rooms as Watson descended the stairs and made his way to the back door and opened it.

"Inspector, welcome. Sorry for the inconvenience but Holmes is convinced that our rooms are being watched and that we need therefore to take precautions."

"Yes, he said as much in the telegram he sent me."

Both men walked down the hall and ascended the stairs to find Holmes standing and filling one of his long-stemmed pipes.

"Inspector, thank you for coming around. Please take a seat. Would you like a cigar? I thought as much. Watson might you get the inspector a cigar?"

All three were seated and smoking. Watson in his chair, Holmes in his, and the inspector on the settee. The usual greetings over, Holmes looked at the inspector penetratingly and began.

"This affair of the little worm is far more complex than you may be aware, Inspector."

"Not the bloody worm, Holmes."

"Yes, I am afraid so. I have good reason to believe that the persons behind this affair will act tomorrow evening and that their actions are part of a larger plan to gain access to Her Majesty's most well-kept naval secrets."

"And what would the damned worm have to do with that, Holmes?"

Watson looked at Holmes and decided to intervene. "Inspector, these worms have been specially bred to produce a series of chemicals that bring either madness to the unfortunate victim or make the victim susceptible to suggestion and control. I know it is difficult to believe, but our investigation has led us to that conclusion."

"Thank you, Watson. I believe that the current generation of worm being used is more refined and though the risk of madness is still present, the chemicals produced by the worm are more likely now to induce a state of suggestion and control in the unfortunate victim."

"And how does that happen, Mr. Holmes."

"I would suggest that the evidence is such, I refer to the death of Persano, the worm is introduced to the victim through the nose. It crawls up into the person's sinuses and having placed itself there emits chemicals that once absorbed by the victim's body have the effect of impacting the brain and making the person the virtual servant of the administrator. I do not know how long this effect lasts, but surely as long as the worm continues to live inside the victim's head – which could be a considerable amount of time."

The inspector sat motionless, tugging at his cigar with each breath, and emitting clouds of blue smoke. He looked at Watson, and then back at Holmes.

"And you have come to this unbelievable conclusion how exactly?"

"Consider the evidence, Inspector. It all began with the unfortunate Mr. Holcomb, although I confess, I did not know it at the time. Here is a man, settled in his ways, a good solicitor, but with the unfortunate habit of attending a certain club, which his law partner introduced him to. He discovers certain anomalies in the legal structure of the many shell companies that this club is hidden behind, and likely other information that I am as yet unaware of, and because of his discoveries becomes the unfortunate victim and experiment of those at the Club with reasons to keep secret what happens there and how they are organized. The worm, introduced to Mr. Holcomb, had the almost immediate effect of driving him mad. He escaped his rooms, ran out into the street, and was run over by a carriage and horses.

"From the evidence at the scene, I know that a woman and a man were present with Mr. Holcomb just before he met his demise. A visit to the law firm revealed that both Mr. Holcomb and his partner were members of the Gemini Club. I visited that Club, Inspector, and the owner and manager is very unusual. Unusual because the owner and manager is a woman, a Miss Rebecca St. John.

"I admit that there is little to no evidence to link her to Mr. Holcomb, except for his membership in her Club. Other circumstances of a private nature, led to further evidence that this Miss St. John was not an ordinary club owner. Which brings us to Mr. Persano. A reporter who most recently has been writing exposes about London's many clubs. His rooms are burgled and when we arrived, we found the man mad and a small white worm in a box on his kitchen table. A worm that you so unfortunately discounted and believed had nothing to do with the crime.

"Persano's madness appeared to be of limited duration and what remained afterward was a man very susceptible to suggestion and control. You were there, Inspector, you saw how Persano acted when I interviewed him. You saw that I was able to get him to do anything that I suggested. A little over twenty-four hours later, Persano was dead having torn away his nose and half his face trying to get at something lodged there. And the doctor at the scene found what Inspector?"

"A small white worm...but why Mr. Holmes? What could be the purpose of so macabre and grotesque a plan?"

"That is exactly what vexed me, Inspector. Until I learned through other channels unnecessary to reveal to you, that certain inquiries have been made of junior clerks who worked in naval armaments at the Admiralty. Then through a series of other events and deductions, I have learned that the First Lord of the Admiralty, recently lost a son. The First Lord's wife, who is taken with mediums and spiritualism, is seeking to contact her son from the other side. And the medium whom she has chosen to use for this attempt, is none other than the friend and business partner of Miss St. John, the owner of the Gemini Club."

The inspector sat with his jaw agape and his cigar in midair. He closed his mouth. He stared at Holmes and then put the cigar back in his mouth and appeared at a loss for words.

"I must admit, Mr. Holmes, this is one of the strangest tales that I have ever heard. Even from you, sir. But your logic is sound. The chain of deductions is true and strong. I can see no weakness in any link. So what do you propose we do about this?"

Holmes smiled. "I propose that we catch them in the act, Inspector."

"But that will take the cooperation of the First Lord of the Admiralty and his wife, Mr. Holmes. Not something easy to obtain."

Watson looked at Holmes with pride and then said, "I believe that we have achieved that particular part of the plan already. Is that not right, Holmes?"

Becca alighted from the hansom in front of her old lodgings and business. The art store had long been closed, but the apartment above the store she had kept in perfect condition. It was her private sanctum and place of safety. She walked up to the door, unlocked the same, and walked into the now empty art store. She looked around and saw that nothing had been disturbed. She closed and locked the door and proceeded to the back of the small store and the door leading to the stock room. It was the same as the front of the store, empty. She walked over to the stairs and ascended to her old apartment.

There she sat in front of the cold fireplace and thought. Memories flooded into her mind. Memories of who she had been when she rented these rooms before she purchased them later. Memories of the whole affair of the Green Dragon and of Moriarty. She had been lucky to escape the purge brought on by the Professor's death and the disappearance of Holmes himself. She remembered her meetings with Moriarty and meeting Lilith. She remembered going to pick-up Lilith as she was released from custody by Scotland Yard. So much had happened in the years since.

She stood, enough of these meaningless thoughts and memories. She had problems that needed her full attention now, and she knew what she was going to do. She walked back into her bedroom and taking out a large suitcase from under the bed, she began to place the clothes, makeup, and sundries she would need in case escape was required. She laughed to herself. The man about town and the old, retired nun might make one last appearance as a kind of curtain call to her escape, if need be. She was confident it would work.

Chapter 25

Wednesday had arrived, but nothing was unique or special about the morning. Holmes had left early, and Watson was left to have breakfast and to read the morning paper alone. Watson expected that Holmes was making last minute arrangements and seeing that everything was in place. Watson thought about the case and how strange the facts were, but he was not particularly nervous or anxious about what would happen that evening. He knew that his role was to ensure that the constables did their job at the séance and that the First Lord and Lady were unharmed.

Mid-day had come, and Watson was wondering how long Holmes would be when he heard his familiar steps on the stairs leading to their rooms.

"Holmes. Where have you been this cool and cloudy morning?"

"Watson, good morning, or rather good afternoon. All is organized at Scotland Yard and MacDonald is prepared with two groups of men he has specifically chosen for this evening's events. I even stopped by the Diogenes Club this morning to catch my brother at breakfast. He was none too pleased by my unannounced visit, but it was important that I speak with him. I need him to put in place alternative plans if the outcome this evening is not as we plan. He has likely already worked with the Lords of the Admiralty and set those plans in motion."

"You have been busy, Holmes. What plans?"

"Yes, and now all there is left for us to do is to wait. Our trap is set, the bait will be placed, and we sit in the tree ready to bag our tigress. Have we had a visit from Wiggins yet?"

"Uh, no Holmes. Why?"

"He should be here shortly. I placed my marks on the side buildings notifying him to meet. He should be here soon. We may have need of him and the Irregulars this evening."

"What plans, Holmes?"

Holmes ignored Watson again and went to his bedroom and changed into his mouse grey dressing gown, walked briskly back into the sitting room, took a pipe from the mantelpiece, filled it with tobacco from the Persian slipper, and flopped into his chair by the lit fireplace in a fit of nervous tiredness. Leaning forward he took the tongs and choosing a red-hot coal, he lit his pipe and threw the coal back into the fire, allowing the tongs to fall to the floor beside the fireplace. He took a long drag from the pipe and let out an equally long exhale filled with both smoke and breath.

"It has been an interesting case, Watson. Not one I think you will publish anytime soon. Too macabre and almost unbelievable. Not to mention, no good can come from giving the members of the criminal world ideas, hey, old fellow?"

"Well, that all depends on the outcome, Holmes. You have done masterful work in bringing what looked to be unrelated threads from separate incidents into one coherent case. Another masterful piece of work."

Holmes's eyes shined at Watson's praise. "As you say, it all depends on the outcome of our plans for the evening. The conundrum may be solved, but we still need to bag our prey."

The bell rang below, and Holmes leaped from his chair, all energy again, and bounded over the settee, opened the door to their rooms, and shouted downstairs for Mrs. Hudson to let up only Wiggins.

The lad soon appeared. Taller and older now. It was hard to put an age to the young man. He was very thin and gangly. His clothes were old and torn in places and other places were patched by cloth that didn't match the color or texture of the garment's original material. His hair was unkempt and unruly. His cheeks ruddy and red with sunburn. His face was dirty, as were his hands and fingernails. His shoes were too big and had holes in the souls that were covered with newspaper from the inside. He took off his cap and gave a little bow.

"I saw your sign, Mr. Holmes. I came as soon as I could. What can we do fer you, gov'na?"

"How are you getting along, Wiggins? You look a bit thin."

"I'm doing fine, Sir. I gets along just fine. Don't you worry nothing about me. I takes care of me self."

"I have a little job for you. Higher scale of pay than usual. I need you to watch the alleys and dark streets around the Gemini Club. Do you know it?" Wiggins nodded. "Good. I plan to be there before ten this evening and it may be a late night. I want you to post your boys around the area and be ready to report to me if you see anyone leaving the club from a back way. Anyone that might look suspicious or who looks like they do not want to be seen. Understand?"

"Yes, guv'na. Man or woman?"

"Woman. Usually finely dressed. Petite and pretty. Just above five feet tall. Hair is auburn with reddish hints. What you might recognize as a lady. Can you do that for me?"

"No problem. Lady, auburn hair with reddish streaks, small, and a good-looking bird. Got it." Wiggins had a sly smile on his face.

Holmes was suddenly very quiet. Lost in thought. Watson and Wiggins simply waited for him to speak again. Several minutes went by without Holmes uttering another word nor seeming to notice the presence of either Watson or Wiggins.

"Anything else, Mr. Holmes?"

Holmes suddenly stood and walked briskly toward his files against the wall by the window facing Baker Street. He opened several different drawers and began to throw papers about until he found the file folder he was looking for. He took the file to his desk between the two windows and began to look through it. He took out of the file a folded piece of brown paper and carefully opened it. He gently picked something up from inside the brown paper, picked up a magnifying glass from the desk with his free hand, and walked to the window looking carefully at whatever he was holding in the light from the window, using the magnifying glass to see closer still.

"What have you there, Holmes?"

"Watson, sometimes I am as dull as a stone. Of course. It all makes sense to me now. Even my powers of deduction and memory are not infallible."

Holmes moved back to the desk and carefully placed the item back in the brown paper, folded it, and gently placed it back in the file. He stood, hands in his pockets with his chin on his chest in deep thought.

"What is it, Holmes?"

"What? Oh, just a little intuition of mine proven correct, I think. Would not have changed anything that I have done, but nevertheless an interesting development."

Watson and Wiggins exchanged glances.

"Should I go now, Mr. Holmes?"

"Wiggins, I am so sorry. No. I have amended instructions. I would be on the lookout this evening for a woman as I described or an old, fat nun. Either one. Clear?"

"A nun you say?"

"Yes, Wiggins. A nun."

"All right either the bird you described before or an old nun." Wiggins saluted Holmes with his knuckle and then held out his hat for the expected payment.

"How many will you have with you this evening?"

"Don't need more than six in all, counting me."

Holmes reached into his pocket and counted out six sovereigns and dropped each, one at a time, into Wiggins's hat. Wiggins's eyes grew big and a large yellow toothy smile creased his dirty face.

"I will see you this evening, then. Be sure to have someone stationed so they can see me signal that I want you. Now run along."

"Thank you, Mr. Holmes." With that, Wiggins ran out the rooms and down the stairs, slamming the door as he made his way back to Baker Street.

"A nun?"

Holmes looked at Watson and began to laugh. "It is a small world, Watson. A very small world indeed." And he continued to laugh.

Lilith had not seen Becca all day and she was worried about the evening. It was afternoon and she had gone over the script for the evening with little enthusiasm. She knew what she needed to do, and it was simple, but still she did not have a good feeling about the evening. She wondered how Becca could have such confidence. She was still unaware of Becca's larger plans for the First Lord and what effect the worms would have when put in a man's head, and that made her feel sick. She kept asking herself why Becca would do such a thing.

Lilith was comfortable with her role as medium and conducting seances for the rich. That was easy money, and no one was hurt by it. She even convinced herself that she provided a service that gave grieving people some relief and, in many ways, helped them. But this thing that Becca was doing, it did not seem to be doing anyone any good, except perhaps Becca herself. She was deeply troubled by what was going to happen in just a few short hours. She comforted herself with the thought that her role in the process was very limited. Still, she would be present and had to watch it happen.

Becca was at the club and trying to fill the hours before the event with busy work. She had reserved one of the rooms on the third floor for her use that evening. She had her disguise prepared in case she needed to make a quick escape. She had Scott hire some men to be on watch outside the club and to look for anything unusual. They would be in place well before the séance was to begin. Steven had a man prepared to help him secure the house. Lilith was prepared, at least Becca hoped so. All was ready.

Becca thought about how this evening would begin a new chapter in her life. An important step toward bigger and more complicated criminal activities. She smiled to herself as she thought about the secrets she could steal and the money and power that those secrets would bring. She thought of herself as becoming the madam of the London criminal fraternity. No more a profession just for men, she would break through and become a force to be reckoned with. She looked forward to having power over men and of the pleasure that would bring her.

There was still the nagging worry of Holmes. What did he know? There was little sense in dwelling on it, she thought. His rooms were watched and nothing unusual was happening, Scott had assured her as much that morning. She had her plans, had trustworthy people to carry them out, and an escape plan if things went awry. She cared little for what would happen to Steven and Lilith. They were simply pawns in the game. She was the queen. She was the one piece that was important. She would succeed.

Chapter 26

It was dark and as the day had been cloudy and cool, the night was wet with a fog rolling in. Holmes, Watson, and MacDonald were at Baker Street making last minute preparations. Watson had his army revolver loaded and in the pocket of his overcoat – such was the temperature outside. Holmes did not carry his revolver, as was his usual custom. MacDonald was armed with both revolver and club.

"Gentlemen, we are prepared. Watson, do be careful this evening. We are not expected, and we have the element of surprise, but that also adds to the danger of the evening."

"I am ready, Holmes." Watson stood almost at attention as he gave Holmes a confident nod of his head.

"Mr. Holmes, this isn't my first parade. My men and I are as keen as iron." MacDonald clicked the cylinder of his revolver in place with a flip of his wrist and tucked it into his coat pocket. "You just take care of yourselves."

The three men exited one at a time via the back door into the alley behind Baker Street. Holmes and MacDonald went in one direction and Watson in the other. Watson had the alert and nervous feeling he was so accustomed to when engaged in one of Holmes's plans. He felt keen and ready. His mouth dry, but his eyes sharp. His reflexes on the edge, ready to react at a moment's notice. He walked down the alley being careful to be quiet and to stay in the darkest shadows of the near-black dark alley. He made his way two blocks and then turned right toward Baker Street. The fog was thickening, and he was happy for the additional cover it provided but also worried because the fog effectively blinded him to who was on the street. He could clearly see only ten feet in front of him.

Watson arrived at Baker Street and the hansom that the inspector had arranged was waiting. He got in and the driver immediately whipped up the horse and began the treacherous drive to Kensington Court. Watson knew the constables were likely already in place. He would meet the sergeant at the park bench across the street from the house.

Holmes and the inspector made their way down the alley for three blocks and found the waiting hansom on Baker Street going in the opposite direction of 221B. As Holmes settled into the hansom, he was confident that the darkness, the fog, and the route he and the inspector had taken meant that the beggar watching his rooms was very likely unaware of their movements. As far as the beggar was concerned, he and Watson were still in their rooms on this cold and foggy night. The hansom ride wasn't a long one and neither Holmes nor MacDonald spoke as they went.

"That's the alley, Holmes. Driver, stop here." MacDonald jumped from the still moving hansom and looked around cautiously. Holmes alighted and the two men proceeded down a dark, dank alley – the same that Holmes and Watson had used when they had kept watch on the club just a few nights earlier.

Holmes stopped and pressed himself against the building that formed one of the walls of the alley. He carefully looked out and could just make out the lights of the Gemini

Club across the street and at an acute angle to his position. He immediately noticed that there were three men loitering in and around the entrance to the club. One in front smoking, and the other two to either side of the building doing the same.

"She has lookouts," Holmes whispered to MacDonald who shifted places with Holmes and did his own careful inspection of the scene.

"Not to worry, Mr. Holmes. I have men in place to take care of them. I blow my whistle and they will be on them in a flash. Did you see the drunk beggar lying in the gutter across the street from the Club?"

"Yes, and the other two men sharing a bottle and arguing. Those are your men?"

"Yes. And I have others behind the Club as well."

"You have done well, Inspector. Now we just wait."

The inspector took out his watch and brought it close to his face but could not tell the time. He knelt with his back to the street behind Holmes, and used his coat to hide the light from the match he lit. It was a quarter pass ten and things at Kensington Street should be starting now. He blew out the match and stood, putting his hand in his coat pocket, he felt the cold steel of his revolver.

Watson sat on the park bench with the detective in charge. He was cold. It was a wet, cold that seemed to seep through his coat and into his bones. He was uncomfortable, cold, and impatient for the evening to come to its inevitable end. As he was thinking about the warm fire of Baker Street, the First Lord's carriage arrived and in the dark and fog he could just make out the First Lord as he exited and helped his wife alight from the carriage. They both approached the front door to the house and the door was opened. He could barely discern the servant in the dim light of the house assisted by the yellowish streetlight. Then the door closed.

Watson and the detective both stood and that was the signal for the constables to move into position. They seemed to appear out of the darkness and fog as they surrounded the house. The order of events had been well-choreographed, and timing was critical. No one, especially Watson, wanted to leave the First Lord and Lady exposed to harm for any longer than was necessary to catch the perpetrators in the act.

After fifteen minutes the first wave of constables entered the house through the locked door of the cellar. One constable, using a strong set of snips, cut the lock from the door; and as soon as the lock was cut, five constables made their way into the cellar with dark lanterns now blazing in the night. Five others almost simultaneously broke through the front door with their own dark lanterns blazing. Watson and the detective ran across the street and brought up the rear.

As Watson entered the sitting room, he saw the First Lord and his wife over to the left, as the First Lord protected his wife. In the middle of the room, the chairs around the table were awry and the constables were fighting with two large men, while two other constables had what Watson took to be the medium in custody. The detective immediately joined the scrum of constables trying to subdue the larger of the two men, and using the revolver he held in his right hand, he struck the large man in the back of his head, causing the man to immediately fall to the floor as the constables put the darbies on his wrists. The other man stopped resisting and was then easily cuffed and put under the control of the constables.

The remaining constables came from downstairs with three young men, boys really, each looking forlorn and themselves in darbies. Watson approached the medium.

"Are you Lilith who goes by the professional name, Lady Tabitha?"

She looked at Watson with tears in her eyes and fear written across her face.

"I am."

"Where is Miss Rebecca St. John?"

Lilith looked around the room as if dazed and back again at Watson.

"She is not here."

The detective ordered the house searched and one of the constables approached Watson and the detective holding a small matchbox and with his finger was digging about the soil it contained, revealing two small worms.

"This was in the hand of the larger man, the one unconscious on the floor, detective. What do you make of it?"

"Be very careful with those worms, Detective. They are not what they seem." Watson took the matchbox and closed it, putting it safely in his coat pocket. "My Lord and Lady are you unharmed?"

The First Lord stood very straight and nodded to Watson.

"We are fine, Dr. Watson. I must say, this was handled with the utmost professionalism and dispatch. Your timing could not have been better. As Mr. Holmes instructed, we had both been offered sherry, and both of us declined. Lady Tabitha was most insistent that we partake, and we declined again. It was at that moment that that large man came out of the darkness with the other, and they were about to force themselves upon us when you all arrived. I am very grateful Detective to you and your men."

Two constables came back into the sitting room and reported that the house was empty. Steven, handcuffed and bleary eyed, began to wake up as his head pounded. As he stirred the constables around him helped him to his feet.

"And you sir, what is your name," asked the Detective.

"My name is of no consequence to you and yours." Steven looked defiant and angry.

"I will ask you again, what is your name?"

"My name is Steven Sobotta and that is all that I will say. I know my rights, gentlemen. Under what charges do you pretend to hold me?"

"All that will be addressed later at the Yard. For now, understand you are in Her Majesty's custody and that anything you say will be taken down and used against you at the inquest. Take them away, Constable."

"If I may speak with Lady Tabitha?" Watson asked.

"Of course." The Detective made a sweeping motion with his right arm.

"Lady Tabitha, or may I call you Lilith, please sit down?"

Lilith took her seat at the table, flanked by two constables, and Watson lifted a chair and sat beside her. She looked around the room innocently and fearfully. The other constables were busy with their charges, taking them from the scene and out to the now waiting police carriages.

"What do you know of this affair?"

"I know almost nothing of the affair except my part in it."

"And what was your part in this affair?"

"It was to hold a séance. It was to get the First Lord and his wife to drink the sherry. Nothing more."

"What do you know of the worms?"

"I know almost nothing except that they are disgusting and that once administered they make the victim more subject to control and suggestion. I know nothing more. Am I under arrest?"

The Detective stepped in, "Yes, you may consider yourself under arrest, and I must warn you that what you say will be taken down and used against you at the inquest."

Watson waived the detective away. "Why are you involved in this?"

The Detective was busy getting the remainder of his men to secure the house both inside and outside. Barking orders and demonstrating that he was in charge.

Lilith looked around her and back at Watson. She looked down at her hands clasped in her lap. When she looked up her eyes were filled with tears, as her face became wet with streaks of tears, she began to shake and tremble uncontrollably.

"I do not know. I simply do not know. Oh God, I do not know." And she wept bitterly and uncontrollably.

Becca sat in her office at the club waiting for news of the successful introduction of the worm to the First Lord that would signal the success of the evening and her departure for Kensington Court. As she considered her future, there was a sudden loud knock on her office door and Scott came in hurriedly.

"There is an unusual number of men on the street and around the club, Madam. I suggest that if you have plans that you activate them immediately."

Becca stood. "Scott, I suggest that if you have a plan of escape that you do so now. As for me, I will go first upstairs and then exit with the crowd of club members. Go now. Go away fast."

Becca's heart was racing, and her spirit was dismayed. She had failed. Scott bowed and left immediately, and she made her way to the room she had arranged and began to change into her disguise. She was now dressed like a man in evening dress and as she applied her make-up, including false beard and wig, she noticed that her fingers were shaking. She stopped as she looked at herself in the small mirror and was surprised to find fear in the eyes that looked back at her. She could hear noise from the floors under her.

MacDonald and Holmes had been waiting in the alley and MacDonald sensed that it was to make their move. He looked at Holmes.

"It is time to act, Mr. Holmes. No more waiting."

Holmes nodded and the two crossed the street as the plain clothes constables and detectives took their crossing the street as a signal to act themselves. The men Holmes and the inspector had seen lying about were immediately subdued and a whistle was blown by one of the constables signaling the others to act. Holmes took off his hat and waved it in the air as he crossed the street, signaling the Irregulars to act and for Wiggins to report.

As the constables entered the club, they were surprised to find no resistance. They secured the ground floor which was mostly empty and began their way to the second floor.

Becca could hear the constables below shouting orders. Her disguise was finished. It wasn't perfect, but she had no time to make it so. She walked out of the room and saw clients and the working girls coming out of the other rooms and looking around. She called to one of the girls.

"You will come with me now." Becca took the confused girl in her arms and began to kiss her as the first of the constables made their way to the third floor. She whispered in the girl's ear, "Act as if I am a man and one of your customers. Do not let it be known who I am. Play your part well and you will be rewarded." The girl nodded.

Clients and club members began to leave as quickly as they could. The constables were not interested in the members. They were looking only for Miss St. John. As they made their way from room to room they shouted, "Where is Miss St. John?" But no one knew where she was.

The constables separated the inebriated man (Becca) from the working girl, who played her part well. "Hey, what are you doing? This is a private club. That is my date for the evening. You there, stop it."

Becca made her way downstairs and separated herself from the now growing crowed of men and working girls leaving. She made her way to the back of the Club and out a door into the alley. There she was stopped by three constables.

"You there, sir. Where do you think you are going?"

Becca acted as if she were drunk. "Do you know who I am? Take your hands off me. I was simply at my club when you ruffians invaded my privacy. I have a carriage awaiting my attendance. Let me go at once!"

The constables complied. They were looking for a well-dressed woman with auburn hair, not a member of the aristocracy and a man. Becca made her way swiftly down the street and hailed a hansom.

Holmes and the inspector were in Becca's office looking about. Holmes left quickly and began a quick search of the rooms on the second and third floors as the crowd of men and working girls were making their exits from the club. He went room to room and finally on the third level he found Becca's dress and the theatre make-up.

"She is gone," he said to the Inspector who was just catching up with him. "She is in disguise. She may be dressed as a nun. Ask about and learn if anyone has observed a nun leaving the premises, likely from the back of the Club."

The Inspector left the third floor and followed Holmes's instructions. Holmes looked around the room for any signs that might hint at Becca's disguise but found only empty wooden hangers on the bed. He looked at the hangers and immediately recognized that each was used for men's clothing and not the heavier clothing of a woman or a nun's habit.

"She is disguised as a man," he said to himself as he left the third floor and made his way swiftly to the ground floor and the back exit.

As Holmes arrived the inspector was reentering the Club through the back door.

"No one saw a nun, Holmes. No one has seen a lady of Miss St. John's description. She wasn't here."

"Yes, she was here, and she changed clothes in one of the bedrooms on the third floor." Holmes opened the door to the alley and shouted to the constables standing about, "Did a man, in evening dress, looking drunk and belligerent come through this door and exit the building?"

One of the constables approached Holmes. "Yes, three men exited through the alley way."

"Was one of the men particularly small and thin?"

"Uh, yes. One of the three was a small fellow. Light of bone and not more than five feet tall, there abouts."

"Which way did that man go?"

"I'm not sure. Down the alleyway I think."

Holmes stood straight and looked about. Except for the half dozen constables in the alley, it was empty. He took his hat off and waved it in the air. The Inspector was standing speaking with two or three constables at once.

"The club is empty, Mr. Holmes. She isn't here."

"No, she has deftly escaped in the guise of one of the men here this evening. We have failed, Inspector."

Wiggins appeared at the end of the alley and was about to be stopped by one of the constables when Holmes motioned for the constable to let him through.

"No woman or nun exited this way, Mr. Holmes. Just three men. Two of the men made their way to the front of the club and into awaiting carriages. One of the men made his way down the alley and to the cross street. He hailed a hansom and left the area. I put one of me boys on him, just in case. If all goes well, we should know before morning where the man went, sir."

"Good job, Wiggins. As soon as you know where that man went, come to Baker Street and inform me immediately. Well done."

Wiggins lifted his knuckle to his forehead and left the way he had come.

"In the meantime, Inspector, I suggest that you put your men at every rail station and be on the lookout for a woman of Miss St. John's description, or of an old nun. I doubt she will use the same disguise twice. I do not think we will be looking for a woman disguised as a man."

The Inspector nodded and began to shout orders to several constables to secure the building and to alert Scotland Yard to make the arrangements for detectives at the rail stations. Holmes stood with his hands on his hips thinking when Watson suddenly arrived.

"It went well, Holmes. We have everyone at the house in custody. How did it go here?"

Holmes looked at Watson and slapped his hat against his right leg.

"Not well, Watson. Not well at all. Miss St. John has escaped our net and is at large."

"But it was all planned so well, Holmes. How did she escape?"

Holmes turned and did not answer at first. "I am afraid that your hunt went much better that my own, Watson. We need to ensure that the rest of the worms in the cellar of the house are secured."

"I have taken care of that, Holmes. We have constables guarding the entrances both outside and inside the house and the worms are secure. Do you think Miss St. John will return to the house?"

"No, she is too smart for that. She will be somewhere else at present. Somewhere we do not know about. Our best bet is to secure the rail stations. If I were she, I would make for the Continent.

"And the First Lord and Lady? Are they safe?"

"Yes. The First Lord sent his wife home and is likely awaiting us now at Baker Street."

"Good, Watson. You have done it well. Much better, I must confess, than we have here. Let us return to Baker Street."

Chapter 27

Becca was at her apartment. She had instructed the first driver to take her on a circuitous route through London and made several stops and changed hansoms twice along the way. She was sure that she had not been followed. She sat now in front of the fireplace warming herself and thinking about her next move. She had consulted her copy of the train schedules that would take her from London to the Dover coast and the boat that crossed the Channel to France.

She knew that she could not take the train in her own person, and the only disguise she had left was that of the retired nun. She would need to use that disguise to make her escape to the Continent. She had time. Patience is what was needed now. She was sure that Holmes and Scotland Yard would have men at all the London train stations to stop her escape via train from London. She had to make her way out of London via carriage and to an adjoining village along the train route to Dover. It was only there that she would have any chance of escape. She decided to rest, to sleep, and to make her way to an adjoining village in a planned and controlled manner. She never spared a thought for Steven, Scott, or Lilith. She was entirely focused on her own escape.

Holmes and Watson were back at Baker Street with the Inspector and the First Lord. All four men were smoking, and each had been fortified with small sandwiches and brandy. Mrs. Hudson was ever resourceful and had provided both, to Watson's relief.

"We have the London rail stations all being watched, Mr. Holmes. She won't escape London that way."

"Yes, and I am sure that she has predicted that and is making other plans to escape. We are dealing with a very intelligent and resourceful woman."

The First Lord cleared his throat. "Gentlemen, I have my responsibilities to attend to. I thank you all for your excellent work. You have everyone in custody except this Miss St. John. You have done it well. Mr. Holmes, I will never underestimate you again. My wife has a story to tell at tea for many years to come, and I have escaped a fate worse than death, thanks to you Mr. Holmes."

Holmes looked at the First Lord and bowed slightly and then turned to face the fire. The Inspector smiled and Watson looked at Holmes with pride.

"I am afraid that I cannot accept your congratulations, my Lord. The big fish has escaped our net for the moment, and I confess that the odds of us catching her are slim at best.

"I am convinced that she will make her way to the Continent via one of the steamers across the Channel. The question is which one and at what time?" Holmes turned to face the First Lord. "Would your Lordship make a ship available for our use to stop any crossing steamers if we can identify one making that crossing?"

"Of course, Mr. Holmes. You have but to ask. The more time that you give me, the better."

Holmes nodded and turned to face the fire again. The First Lord stood to leave. Watson bowed and shook the First

Lord's hand. The inspector did likewise. Holmes, his back to the First Lord, stared into the fire in deep thought.

"Thank you, again Mr. Holmes. I will await word from you before I act."

With that the First Lord left the sitting room and made his way to his waiting carriage on Baker Street.

"Gentlemen, I have reports to write. I am afraid I am needed at Scotland Yard. I will make my exit as well."

The Inspector stood and shaking Watson's outstretched hand he left Baker Street as well, saying nothing more to Holmes who still stood like a statute starring into the fire.

"What now, Holmes?" Watson sat in his usual chair, the very image of exhaustion.

Holmes turned his face toward Watson but did not answer his question. He took a pipe from the mantle, stuffed it with tobacco from the Persian slipper, lit the pipe with a match, and threw himself into his usual chair beside the fire.

"We think, dear Watson. We think and we wait."

Holmes sat and thought for the better part of two hours. It was now early Thursday morning. The sun was out, and Watson had fallen asleep in his chair by the now-dying fire. The bell rang below, and Holmes could hear Mrs. Hudson as she answered the door. Holmes looked at the sleeping Watson. He knew the bell was likely rung by Wiggins and thought that it would not be good news. As he looked over to the door to his rooms, Wiggins knocked and entered.

"Mr. Holmes, good morning, sir." Wiggins looked worn and tired. He did not look happy.

"Wiggins, thank you for coming so soon. What news?"

Wiggins held his hat in front of his belt and looked down at the floor. "We lost the man, Mr. Holmes. The hansom took my man all over the West Side and he lost him when he changed hansoms. I am afraid we failed you, Mr. Holmes."

Holmes stood and looked at Wiggins. "You did not fail me, Wiggins. On the contrary, you and the Irregulars gave us the only lead coming from our rather disastrous watch of the Club." He put his hand into his trouser pocket and pulled out another sovereign. "This is for you, Wiggins. Thank you for your efforts. Now, run along and get some rest."

"Thank you, Mr. Holmes. I will indeed." Wiggins took the sovereign and tucked it away in his jacket pocket. He turned and left Baker Street the way he had come. Disappointed but happy with the coin that bounced in his pocket as he ran down Baker Street.

Holmes woke Watson with a tug at his jacket. "Watson, wake up."

Watson aroused himself and looked at Holmes sleepily. "Any word from the Irregulars?"

"Yes, just now as you slept. I am afraid they lost Miss St. John. Not surprising really."

Watson stretched himself and wiped at his eyes. "What now, Holmes?"

"She will stay put wherever she is for the next day or so. Then she will make her way out of the city via carriage, likely in disguise, to one of the villages along the route to Dover and her escape via steamship across the Channel. In the meantime, we need to make our way to Scotland Yard and see what we can learn from those we were successful capturing.

"Come along, Watson. No rest for us until we have our bird in hand."

Holmes moved toward his desk, rather than the door and began to complete a telegraph form.

"We will drop this off at a telegraph office along the way."

Watson was still stretching and trying to wake up as Holmes moved toward the door and retrieved his walking stick and hat. Watson watched Holmes with weary eyes.

"Do we have no time for breakfast, Holmes?"

"I am afraid not, Watson. The game is afoot."

Becca was packed and had several trunks and a large carpet bag with the makeup, theatre glue, prosthetics, clothing, and other things she would need to sustain her disguise as Sister Mary Brendan and change disguises during her journey, first by rented carriage, and then by train to Dover, and finally the Channel crossing to Calais, France.

Her disguise as Sister Brendan was laid out on her bed. She had gone out that day dressed as a man and had made the arrangements and paid for the carriage and the train tickets. She was careful to avoid the train stations and had used the services of an agent to get what she needed. The tickets and itinerary had been delivered by a confused messenger who saw the closed art store and at first was unsure about what to do.

She still had several hours before the carriage arrived to take her fifty miles north and to a village where she could then get on the train for Dover. The carriage would travel through the night, stopping several times to change horses and would get her to the train station before sun rise. The train would take her to Dover and potential freedom.

She planned to get on the evening Channel steamer in her male persona, leaving her nun disguise and other things in Dover, preferably in a trash heap. After getting on board and ensuring that all was safe, she would allow herself the comfort of changing into her own clothes and to be her own self – getting off the boat in Calais as herself.

She decided to rest before she started the laborious task of becoming a short, fat, old nun. The disguise was heavy, uncomfortable, and required her to be both bent at the knees and at her waist for long periods of time. She knew she would be exhausted by the end of her trip to Dover and happy to be out of the heavy disguise.

Holmes and Watson arrived at Scotland Yard after stopping to send the telegram to the First Lord. Holmes had written the First Lord to ask him to send one of her Majesty's Channel fleet to waylay the night steamer in mid-crossing that late evening or early Saturday morning, and to look for either a nun or Miss St. John herself on board. If found, he requested that she be detained, arrested, and brought back to London to face charges for the murder of Mr. Isadora Persano, treason, espionage, the attempted murder of the First Lord, and a litany of other potential charges Scotland Yard wished to bring against her.

Holmes and Watson waited in an anteroom for Inspector MacDonald to arrive and give the permission required for Holmes to interrogate the prisoners. He arrived looking disheveled and tired.

"Mr. Holmes, can this not wait until later? I am not finished with my paperwork, and I wish to go home and get some rest."

"I am afraid not, Inspector. We must strike while the iron is hot. I would like to see the man you apprehended at the house."

"You mean Mr. Steven Sobotta?"

Watson answered, "Yes."

The inspector gave the necessary permissions for Holmes and Watson to speak with both Sobotta and Lilith. Three constables led Holmes and Watson to Sobotta's cell and unlocked the door after warning the prisoner to make no sudden moves. Each constable carried a large wooden club. Sobotta did not appear to be in any mood to give the constables a fight.

"I will not resist," he said as he laid in a pile of hay to one side of the smelly cell.

"Mr. Sobotta, I am Sherlock Holmes, and this is my colleague Dr. Watson. It will go well for you if you cooperate with us."

Inspector MacDonald appeared behind Holmes and Watson and looked over Watson's shoulder at the reclining Sobotta.

"Get up off the floor, Sobotta, and talk with these men."

Sobotta rolled over and looked in the direction of the Inspector. "I have nothing to say to anyone, about anything. Go away and leave me alone."

MacDonald pushed aside Holmes and Watson and taking one of the constables by the wrist, came aggressively into the room toward Sobotta.

"I am telling you one last time to sit up and cooperate with Mr. Holmes. Do it now or feel my boot in your arse."

"That will not be necessary, Inspector." Holmes stepped further into the cell. "Let me tell you what I already know Mr. Sobotta. You and your twin brother, who appears to have escaped, worked at the Gemini Club and for Miss St. John in many different capacities. The two of you are enforcers for Miss St. John and I would venture to say, have records with Scotland Yard for a sundry of small crimes. Am I correct so far?"

"Go on Mr. Holmes, I will not give you any information." Sobotta had rolled over and was now sitting with his legs crossed looking from Holmes to MacDonald.

"You knew and were likely involved in the managing of an unfortunate entomologist who worked tirelessly under the control of Miss St. John to breed the worms that you eventually used to kill two men. First Mr. Robert Holcomb and later Mr. Isadora Persano. I unfortunately cannot prove that you killed Mr. Holcomb, but I know that Miss St. John and perhaps either you or your twin brother were in his rooms and administered the worm that drove him mad and into the streets to meet his death."

Sobotta looked at Holmes with barely veiled surprise.

"Yes, that is right Mr. Sobotta. I know that after you administered the worm to Mr. Holcomb, his reaction was a surprise to you. That he overturned chairs and became violent and mad. In his madness and the strength that comes to men in such a state, he made his way out his apartment door before you, or your twin brother, could subdue him. Miss St. John, and either you or your brother, then left the building through the back alley, where you had a waiting carriage. Tell me Mr. Sobotta, was it you or your brother?"

"I am not going to say anything to you, Mr. Holmes. You weave an interesting tale, but that's all it is. A tale. You have nothing on me. You don't even know if it was me, my brother, or someone else. You don't have anything on me."

"Perhaps not. As I said, I cannot prove that you were involved in Holcomb's death, but we do have a witness to Mr. Persano's death. It will be interesting if he identifies you as one of the two men who broke into Mr. Persano's apartment and administered the worm before he interrupted you. It was then that you, or your brother, made the capital mistake of leaving one of the worms, in a matchbox, on the table.

"Let me get to the point, Mr. Sobotta. Where is Miss Rebecca St. John?"

Sobotta laughed until he choked. "I do not know, and if I did, I would not tell you. She is likely a long way from London, I can tell you that. Somewhere you will never find her. Don't sleep easy, Mr. Holmes, because at a time that fits with her plans, she will find you and when she does, well let's just say you will not be solving any more mysteries."

It was Holmes's turn to laugh.

"I have been threatened before, Mr. Sobotta. And yet, here I stand. Do not underestimate me, Mr. Sobotta. I know that Miss St. John is likely on her way, via carriage, to eventually catch the steamer across the Channel. I know she will likely catch the Channel train somewhere north of London. I know that she is adept at disguises, including as a man and as an old nun."

Sobotta looked at Holmes with surprise and for the first time, with fear in his tired eyes.

"Yes, Mr. Sobotta, I know these things. Please believe me when I tell you, she will be brought to justice."

Holmes looked at the Inspector and said, "I have nothing more to discuss with this man. Please take me to see Lilith, the unfortunate medium." Holmes turned on his heels and quickly left the cell leaving the Inspector, the constable, and Watson standing.

Lilith was in a different part of the prison, being held in a cell in the women's section of Scotland Yard. The women's cells were cleaner and nicer because they were seldomly used for anything other than holding prostitutes until they were released after their inquests. As they walked to Lilith's cell, Watson told Holmes what he had learned from his conversation with Lilith during her arrest. As the door to her cell was opened by the constable, Lilith stiffened and sat upright, expecting the worse.

"Do not be afraid, Lilith. I am Sherlock Holmes, and this is my colleague, Dr. Watson. Are you in need of any medical help at present?"

Lilith shook her head and stared at Holmes and Watson, looking over their shoulders at the constable and Inspector who were standing just outside the door to her cell.

"I know from what Dr. Watson has told me, that you know very little of the details of this affair. Your role in this was to hold a séance and to convince the First Lord and his wife to drink the sherry that was likely mixed with laudanum. Am I correct, madam?"

Lilith nodded.

"Do you know where Miss St. John is?"

"I do not. She never told me her plans, and I haven't seen her for two days." Lilith trembled, but her voice was under control. "How…how did you know about the séance and Becca's plans?"

"It is my job to know what others know, Madam. I have many ways of learning what is in the minds and hearts of others. Sometimes by intimate conversations between two people on a sunny morning, on a park bench."

Lilith's eyes grew large, and her mouth was agape.

"It was you then? You were the kindly priest who spoke with me on the park bench?"

"Yes, it was I. You should have followed my advice when I quoted our Lord and told you to 'go forth and sin no more.'"

Lilith looked down at her hands in her lap and began to cry.

"I have never followed that advice, Mr. Holmes. I have had many opportunities to make different decisions, but each time I have stayed my course and continued as before. You were kind to me that day so allow me to repay you with this warning. Becca will not stop until you are dead, Mr. Holmes. She is singular and she never quits. As long as there is breath in her body, she will come for you. She has a strong hatred of men, and it is even stronger for men who cross her.

"Even now, as I sit here, I tremble with fear, Mr. Holmes. I cry, not because of what awaits me here in this prison. I have suffered worse. No, I tremble out of fear that she will find a way to get to me. Yes, even in this cell. I am frightened even unto death for what she will do to me, when she finds me." Lilith's crying became more pronounced, and she began to tear at the air with her clawed hands. She stood and threw herself against the stone walls of her cell. "She will kill me. She will kill me," and she began to tear at her hair.

The constable and Inspector moved past Holmes and Watson and each grabbed ahold of Lilith as she threatened to tear herself apart. Watson backed away and called down the corridor for one of the constables to bring a straitjacket, a syringe, and a bottle of sedative. It took several minutes for his request to be fulfilled and as he waited, Holmes knelt down next to the restrained Lilith and calmly caressed her face and slowly stroked her hair.

By the time the straitjacket arrived, Holmes had convinced Lilith to calmly allow the jacket to be put on her. Watson took the syringe and sedative, and administered a strong dose to the poor woman, who quickly went to sleep. The constable and Inspector lifted her up and laid her softly on the bed of hay in one corner of the cell. MacDonald looked up at Holmes as if to say, "Thank you."

Homes looked at Watson with compassion and sadness in his eyes. "Inspector, I think we are finished here. Thank you."

Chapter 28

Sister Brenan was now at the train station where she would catch the boat train to Dover. It had been a long trip by carriage, and she was tired and weighed down by her disguise. She was standing alone at one end of the platform, surrounded by her trunks. She was looking for an opportunity to change her disguise before the boat train arrived. It was late and dark, and no one was at the station except her and the ticket master. She looked around for the water closet when a constable appeared shining a dark lantern in her direction.

"Mam? Say there. Please stay where you are."

Becca stiffened but immediately regained her composure and turned slowly in the direction of the voice and the light.

"Oh young man, you are sent by God, you are. I am so tired, and these weary knees will not cooperate with me tonight. Can you please help me to the bench so that I may sit and rest?"

The constable continued his approach, shining the light around the old nun.

"Where are you traveling tonight?"

"Oh, just to a historic church not far from here. I missed my train and now I am forced to travel so late at night. Just one more train ride and I will arrive. But what the priest will say when I come knocking on his door so early in the morning…well, I shouldn't want to even imagine it." The nun smiled at the young constable.

"We have been notified to be on the lookout for a woman. A woman perhaps dressed as a nun. Who are you?"

"I am Sister Mary Brenan. A woman dressed as a nun; you say?" Becca laughed. "Whatever for?"

The constable stopped just three feet from Becca and shined his dark lantern in the nun's face.

"Oh, please stop it. That light is so bright, and my tired eyes just cannot take it. Now see what you have done, I cannot see anything now."

Becca began to move toward the constable in a lost, back and forth fashion. She appeared unsteady on her feet and almost tripped. As she did, her right hand went to the back of her head and without the constable noticing, she pulled a long sharp hair pin from her wig. The constable reached out to prevent the old nun from falling, and that was the chance that Becca was waiting for.

Becca fell into the constable's outstretched arms as he dropped the dark lantern to the platform, and with one swift motion, she plunged the long hair pin into the base of the young man's neck, just below the skull. She moved the sharp pin back and forth until the young constable's body went limp. With a strength that no one would have imagined she had, she deftly moved the constable to the bench and arranged his body so that he appeared to be asleep.

Becca quickly picked up the fallen dark lantern and closed the shutters and set it beside the dead constable. She waited for her eyes to readjust to the darkness and leaving the dead man and her trunks on the platform, she took the carpet bag and made her way slowly into the station. She found a drowsy ticket master in his cage and motioned to use the water closet. The man simply nodded and leaned his head back on his hands dreamily.

After changing her costume to that of a man, she stuffed the habit and accoutrement of the nun in the carpet bag and left it in the water closet. She looked at herself in the mirror. Her new appearance was good. The beard, hat, and man's clothing made her look the part. Her posture and demeanor changed, and she took on the air of the confident young man she appeared to be.

She slowly opened the door and saw that the ticket master was asleep and quietly made her way back to the platform and her baggage. It was only a short half hour before the boat train arrived and she was on board. The stop was short, and no one bothered to awaken the sleeping young constable lying on the bench.

Holmes and Watson had returned to Baker Street several hours earlier after their visit to Scotland Yard, and Watson was asleep in his bedroom. Holmes could not sleep and though it was late, and he was very tired, his mind would not let him rest. He berated himself for allowing Miss St. John to escape the club but hoped that his directions to the First Lord would eventually resolve his error and bring a final successful conclusion to the case.

It was half past six on Saturday morning when the bell rang below. Holmes was up in an instant and made his way down the stairs to the front door before Mrs. Hudson could be aroused. At the door was a messenger with a telegram. Holmes grabbed the telegram and closed the door in the face and outstretched hand of the messenger. He bounded up the seventeen steps and into his room. He tore open the telegram, read it, and snarled to himself.

It was from Scotland Yard. The body of a young constable had been found at a train station along the route of the boat train. The ticket master had not seen or heard anything and could only say that an old nun had been on the platform and used the water closet earlier that morning.

Holmes wadded the telegram into a ball and tossed it disgustedly into the fire. He threw himself into his usual chair and stared absently into the burning coals watching the telegram as it was consumed by the flames. Only one more chance to catch her before she arrived in Calais and disappeared into the Continent.

Miss St. John was herself, a beautiful and smartly dressed young lady. She had changed clothes in her first-class cabin and thrown her costume overboard. Most of the passengers were in bed asleep and she was alone on deck, except for another young lady with long beautiful brown hair who stood several feet away. The second young lady looked remarkably like Becca, was similarly dressed, and appeared to walk about aimlessly.

Becca looked at the first bluish lights of morning as the still hidden sun slowly began to give its light to the waters of the Channel. The crossing had been relatively smooth, with only large swells that slowly rocked the steamer from side-to-side. She was feeling relieved. She was halfway to the Continent and her freedom. Becca's hair was short, and she had dyed it a dark black almost immediately upon coming aboard. She wore the dark glasses of the blind, now pushed down her nose so that she could see. She carried a white cane to complete the effect.

As the young lady looked out over the water from the starboard side of the boat, walking about aimlessly, she heard the waves from the port side of the steamer suddenly change. She could not see the port side of the vessel as the staterooms blocked her view. She felt a strange tickle in her nose and rubbed at it. The voice in her head repeated, "Jump!"

As she stood wondering what the change in sound meant, she saw a beautiful young woman with short black hair open the door to her stateroom and go inside, closing the door behind her. She heard the voice inside her head, demanding, "Jump," and she heard a man shouting across the waves.

"This is Her Majesty's ship *Majestic*. You are ordered to heave to and come about. Comply immediately."

She froze. Her mouth went dry, and she felt a cold chill run through her body. She felt the steamer's engines stop and the heavy vessel immediately begin to slow. She raced around the staterooms so that she could see the port side of the steamer. As she did, she saw a bright search light focused on the front of the vessel and several of the ship's crew running out on deck. The search light came from a large naval vessel of war not five hundred yards from the side of the steamer.

"Heave to and prepare to be boarded!"

Her mind raced. She felt trapped aboard the steamer in the middle of the Channel, and it was clear to her that the men aboard the *Majestic* meant to harm her. She looked around like a rat trapped in a cage. The voice repeated in her head, "Jump!" Passengers began to open their stateroom doors and come out on deck in their night shirts and robes; but not the beautiful young woman who had gone to her stateroom – she did not come out. The crewmembers were busy trying to catch a line that had been shot from the deck of the *Majestic* to the now stopped steamer. There was nothing to be done but obey the voice in her head.

She looked around for something heavy. There was a large spanner hanging from the side of the superstructure of the vessel and she ran toward it. It was very heavy. She lifted it off the wall where it hung, barely able to carry it, and slowly dragged it and herself to the side of the vessel. The search light moved, and she was in its full glare.

"You there, stop what you are doing. Stop at once." The voice called from the darkness on the other side of the bright search light. "I repeat, stop at once."

She didn't stop but continued to half carry and half drag the large spanner to the edge of the deck. The passengers that had exited their staterooms began to yell at her to stop. A crewman from the upper deck of the steamer, shouted down as well. But it was all just noise and chaos. She only responded to the voice in her head, "Jump!"

Tears began to wet her cheeks as she stood on the edge of the deck hugging the large spanner to her chest. She shook with cold and fear. Her tears became a torrent as she looked around at the distant faces of the passengers as they watched in horror. Everything slowed down. The *Majestic* was near the side of the steamer, toward the bow, and a gang plank was being positioned between the *Majestic* and the steamer. The steamer was about to be boarded by the sailors onboard the

Majestic. The voice in her head demanded obedience, "Jump!"

She shook in the cold. She looked down at the dark waters of the Channel and out again at the *Majestic*, the search light, and the ever-lightening skies. Her mind raced in its madness, "Jump!" She took one last look at the now reddish sky and leaped over the side of the steamer into the cold waters of the Channel, hugging the heavy spanner against her body. And as she sank, her long brown locks floated, for just a second, in the cold embrace of the Channel.

She sank quickly, weighed down by her clothing and the spanner. The voice inside her head was quiet now. And as she sank deeper, her life ebbed away until all that existed was the cold of the sea and the blackness of death.

It was mid-morning and Holmes had not slept all night. Watson made his way downstairs to his waiting breakfast. As he entered the sitting room, he saw a tired and weary Holmes sitting by the fire in a posture of dejection and defeat.

"Any word of Miss St. John?"

Holmes looked over at Watson and shook his head. "Nothing as yet, Watson. Nothing."

Watson sat at the table and began to serve himself breakfast.

"Will you have something to eat, Holmes? You are exhausted and look as if you have not slept. Please join me and eat something."

Holmes stood and walked slowly to the table and sat across from Watson.

"Just some tea. I cannot eat anything at present."

Watson poured Holmes a cup of tea and pushed the cup and saucer in front of him. Each man sat in silence. Watson eating his breakfast, and Holmes occasionally sipping at his tea.

"I am afraid that I have failed miserably, Watson. Early this morning I received a telegram from Scotland Yard informing me that the body of a young constable had been found dead at a railway station along the route the Boat Train takes. Another victim to add to her long list of victims, I am certain of it."

Watson stopped eating and looked at Holmes. He looked defeated and depressed.

"There is nothing else that you could have done, Holmes. You stopped her plans and rescued the First Lord from a horrible fate. Not to mention, prevented the Crown from the loss of invaluable naval secrets. You have all her accomplices in custody. You have solved a most confusing and difficult mystery. Miss St. John may have escaped, but the case is a success."

Holmes let out a grunt and pushed his tea away. "I have acted like one of Scotland Yard's detectives, Watson. I am indeed an amateur detective, as so many are fond of saying about me. No, this morning I am ashamed and disappointed in the outcome of this case.

"After learning of the dead constable, I left our rooms and dispatched a telegram to the First Lord. I aroused a rather sleepy telegraph man at his post. If she is on the night steamer, which I deduce she will be, we will have her. The First Lord is sending one of the Channel fleet to waylay the steamer as we had discussed. That is my last move in this wretched game. I returned home and you see me as I am now."

Watson pushed his breakfast plate aside but was at a loss for words. Both men sat starring at the table. The bell rang below, but neither man moved.

"Send them away, Watson. I want no company this morning."

Watson waited and then stood and walked toward the door just as Mrs. Hudson arrived with a telegram.

"Dr. Watson. A messenger delivered this telegram for Mr. Holmes." Mrs. Hudson looked past Watson and into the sitting room. "He looks terrible this morning."

"Thank you, Mrs. Hudson. I am sure he will be fine with time. It is just the outcome of this case. It has not gone as Holmes wished."

Mrs. Hudson turned and began the slow walk down the stairs, mumbling incoherently to herself. Watson walked over to the table and set the telegram down in front of Holmes.

"Watson, I haven't the strength to read it. Can you do so, please?"

Watson, standing beside the table, leaned over, and picked up the telegram and carefully tore it open.

"It is from the First Lord." Watson read the telegram and then continued. "The First Lord dispatched the HMS Majestic, at your request, and intercepted the Channel steamer early this morning. A young woman, believed to be Miss St. John, but who has not been positively identified, threw herself overboard and is presumed dead. The vessel was searched and no one answering to Miss St. John's description was found. After the search of the vessel, a man was found to be missing and his whereabouts are unknown. Scotland Yard believes he likely simply missed his boat. Miss St. John's fate cannot be positively determined, but it is highly likely that she was the young woman who died at sea. The First Lord offers his congratulations at a job well done, and warmly thanks you for your efforts both for him and the Crown."

Watson sat the telegram down in front of Holmes. Holmes picked it up and read through it quickly.

"A missing man. She was on the boat, Watson. She came on board dressed as a man. The man is missing because she changed her disguise. Jumping overboard into the waters of the cold Channel. I wonder..."

Holmes slowly rose from the table and walked sadly to a small table beside the fire and retrieved his violin. He stood in front of the fire and began to play a sad and melancholy tune.

Epilogue

It was Sunday afternoon. Holmes and Watson were at the home of Mrs. McKinnon. Mrs. Snyder was present and the four were enjoying an early tea as they sat across from each other around a small table in the garden. The air was warm, and the sky was clear.

"And so, Mrs. Snyder, Mr. Holcomb was the unfortunate victim of a much larger plot. There is very little that the law can do by way of his partner, but I have dispatched a telegram to the managing solicitor at this firm, which he should read tomorrow. I will be very much surprised if Mr. Gurel is employed as a solicitor at that firm by this time tomorrow."

Mrs. Snyder wiped a tear from her eye and reached out with her gloved hand and touched Holmes's hand. "Thank you for saving his honor, Mr. Holmes. It was so important to him."

Holmes moved his hand from under Mrs. Snyder's gloved hand and gave a little bow as he took a sip of tea.

Mrs. McKinnon hugged her niece and looked at Watson and then Holmes with a smile. "I cannot thank you enough for what you have achieved, Mr. Holmes and Dr. Watson. I am prepared to cover any expenses and your fee, if you will send an invoice to me later this week."

Holmes smiled. "My bill for my services and my expenses is being covered by Her Majesty's Navy. As for your case, my work is its own reward."

Mrs. McKinnon smiled at Holmes. "Then you must allow me to take you to dinner, Mr. Holmes. Surely you will not deny me the pleasure of your company for dinner?"

Holmes stiffened and looked away from Mrs. McKinnon and at Watson.

"Well, Holmes? Are you going to turn down the request of so lovely and fine a lady?" Watson was all smiles.

Holmes was at a loss for words.

The guard was making his rounds checking on the female prisoners. It was something that he did four times during his eight-hour shift. He walked swiftly from door to door, opening the sliding door and calling out the names of the prisoners as he went. Each prisoner was obliged to answer, "Present."

He arrived at the door of a prisoner known only as Lilith. He knocked and slid open the small door and called in, "Lilith." He immediately slid the door shut, being so accustomed to the immediate "Present," but this time no answer came from inside the cell. He stopped and opened the small sliding door again and called a second time, "Lilith?" There was no answer.

"Don't make me open this door. Now I say once again, 'Lilith.'" There was still no answer.

"I am unlocking this door and coming in. Please stand with your face to the far wall and make no sudden moves."

The guard unlocked the door and opened it. The cell was darker than the hallway where he stood, and it took a few seconds for his eyes to adjust to the relative darkness of the cell. He did not immediately see Lilith. She was not standing, facing the opposite wall, as he had instructed, and he looked around the small cell to see where she was. When he saw her, he nearly retched.

In the darkest corner of the cell was Lilith's body. She had escaped the straitjacket she had been in and had used it to hang herself by one of the eye bolts placed in the wall to secure restraining chains. The eye bolt was barely six feet off the floor of the cell and it must have been difficult for her to reach it. Lilith hung from the straps of the straitjacket; her bent legs were just touching the floor of the cell at an awkward angle. Her knees intentionally bent to allow her to suffocate. She had hanged herself in a most deliberate manner and after falling unconscious, the weight of her body had finished the job. Lilith was dead. She would suffer no more.

Scott had escaped Holmes's raid of the Gemini Club and had been in hiding with a friend in a darker part of London. He knew that his brother was being held by Scotland Yard and was himself a wanted man. He had decided to leave London at his first opportunity and was at this moment standing at the train station awaiting a train to Scotland. He would start his life again. He had taken his and his brother's savings and planned to buy a pub in some small village in Scotland and there take advantage of his experience.

As he waited for his train, he looked around cautiously. He wasn't sure if Scotland Yard was looking for him, and he avoided eye contact with the others who waited with him for the train. He was dressed unremarkably and hoped that he would not be noticed or remembered by any of the people on the platform.

As the train arrived, he quickly got on board and found his seat amongst the many others who could only afford the lowest priced seats on the train. He did not want to risk attention by purchasing a more expensive berth. He sat next to a window on the train and looked out at the now empty platform. As he waited impatiently the train lurched forward and slowly left the station. As the speed of the train increased, his hopes increased, and his fears subsided. He had succeeded and he was on his way to freedom.

Several weeks had passed and Steven was moved from his cell to court for his criminal trial. He was in an anteroom alone waiting for his attorney to join him. It wasn't long before Mr. Gurel joined him in the anteroom.

"The club is closed. Miss St. John has either escaped or is dead. I do not know which. Your brother, Scott, is nowhere to be found. You, the other chap and the boys from the cellar are all that remain. The boys have been released, there being no real evidence that they were involved in anything more criminal than fooling the rich by staging seances."

Steven grunted. "If my brother is smart, he has long left London and has started a new life far away from here. As for Miss St. John, I would bet a week's pay that she has escaped and is somewhere on the Continent. What is to happen with me?"

"As you know, the First Lord of the Admiralty and Sherlock Holmes both provided testimony at your inquest." Gurel sneered as he mentioned Holmes's name. Because of Holmes he had lost his partnership and was now on his own, making a living as a solicitor representing clients in criminal matters. "It is impossible to escape the testimony of two such distinguished members of society. The trial today is merely theatre. You will be found guilty of the death of Isadora Persano."

Steven started to protest, but Gurel stopped him.

"I know, you say it was your twin brother, but you were identified by Persano's neighbor, and there is no escaping that. I am afraid that after today's trial you will be sentenced to hang for both the murder of Persano and the attempted murder of the First Lord of the Admiralty. I have no doubt about it."

Steven sat in silence staring at the table in front of him. Everyone had escaped justice he thought except himself. He had been left holding the bag. He thought about his brother and smiled to himself. His twin would live and in a strange way, that meant that a part of him would live as well.

"Let's get this over with."

A beautiful young woman with short black hair walked in the sunshine through the streets of Paris. It was a beautiful day, and she was on her way to the newly opened art store she had purchased not far from the *Champs-Elysees*. She had just left her apartment where she spent her evenings when she wasn't on the streets and in the salons of Paris, learning the area and meeting men of standing and wealth. There was a small room just off her bedroom; a room she kept locked. It was there that she carefully cultivated the four worms she still had left.

The End.

Milton Keynes UK
Ingram Content Group UK Ltd.
UKHW020901110624
443837UK00013B/395

9 781804 244562